The Ruby Realm Book Two
# Wilting Captive

## Abigail Manning

D0840831

The Ruby Realm: Wilting Captive
© 2022 Abigail Manning

Cover design by Karri Klawitter

Edited by Silvia Curry

# Authors Note

In this tale, you'll find depictions of the immune disorder, Celiac disease. Those with Celiac disease are triggered by consuming food that contains or has come in contact with gluten. Celiac disease was not officially identified until the early 1900's, much later than the approximated time period of this story. In order to accurately portray the lack of knowledge available on Celiac, the characters in *Wilting Captive* refer to this ailment as an "allergy to wheat" or simply an illness.

With that being said, Celiac disease is far more than an allergy and affects approximately 1% of the world's population. Many affected often live undiagnosed, and suffer daily without knowing why. This book is dedicated to all those who suffer from Celiac disease, and those who have yet to be diagnosed.

# prologue

Tufts of half-melted snow spotted the path, drenching my boots in the icy frost. The forest canopy had thinned with all its leaves littering the ground, allowing patches of sun to blind my eyes. My calves burned from the last two weeks of endless walking, but I'd been through worse before.

My skin itched along the long scars hidden beneath my tunic. With gritted teeth, I ignored the urge to acknowledge their existence... to acknowledge my failure.

The muscles that burned along my arms and legs clenched with frustration as the word seared into my mind like a red-hot branding.

*'Failure... Failure. You've failed me yet again.'*

I stomped on a cluster of twigs, relishing in the satisfying snap as I imagined I had broken the word in two. A rush of oxytocin spread up through my leg and settled warmly inside my chest like a sip of fine wine. It wasn't my fault I had failed; it was the beasts' fault. They were sloppy and arrogant, and they were the ones who were foolish enough to bow to a king instead of forging their own path.

*'Yes, but you followed them... So, what does that make you?'*

"Shut up!" I shouted into the forest and slammed my fist into the nearest tree, sending a shower of decaying leaves and broken twigs onto my head. I took in a seething breath as I pulled my bruised knuckle away from the tree, then froze.

*Snap.*

Someone was here...

I whipped out the dagger from my belt, flipping it around in my hand to get a more lethal grip before turning toward the sound with the vicious point greeting them. "Show yourself." A growl rose in my throat as I spoke the words, recalling that no one in this realm actually spoke my language. My free hand twitched, feeling the two golden talisman bracelets shift across my skin.

*They can't understand me unless they take one of my bracelets. Oh well, I was never one for negotiating, anyway.*

No sound followed, but I wasn't convinced by the quiet. I held my position, shifting my foot so it was free to spring into action if needed. Despite only living in this realm for a few months, I had already acquired a lengthy list of enemies. But that was fine by me. I didn't need the people here to like me... only bow to me.

Another crackle of leaves and twigs pierced my senses, alerting me that there was definitely more than one individual. *Excellent, a proper fight, then.* I steadied my blade, preparing to lunge at the first baffled face I saw, but stiffened at a single word.

"Wait." The voice was firm and female, reminding me of the prudish older servants I knew growing up in my kingdom. Not only that, but it was in my language... A hand burst out through a cluster of bushy leaves and twigs, holding up a flat palm to signal me to stop.

I froze, but didn't lower my weapon as I recognized a golden charm bracelet, identical to mine, on the tanned wrist.

*They worked for the Golden King...*

The trees and bushes bristled like the sound of crinkling paper as a cluster of men and women pushed through the foliage. I watched with slitted eyes as they lined up in a neat row, as if they were observing a penned dog. The woman in the center of the group was definitely the oldest of them all. She had slender features—a long narrow nose and hollowed-out cheeks that displayed her cheekbones in full view. Her hair was thick and gray with age, tied off in a tight braid that hung down her shoulder, held together with a strap of worn leather. At the end of her long, fragile-looking arm was the golden charm bracelet, alight with magic that translated her voice into the only language I could comprehend.

"We've been looking for you, beast." The woman's eyes were slanted, her lids only open enough to reveal a vibrant blue that could rival a diamond.

I tensed, feeling my muscles constrict around my spine and shoulders. "I'm not a beast anymore," I growled. My knuckles tightened around the blade, causing them to grind against each other. "Haven't you heard? The beasts are dead. Their *fearless* leader was found dead in the Omairan forest, and the rest of his pathetic followers were imprisoned."

*Ridiculous.*

The woman seemed completely undeterred by this news, her wrinkled features remaining as emotionless as an abandoned marionette. "But you still walk free, don't you?" She held out her hand to the nearest man who stood beside her, a younger gentleman with the soft shadow of a beard adding age to his face. The man pulled a piece of parchment from his coat pocket and passed it to the woman without separating his gaze from me. Wordlessly, the woman unfolded the paper and turned the inked side to me so I could take it into full view. Knowing that I couldn't read the foreign script, she read the words aloud as I narrowed my eyes on the scribbled print.

*Wanted Dead or Alive:*

*Conan Leander*

*For Association With The Criminal Group Known As 'The Beasts'*

Beneath the description was a detailed sketch of my marred face, accurately depicting the hideous scars that traced down my right eye to my lower cheek, across my nose to the edge of my jaw, and straight across my neck like an invisible noose. The image curdled my stomach with a feverish rage, urging me to slice through the offending poster.

*The beasts... How fitting that the group who humiliated themselves have bound me with their insufferable title. That's what I get for relying on anyone but myself.*

"It would seem you've made quite the impression on this realm..." the woman raised her thick brow as she folded the poster to return to her lackey, "and also, a strong impression on our king."

My jaw clenched tight enough to bite through steel. "You're another group of his dim-witted followers, aren't you?" I spat, recalling the various organizations the beast's leader had taught me when we first met. "Who are you? The dragons? Or the bird monster things?"

"We are the king's griffins." The woman bowed her head, and her entourage followed, as if their title deserved some form of odd respect just for being spoken. "We have been sent on behalf of our king to make you an offer to join our ranks and receive the blessings of our benevolent ruler."

I rolled my eyes and lowered my dagger with a squeeze on the hilt. "Not this rubbish again." I fastened my gaze on the older woman, digging into her eyes like a starving viper ready to strike if she dared press me further. "I've already done my time with your king's play-things, and I wasn't exactly sold on the job. You can tell your *benevolent* leader that I don't give my respect to a man who works from the shadows." I backed away from the group, only now feeling the burn of their beady eyes as their offense seeped in.

"You had better watch that pride of yours." The woman's tongue flicked like a whip, her eyes slitting so thin I could barely see her pupils.

I chuckled, feeling the same pride she was warning me about trickle through my blood like a flush of endorphins. "I don't need your warnings, you old hag, and I don't need your king either. Once I arrive at Dhurin, I'll take the province for myself, and then overtake the empire your king so foolishly has left standing." I smiled wickedly, catching the gleam of my pearly teeth in the reflection of my dagger. "Unlike the golden imp, I don't need a collection of toy soldiers to do my bidding."

The woman's features tightened, but otherwise, showed no reaction to my unapologetic words. "We shall see what you do and don't need from our king." She slipped her frail, wrinkled hand into her pocket, and oddly enough, pulled out a small golden key. The key looked oversized in her small palm, but otherwise, it looked the same as any other skeleton key, aside from the fact that it was glittering with magic. "The king warned us that you'd be unlikely to join our ranks, so he requested that we offer you this gift. He hopes its usefulness will sway you into seeing the power and influence he possesses. If you do decide to change your mind, there will always be a place for you among the griffins." She stretched out the key to me with a slight tremble in her old hands, placing the key in a beam of light so its festering magic glittered like a trapped galaxy of golden stars.

My instincts warned me to avoid any further gifts from this metallic monster, but at the same time, the greed in my heart burned with desire. My gaze shifted to the golden charm bracelets that glittered on mine and the hag's wrists. *His gifts have certainly proven useful before...* "What's the catch?" I huffed impatiently, trying to keep my hungry eyes from giving away my interest in the magical trinket.

The woman's thin lips curled up into an almost motherly smile. "No catch, my dear beast. All the king asks is that you remember where such power came from." She reached out the key to me, holding it by only the end as she waited for me to accept it from her teetering grasp.

I hesitated for a moment, but in the end, I couldn't restrain my curiosity for another dose of magic to claim as my own. I swiped the key from her hand and stuffed it deep into my pocket. "Fine. I'll accept his gift, but this changes nothing." I turned on my heel, scuffing up dried roots and leaves as I skirted my heavy boots across the forest floor.

"Where will you go, then?" the woman called, none of them moving from their rooted stances. "How do you expect to take over a whole province as a lone beast?"

A devilish smirk tightened my lips, and I couldn't resist turning back to show the pesky griffins just how powerful my pride could truly be. "Why, I'm going straight for the castle, of course."

# *chapter one*

"Mirabel, darling, try not to slouch so much. You wouldn't want the duke's first impression of you to be a saggy one, would you?" Mother pursed her plump lips with the slightest curl of a smile, accentuating the slender point of her delicate chin.

I turned my attention from the carriage window, checking my smile in its reflection to ensure it hid my gritted teeth before turning back to face Mother. "Are dukes truly that invested in a young lady's posture? I could have sworn that interest was reserved for finicky grand duchesses." I raised a thin, dark brow at my mother, keeping my face as innocent as a newborn lamb.

"Mira..." Father warned as he glanced up at me through his spectacles. He had been engrossed in a book on Dhurin's etiquette and cultural traditions ever since our journey began three days ago. "Heed your mother. You know how imperative it is for this union to proceed without a hiccup. If your mother believes your posture might impact the young duke's perception of you, then there's no need to fiddle with questions." With his fatherly scolding complete, he burrowed his nose back into his book, shifting his eyes in rhythm to the thump of the carriage.

My face itched to flex into a scowl, but I knew that doing so would only earn me another lecture, so I put on my pretty smile that the province adored and straightened my shoulders with an overly exaggerated flutter of my lashes. "My apologies, Mother." My tongue was dripping with sweetness as I added a pompous flair to my tone. "I'll be certain to appear as flawless as porcelain when meeting Duke Ian. I certainly wouldn't want him to judge my *character* before we're wed. It's clear to me now that a bride's worth is in her unattainable beauty."

Mother's face twisted in displeasure at my sarcasm, causing frown lines to scrunch up her smooth ebony forehead. As I was a twenty-one-year-old grand-duchess-to-be, she knew she could only do so much to tame my tongue, but that didn't mean she wouldn't try.

"Mirabel, sweetheart." She folded her satin-gloved hands in her lap, delicately fiddling her pinkies together as she tried to appear stern through her poised mask. "My concerns aren't that the duke won't find you attractive. After all, he already confirmed his agreement to becoming your betrothed after seeing your portrait. I'm more concerned that he won't think you're pleased with the arrangement if he sees you looking so disinterested in giving a good impression." She tilted her head at my crossed arms and rigid clenching, raising a freshly plucked brow.

I shifted uncomfortably in my seat, suddenly feeling like there were ants crawling beneath my dress. "Fine," I clipped, averting my eyes from her sapphire-blue gaze. "I'll do my best."

Mother's skewering glare lessened, allowing a breath I hadn't known I was trapping to seep out of my flared nostrils. She knew I didn't want to marry the duke. There was no hiding my dislike of the situation to her, but despite my hatred toward the arranged marriage, I knew this was the only chance I had at ruling my province. It was just a sacrifice of fulfilling the duty my brother passed on to me.

I let out a quiet sigh and turned back to the window, this time ensuring my shoulders stayed squared and level. My thoughts drifted to my brother and his darling new wife, causing me to wonder if I had made the right decision inheriting his birthright. Ever since Zac and I were children, we had always dreamed of protecting the realm from evil and fighting off the mysterious Golden King's forces. We were going to study under the emperor's finest soldiers and train to become some of his most elite spies capable of any command. But that dream only came true for Zac...

"Are you hungry, dear?" Mother's voice cut through my thoughts, and I turned to see her extend a bag of dried fruit to me. "We should be arriving at the castle soon, and I'm not certain how long it will take for the chefs to accommodate your dietary needs. It might be wise to eat a little something, so you're not tempted to snack during the betrothal ball."

I eyed the candied fruits with disinterest, then smiled kindly at my finicky, yet caring, mother. "No, thank you. I ate a large breakfast, so I think I'll be fine."

Mother pulled the bag back with a look that bordered between a worried mother and an unconvinced grand duchess. "Very well. Just be cautious with what you eat at the castle, dear. We've informed Grand Duke Simeon of your ailment, but I'm still not certain if they understand the severity of your allergy. The last thing we want is for you to start upheaving—"

"I understand, Mother," I cut her off with a tart snip in my tone, effectively silencing her before she could get too far into the gory details. "I'll be cautious."

Mother settled back into her seat like a mother goose fluffing out her feathers while watching her gosling take its first plunge into a pond. Having such peculiar needs had caused a lot of worry for my parents when it came to finding a proper match for me. Despite being an heiress to a province, it was difficult to market a potential wife who couldn't come in contact with nearly half of most provinces' food supplies. To my parents' relief, Duke Ian didn't seem to have any problem accepting my generous dowry and self-imploding bodily functions. Well, not that my parents went into extreme detail on said functions. I don't think any right man would find a girl attractive after having that information disclosed.

*Although, he did seem rather smitten with my portrait...*

I stared at my reflection in the glass, watching as the

trees and fluttering leaves cut through my features. My brown eyes mirrored the dark walnut trees that lined our path. Long, dark lashes clung around my eyelids, emphasizing their smooth almond shape and sculpted brows. My nose was petite and slightly upturned, and my heart-shaped face was framed by thick black curls that hung loose from my updo around my cocoa-toned skin. It had taken a while for my hair to grow back to its former glory after dealing with the after-effects of my ailment, but now it looks even sleeker than it had before.

If it wasn't for the fact that my parents were too fearful of my allergy to let me venture out into the town, I likely would have had suitors lining up at our castle doors ages ago. It was no wonder Duke Ian had been so eager to meet me. I just had to hope that he liked what was beneath my skin, too.

The trees outside the glass grew sparser and sparser until they had been completely replaced with stout cottages, bustling taverns, and a chaotically cheerful marketplace. The dirt path shifted into cobblestone, causing my tailbone to bounce uncomfortably against the thinly padded bench. A large market square centered around a bubbling fountain that still sputtered chunks of ice from the dwindling winter. It was flooded with diverse citizens, young and old, all sporting long, cozy cloaks to fend off the chill of the lingering season. We swerved around the circular town center, directing our carriage down a wide lane of tall estates with curved roof tops, elongated windows, and luxurious curtains with hand-printed patterns on full display through the glass. If there was any doubt that this section of the province was occupied by nobility, a finely dressed woman with a short, white-haired dog—that looked more like a rat than a canine—confirmed my suspicions with a prudish tilt of her pointed nose.

I craned my neck to look toward the front of the carriage and nearly gasped when I saw the grand castle of the Dhurin province. I had been fully raised in the Omairan castle, so I was no stranger to finery and overly-embellished architecture, but this... This was what I had envisioned the emperor's palace to look like.

Tall, black stone towers stretched skyward, only stopping when they kissed the bottom of the graying snow clouds. A large gate, stretching all the way to the edge of a red brick estate, spanned the entire circumference of the castle, blocking off its entrance with iron bars that twisted into decorative vines and ravens at the top. Beyond the gate stood two massive doors, at least two-stories tall, that accented the front of the dark stone walls. The doors glittered with what looked like silver and onyx, crafting a mosaic of a blooming rose—the official flower of Dhurin. Skinny turrets framed the door, speckled with beautiful stained glass, but it was too distant to see what images they displayed. As we pulled through the gates, I was finally able to see the flourishing gardens that were filled with jewel-toned blooms, vivid enough that I could almost smell their sweet fragrance from within the carriage walls.

We pulled around to the front of the extravagant doors, and I fought the urge to press my face against the glass so I could get my first look at my husband-to-be. From my elevated angle, I could see at least five pairs of legs, one in a voluminous turquoise skirt and the others in tailored pant legs, all of which seemed to vary between guard uniforms and the grand duke with his son.

I snagged a tight breath, allowing it to burn in my lungs for a moment before setting it free. I hadn't expected to be so nervous about meeting my betrothed, but I suppose it shouldn't be shocking that I harbored stress, considering I was meant to spend the rest of my life with him.

*Please don't be a spoiled brat...*

My hopes seemed almost futile as the footman pulled the door open with a flourished wave. I only caught his uniform for a brief moment, but the dark gray coat and embroidered gold tassels made it difficult to believe that my betrothed contained much humility. I bit down on my tongue, forcing my thoughts into submission as I reminded myself not to be so judgmental. After all, I was a duchess, too. It was very likely that he was just as fearful about my personality as I was about his.

Father stepped out of the carriage first, causing the cabin to shift awkwardly as his weight pressed down on the step. He turned back to the door to offer Mother a hand, who placed her gloved hand into his with a dainty lift of her skirt hem. I shifted behind her, stuffing my nerves into my gut like an over-packed trunk I needed to slam shut. The footman offered me a hand, which I accepted with the same grace my mother had modeled as I gently climbed out of the cabin.

My vibrant teal dress swayed around my ankles as I stepped airily onto the ground, lifting my lashes coquettishly as I looked up into the face of my husband-to-be.

Striking blue eyes, rimmed in a nearly purple border, swept up and down my gown, taking in my appearance with an almost smug smile. His round eyes were shadowed under his thick blonde eyebrows that nearly traced down along the curve of his sculpted nose. His jaw was strong and his chin prominent, mirroring the wide berth of his muscular arms that strained against his red silk coat. His hair looked to be about shoulder-length but was tied back at the nape of his neck in a neat ponytail. He was tall, but not willowy. His height was well-balanced by his strong features and muscular build, making him appear extraordinarily masculine and well-defined. He pinched a freshly cut blood-red rose between his fingers, the bloom wider than a closed fist.

*Well, at least he's attractive.*

"Welcome, Grand Duke Brantley and your beautiful family." Grand Duke Simeon bowed with a perfect bend at the waist, followed by his son as his wife flared out her turquoise skirt with an elegant curtsey. When he rose, I was able to get a better look at his features and saw a heavy resemblance between father and son. He had the same chiseled features, blue eyes, and tied back blonde hair, but his eyes were softer, with crow's feet spanning out from the corners and a slight droop in his lower lid. Wrinkles creased along his smile, showcasing just how often he utilized the cheerful expression that emphasized his flawless teeth. "We are honored to have you as our guests in our humble home, and we greatly look forward to celebrating the upcoming union of our dear son Ian and the lovely Duchess Mirabel."

I took that as my cue to curtsey, being certain to uphold pristine posture to ensure Mother couldn't find even a fraction of a flaw to pester me about later. As I rose, my gaze met Duke Ian's cold blue eyes, frosty enough to curse the realm with another month of winter. I formulated a sweet smile, taking Mother's advice by attempting to give off an impression that could rival that of a foreign princess.

"It's a pleasure to finally make your acquaintance, Duke Ian." I released my skirts with a subtle flick of my wrists, ensuring that the fabric draped elegantly over my curved hips.

The duke's pupils widened, nearly blacking out the blue of his irises. He approached me with two long strides, closing the distance between us in the time it took for my mother to let out a doughy sigh. Duke Ian reached for my hand, encompassing my petite fingers in his muscular grip. His hand was rough and hot, his grip a touch too tight for someone I had just met.

"Believe me, my dear duchess, the pleasure is all mine." He raised my hand to his lips and placed a wet kiss on the back of my hand that lingered for far longer than I appreciated while in front of our parents. His eyes never left mine as he ended the kiss, looking at me like I was the last slice of a decadent cake instead of his future wife. My skin squirmed under his touch, feeling uncomfortable around his tight grip until he finally released my hand and let it drop against my skirts. He extended the ruby-toned rose to me, flicking outward as if it were a concealed trick. "A token of my welcome, to introduce you to the flourishing beauty of our province that is rivaled only by you, my duchess." His flowery words made the rose feel fake in comparison. Before I could reach out to accept his gift, he lifted the flower up into my hair and nestled it into the edge of my twisted updo.

*Uh...*

If he was trying to be romantic, he was doing a wretched job of it. The rose's thick stem scraped against my scalp, snagging my hair on its ridges and pricking my head with its slender thorns. I clenched my smile, fighting the urge to shoo his hands from me like a pesky insect as he traced his hand all the way down my cheek, leaving me with the urge to dip my face in boiling water.

"Thank you," I said stiffly, clearing my throat for another falsified smile. "It's beautiful."

His brows flexed upward as he rested his hand on his lapel, raking his eyes over my soft features. "Indeed, it is." He slyly bit the corner of his lip, ensuring only I noticed it before taking a step backward.

For the first time in years, I felt like I might throw up without having consumed any of my allergens.

*Why is he so... creepy?*

Even after he returned my personal space to me, I could still feel his eyes tracing over me like a detailed scan. I flicked my gaze over to Mother and Father, wondering if they had noticed my discomfort, but they were now completely enraptured by Duke Ian's lavishing attention.

"It is such an honor to be in your company, Grand Duke, Grand Duchess." Ian bowed. I had barely known the man for a full minute and a half, yet he had already abandoned my side to schmooze with my parents.

*After all the grief Mother had given me about making good impressions, my betrothed seems content with eyeing me up and down and flirting with my parents.*

A tense lump started to formulate in my throat, but I forced myself to remain calm. We'd barely even met; surely, things would get better the more I got to know him.

"Grand Duke Brantley, I must say, you have raised the most beautiful daughter. I have courted many fine women in this realm, but none compare to her shining beauty." *I'm sorry, come again?* Duke Ian's voice was thick with charisma. His flashy smile and charming features practically hypnotized my mother, though my father's brows squashed together.

"She is indeed a vision of loveliness." Father cleared his throat, seemingly feeling the discomfort of the duke's unfiltered fondness for my appearance. "However, I do need to remind you of the importance of monitoring her health. While I'm glad that you find her... *ahem,* alluring, I will only approve this union if—"

"If her nutritional needs can be met and monitored at all times," Duke Ian finished with a prideful gleam in his eye that reflected off my father's impressed smile. "Have no worries, sir. I have already arranged for a separate kitchen, entirely dedicated to Duchess Mirabel's needs. Not even a shred of wheat will be permitted in or out, and we have already hired a team of specialized chefs and servers who will monitor and guard her meals from any and all contamination from her allergens."

Mother and Father's jaws practically dropped open, their eyes wide with relief that spanned across their joyful smiles. All ounces of reluctance vanished from Father's face and he latched his hand onto Ian's, giving him a firm shake. "Why don't we just have the ceremony now, then?!" He chuckled, smacking a hand of approval onto the duke's shoulder.

"If that's what you and the Grand Duchess desire, then I'd be more than happy to oblige." Ian laughed with my parents, the three of them buddying up like a clan of hyenas.

I took in a fiery breath, biting back my tongue to keep from spewing out something along the lines of, "Did you think to ask me first?" or "How about you explain the meal plans to me, instead of only my parents?" The more the conversation dwindled on, the more I realized that Ian was only interested in flashing me coy looks and sultry smiles, while directing all the actual conversation to my parents.

He knows I'm meant to be his wife and not a pet, right?

"It sounds to me like Mira will be more than comfortable here." Mother smiled vibrantly, squeezing her gloved hands together with unfiltered excitement.

"Indeed, she shall," Ian said assuredly, with a grin so smug, I knew it would only be two more minutes before I could withhold slapping it away. "Your daughter is very lucky to have me as a betrothed. I can assure you, she won't find anyone in the realms as capable of caring for her fragile beauty in the same way I can."

Okay, make that ten seconds...

"Fragile beauty?" My furious tone bit through the joyful air, cracking everyone's blissful reality like a rock through their stained-glass. All faces turned to me, Mother and Father's particularly red, like the way Ian's would soon be after I struck him. "Listen here, *Your Grace*." I stomped toward the puzzled duke, jeering a finger into his burley shoulder. "I am not *fragile*, or *weak*, or *delicate*. Tell me, Duke Ian, does this feel *fragile* to you?" I raised my hand above his cheek, preparing for the most satisfying clap of sound to fuel my pulsating adrenaline.

But my wrist was snatched mid-swing, and to my horror, Duke Ian had blocked me with a simple, yet strong, block. His polished smile looked the exact same, but there was an added glint in his frost-blue eyes that caused my courage to wilt.

"Why don't you and your family get settled?" he suggested in an oily tone, slick and shimmery with his iridescent grin. "We can visit more later."

# chapter two

The guard fell motionlessly onto the cobblestone, crumpling like a paper soldier, barely capable of saying the phrase, "Hold it right there!" or something similar in his rubbish language. You would think a man would scream a little louder when he saw a face like mine.

*Pathetic.*

The castle shadowed the western wall, flooding the paved garden paths with pointed silhouettes from the elongated turrets. Moss and dark green ivy burrowed into the edges of the wall, feeding off cool darkness and infecting the mortar with its invasive roots. I hooked my grasp underneath the limp guard's arms and dragged him into the bushes, where he could enjoy the sweet fragrance of thyme and mint while he took his lazy morning snooze.

The Dhurin castle had been buzzing since the moment I vaulted over its iron gates. Dozens of carriages trimmed in gold, silver, and platinum rolled up the cobble path, flying silk flags that appeared to represent family crests or other nods to nobility. While I wasn't sure what event had brought on such pomp, I wasn't going to neglect the advantage it gave me.

With so many distinguished guests flooding the doorway, a majority of the guard appeared to be outside, monitoring their arrivals. I lowered my gaze to the resting guard, raking my eyes over the fresh purple bruise on his temple before inspecting his uniform. He looked to be about my size... although the sleeves might be a little tight.

I unfastened the gaudy gold buttons and tugged the jacket off with a less-than-tender yank. The gold embroidery twisted into a blooming rose on the edge of the lapel, glittering against the small specks of light that had pushed through the castle's shadow. The guard's simple black trousers were similar enough to mine that I didn't bother swiping them, although his lacked rips and mud stains.

The coat fit me like a snug corset, or at least, what I presumed one felt like. The soldier had been much smaller than I originally gauged, causing my arms to feel squeezed and my neck half-choked. Ignoring the unpleasant compression, I glanced around the edge of the castle walls, pressing my tense spine against the fluffy lichen and moss. One of the carriages halted in front of the entryway, this one far grander than the rest with gold-trimmed doors, velvet curtains, and a family crest painted on the side, depicting a spread eagle clutching a bundle of grain and an olive branch in its talons. The door swung open and out stepped an older gentleman, whose physique sat on the border between well-fed and hefty. His chin was lost underneath his round cheeks and thick neck, while his broad nose spanned a majority of his features. He wore a crystal monocle and a brown waistcoat with a tan vest that held a rather expensive-looking pocket watch dangling from a brooch.

Behind him came a second man, who looked to be his complete opposite—tall and lanky, with long blonde hair tied in a low tail, which opposed his stout companion's dark comb-over. His features were narrow and long, with a pointed nose and thin brows that seemed to make his forehead go on forever. His gold suit jacket glittered like a burning candle, almost causing me not to notice the simple white gift clutched under his arm.

*A gift? So, it's some sort of christening celebration? Or perhaps a wedding?*

The next passenger to step out of the carriage answered my question for me. A young woman, probably in her mid-twenties, stepped out of the carriage in a blood-red gown. I may not have been around this realm long enough to know more than a few words of its language, but I did know that red was reserved for brides—but also formal events where there wasn't a bride present, and I suppose also the occasional red cloak?

I rolled my eyes, not feeling the need to decipher fashion trends at such a critical hour. Either way, the girl's dress informed me that this wasn't a wedding, or at least, not yet. Conquering the castle may be difficult with so many flashy guests who brought their flashy security. Perhaps it was best to wait until the majority of the guests cleared out...

*Unless...*

The golden key buried in my pocket felt as heavy as lead, forcing me to recall its presence. I gritted my teeth, swallowing back a growl as I dug the cool metal trinket out. Although the key was clearly gold, silver sparks and light radiated from within, the color of magic. I wrapped my fist around the key, squeezing it until my knuckles turned ashen.

*'If you use it, you're bowing to a power that's not your own.'*

I clenched against the voice scraping my mind, recognizing it as one that wasn't my own. The metal key warmed as my heat bled into it, relaxing my muscles until my clenched fist softened. I looked down at the key with balanced thoughts, then turned to the door the guard had failed to protect.

*'Don't be a fool, Conan,'* the voice rasped in my brain, clawing against my skull with a painful scratch. *'He wants you to rely on it, wants you to rely on him.'*

My shoulders tensed, but I wasn't sure if it was from the pressure in my thoughts or the suffocating jacket. I lifted the key to my unscarred eye, inspecting it with a narrowed gaze, as if my future could be seen in its brassy reflection.

"I'm not relying on anyone," I seethed between my teeth,

positioning the glistening key above the lock. "If the king wants to share his tricks with me, then let him be the fool who handed over his crown."

I pressed the key into the lock and it clicked with ease.

*Let's see what his toys can do.*

The door swung open like the *creak* of a widening treasure chest. Light poured through the opening, and my eyes widened like a new moon, slowly being eclipsed by my wicked grin.

*I see... Perhaps a party is just what I need.*

• • • • • • • • • • • • • • • • • • • • • • • • • • • • • • • • • • • • • •

"Mirabel Jada Brantley, do you have any idea the kind of trouble you could have caused!?" Mother jeered a scolding finger a breath away from my nose, her face as red as the itchy rose still nestled in my hair. "After all the difficulty your father and I went through to secure you a husband that was willing to cater to your health, you go off and nearly strike him after having barely made introductions." She flailed her arms up in the air, reminding me of an irritated pigeon, flaring its feathers up before fleeing in frustration.

Father occupied the plush armchair in the corner of the room, eyeing me with disappointment that also masked a touch of concern.

I rested my shoulder against the side of the bedpost as I picked at my brittle nails, sitting half-sunk into the fluffy mattress that took up only a fraction of my enormous suite. "I'm sorry, Mother, but I can hardly apologize," I said frankly, shrugging in the same manner I would to deny sugar in my tea. "He was being rude. If this union is going to have any chance at success, I refuse to sit idly by and let him treat me like a frilly Pomeranian that he can hand off to a servant when it starts to yap and bite." I leveled my eyes, meeting Mother's flustered rage with firm defiance.

Her manicured nails dug into her palms, causing her arms to tremble with an unladylike lack of control. "Mirabel... If I had known you were going to be so *ungrateful,* then—"

"Hold on just a moment, dear," Father interjected, rising from his seat to place a soothing hand on Mother's near combusting shoulder. His gentle gaze turned to me, searching me like a scrambled map he couldn't quite figure out. "Let's all take a deep breath and approach the situation more calmly. You know as well as I do that Mira would never rebel against us without good reason. Before you both start rattling the doors of this suite with a screaming match, let's at least attempt to discuss this civilly."

The tensions that had wound around my chest seemed to ease, allowing a shallow breath to release, long and slow. "Thank you, Father." I straightened, pressing out the wrinkles in my skirts as I mentally smoothed my ruffled emotions.

*Father is right, reacting in anger isn't going to fix this engagement.*

Mother's fury also seemed to decrease as she allowed Father to guide her to the arm-chair he had previously occupied. She sank into the chair with a tight-lipped frown, crossing her arms stiffly over her hardened heart. "Alright," she clipped. "Tell us then, why do you dislike the duke?"

*Let's see... he's arrogant, dismissive, controlling, clearly full of himself...*

"I don't feel that he will respect me as an equal," I answered honestly, but still polished my answer enough to appeal to Mother.

She crinkled her brow, pursing her lips as she shifted against the cushioned seat. "I don't understand. He seemed perfectly considerate to your father and I. I mean, did you even hear how much attention he has put toward your meal preparation? Honestly, Mira, I don't understand how you could find any fault in him."

Fire sparked on the back of my tongue, but I doused it with a cool breath. "Mother, there is more to me than just my ailments. While I appreciate the efforts the young duke has gone to, I feel that they are slightly misplaced." My pulse threatened to elevate, thumping my heart against my ribs with a new rigidness.

"Misplaced? Mira, you've hardly even met the man." Mother flung her crossed arms into the air with a smack against the edge of the chair. "It's not every day that a duke is willing to go to such lengths to acquire the hand of a young woman. You should be honored, not nitpicking his first impression."

My muscles tightened. *Funny... When I risked making a poor impression, I was being a disgrace. Yet, now that he's made one, I'm the one who's a hypocrite.*

"I think your mother has a point," Father chimed in, placing another cooling touch on Mother's arm. I snapped my gaze at him with wounded eyes, wondering when he'd suddenly drawn battle lines against me. "About you hardly knowing the duke, that is... Perhaps you two simply got off on the wrong foot. How about this...? Why don't you head down to the ballroom and mingle with the guests as they arrive? Duke Ian is sure to be there since he's hosting, so the two of you can spend a little more time working out the wrinkles of your... rocky introduction."

The bed I was sitting on suddenly felt far more comfortable than it had before, calling me to snuggle into it and avoid crowds, snobby nobles, and a brutish betrothed. I glanced over at Mother, looking to gage her reaction to Father's plan, and to my regret saw that her settled postured and relaxed jaw meant she was on board.

*Wonderful.*

"Very well." I reluctantly rose from the bed, feeling my achy joints protest the movement after days of uncomfortable travel. "I'll give him a second chance, but if I continue to discover flaws in our arrangement, I should hope that you two would be receptive to hearing my concerns." I gave them a taut glare, digging more into Father's sympathy than Mother's unyielding pride.

"Of course, my dear." Father smiled warmly, his round features wrinkling from the curve in his lips. "We only want what's best for you and our province."

My anxiety eased a touch, releasing some of the strain I had felt in my neck and shoulders as I fluffed out my skirt in the mirror before turning toward the door. When I stepped out into the lavish hallway, my lungs released an irritated sigh. The halls were wide and filled with ornate paintings, tapestries, and crystal floor mosaics, but I still felt suffocated behind the stone.

*It is no wonder my brother decided to give up his title... He likely knew how frustrating an arranged marriage would be.*

My heart clenched as I thought back to Zac and his darling wife, Ro. They had barely been married a month at this point, but it was no doubt their love for each other was already timeless. I'd always known that accepting his title would come with the cost of an arranged marriage, but I'd always placed it in my mind as a bridge I would cross when I arrived at it. Well, it was here now, and the envy I felt toward my brother's happiness was finally starting to gnaw at me.

I adored Zac, I truly did. But between his freedom to marry for love and his health permitting him to work directly under the emperor, I couldn't help but feel as if he was the one living out all the dreams I'd once had. As soon as it became known that my illness was chronic, all my studies of espionage and combat were replaced with diplomatic etiquette and political affairs.

In some ways, it was a gift Zac had offered me of his inheritance, since it allowed me to do more for my province than simply watch from a window. At least now I could put my power to good use and aid in the investigation of the griffins and their branch groups. That is... if my future husband didn't prevent me from doing more than lift a dainty finger.

Eerie silence followed me as I passed through the halls, only striking me as odd when I realized this was the third corner I had turned without seeing a single guard.

*Are they all at the party?*

I halted at the top of the stairs, peering down the banister to look for the bearded guard who had been present upon our arrival.

*No one...*

Maybe it was because I had been thinking about the griffins, or maybe it was because I had just reminisced on my desires to do more than be a duchess, but something inside me pulled at me to investigate the upper halls before descending to the ballroom. I swept back down the way I'd come, this time exploring the branching hallways before coming to the conclusion that there wasn't a single guard on this floor.

*Where did they all go?*

I turned back toward my suite, deciding this was an odd enough occurrence to alert my parents—and potentially even get out of attending the party. When I rounded the corner that I had come from, I nearly tripped over my skirts as I skidded to an abrupt stop. Walking down the hall was a guard.

I could only see his back, but he was definitely wearing the Dhurin uniform with a dark blue jacket covered in detailed gold embroidery. He was tall, and definitely far more muscular than most of the other guards, with black hair and olive skin, but his pant legs were soiled with dirt and what appeared to be grass stains.

I watched him trudge through the halls for a moment, his movements stiff and commanding, more like that of a noble than a castle guard. He didn't seem to be attending a post or even doing routes, but every time he passed a doorway, he stopped and locked it with a chunky golden key. My brow lifted, and I followed him with quiet steps.

*Is this some sort of security protocol?*

One by one, he clicked the key into every door, until he approached what appeared to be a closet that possessed no lock. I side-stepped behind a large marble bust that looked more like a scraggly dog than whatever nobleman it was meant to honor, and peered out to observe the guard. My eyes bulged indelicately as I watched the man place his key above the lockless knob, twisting it in the air until an audible *click* permeated the silence.

*What in the realms…?*

I leaned further out from behind my hiding spot, even more intrigued by the guard's odd task than before. When I latched my gaze back onto him, I saw he was now approaching the door to *my* suite. The suite that my parents were still inside of.

*He isn't going to lock them inside, is he?*

He positioned the key in front of the lock and my will to stay hidden vanished as quick as a candle's flicker. "Sir, wait a moment!" I hitched up the edge of my skirt and waved at the man as I hurried forward. "Please don't lock that door, my family is—"

My breath caught in my throat like a lump of stone as the guard turned to me with the blackest eyes I had ever seen. His dark hair swept over the edge of his forehead, emphasizing the angle of his chiseled jawline and prominent chin. His nose was cleanly angled and tilted down a touch, looking foreign from most Omairans or Dhurins that I'd seen before. His broad shoulders seemed to be nearly splitting the seams in his snug coat, highlighting the defined curves of his muscles and daunting height. He would have been handsome, in a devilish sort of way, if it wasn't for the hideous scars that stretched across his face and neck, adding streaky red veins to the white of his right eye.

I pressed a hand to the edge of my lip as I took in a sharp breath. *Why does he look so… familiar?* I tried to study his face further, but blinked away when I realized how rude my staring must have come across. While my physical abnormality wasn't visible like his was, I knew what it was like to be treated differently.

"I, uh... I'm sorry. I only meant to ask—" My voice broke off with a stunned squeak as the man turned his back to me and proceeded to shove the key into the lock, completely ignoring me like I was a needy child. "I beg your pardon, sir." I placed my hand on his arm to try to spin him around, but his arms felt as solid as steel, and he shook off my touch with barely a flinch.

My pestering at least got his attention because he snapped his onyx gaze to me, the dark color void of any respect toward our difference in status.

*Status or not, he should at least have the courtesy to answer me.*

I tightened my gaze on him, leaving no room for argument as I matched his intense stare. "I demand you unlock this door at once." I pointed at the door with a viperous flick of my wrist, pressing my other hand to my hip. He didn't look away from me, only studying me like I was an unusual moth that had fluttered across his path. His unmoving stare both aggravated and captivated me all at once. *Where have I seen that face before?* "What is your name? I should like to—"

Like a bucket of water being thrown on a flame, my body shriveled. My heart stopped, filling with dread as my brain slowly filled in the missing pieces to this man's identity. Those dark eyes, the way they watched my lips without understanding the sound they made... The scars that striped his face from the vicious claws of a wolf.

His sketched portrait flashed in front of my eyes like a blurred nightmare, the words bold in freshly dried ink.

*Conan Leander*

*Wanted for association with "The Beasts."*

"Y-you're the last beast." My voice wavered as my foot cautiously slid back against the crystal floor. "You're Conan."

His eyes widened at the sound of his name, causing the red veins in his injured eye to dilate and deepen. My first instinct was to run, but he was still standing in front of the door my parents were behind. What was that key going to do to them?

Before I could even attempt to decipher his schemes, he clicked the key into the lock and pushed the door open, rushing inside like a prisoner desperate for escape.

"Wait! Stop!" The danger that had saturated me with fear had converted into pure adrenaline as I watched the beast who nearly killed my brother and his wife dart for my parents.

The door slammed in my face, nearly smacking me in the nose before I managed to stop. Without hesitation, I twisted the door knob, nearly fainting with relief when it pushed open without resistance. I burst through the door like a frenzied animal, barely even looking up until I had passed the threshold.

"Mother! Fath—"

I stiffened. They weren't here, and the beast wasn't here, either. Because this wasn't my suite.

My chest heaved with labored breaths that felt so airy, I thought I might black out. Dozens of stunned and puzzled faces looked up at me, painted with cosmetics and dripping in glitzy accessories.

This was the ballroom.

# chapter three

I spun around on my heel to look back at the door I'd crossed through, only nearly colliding with a footman.

"Pardon me, Your Grace." The footman stepped aside, giving me a full view of the ten-foot-tall ornate door. I practically pushed past the bewildered man, inspecting the door with festering panic.

*Where did...? How did he...?*

The cedar door was carved with delicate leaves and vines, painted in iridescent shades of bronze and copper. My stance wavered as I gawked up at the massive double door, which couldn't have possibly been the same as the simple suite door I'd burst through.

*How in the realms did it lead me here? And where did my suite go?*

I grabbed the oversized handles and leaned back to put all my weight into a hard yank, but froze when an undesirable voice halted my movements.

"Ah, Duchess Mirabel, so glad you could join us." Duke Ian's slick voice split through my ears like the screech of nails against slate. "I do hope the arrangements were to your liking."

*They were when I could find them...*

I released the door and turned to face my betrothed, unsurprised to find a young woman hanging on his arm with a snug yellow dress that left little to the imagination. Behind him were two noblemen, approximately the same age, each with a

31

bubbling glass of rosewater and tonic between their fingers.

"Your Grace, have you happened to see my parents?" I looked straight past the duke and his entourage, searching the kaleidoscope of ballgowns, feathered hats, and jewelry for any chance that my family ended up in here, too.

"Your parents? No, my dear, they have yet to join the festivities." He scoffed with a prudish smile, as if my searching for them was something to find humor in. "Gentlemen, Lady Henrietta, allow me to introduce you to my betrothed, Duchess Mirabel Jada Brantley of Omaira. I truly am a lucky man, indeed."

"I suppose you're prettier than the duke's previous courtships," Lady Henrietta commented in a shrill voice, similar to that of an out-of-tune flute. She released the duke's arm for a brief moment, long enough to lower into a half-hearted curtsey that's true purpose seemed to be to look me up and down. "I must say, Your Grace, you truly do look lovely for someone who derives from Omaira... a far more *rural* part of the realm." She rose to her full height, giving me a distasteful look, as if reigning in a province full of forests meant that I should have had straw sticking out of my hair and manure on my skirts.

"I don't know, Lady Henrietta... I think rural girls can have a bit of charm to them." One of the duke's companions, a stout man with a crooked front tooth and an expensive red tail coat, chuckled with a nauseating wink. "It's like finding an untamed mare. Quite the exotic acquisition." He elbowed the duke in the ribs, and the entire entourage burst into revolting laughter.

I've had my patience tested before; I truly have. But never in my life have I shown as much control as to not stamp on my betrothed's foot, grab him by his ridiculous ponytail, and kick him with my heel until he tumbled over the balcony. That didn't necessarily mean that I couldn't do it later... But right now, I needed to figure out what had happened to my suite, and where the beast had disappeared to. I snapped my attention back to my horrid betrothed, searching his eyes for any sign of seriousness

I could latch onto. Unfortunately, his broad smile and uplifted chin really only showcased enough hot air in his head to sail a ship, without leaving much room for anything of importance. I forced my pride into the deep depths of my aggravated soul, reminding myself that I could always make a second attempt at blackening the duke's eye after my family was safe.

"Ian, please. I need to find my family. Something is—"

"*Duke* Ian," he corrected, snapping his fingers an inch away from my face with a scowl that should have been reserved for scolding a child or a misbehaving pet. My voice choked in my throat, too appalled by his insolence to formulate words. His full lips slid sideways, forming the start of a crooked grin. "We're not married yet, dear duchess. So, let's not drop the formalities, especially in the presence of such fine company." He patted a hand atop the glove of his arm candy and glanced around at his entourage, whose priggish smiles were in full support of their duke's disrespect toward me.

*Why you insufferable, bull-headed, egotistical, spoiled lump of muscles...*

I curled my lips into a poised smile, sweeter than the nectar of a honeysuckle in full bloom. "Oh, but Ian dear, I find that the lack of a title suits you. Since you clearly prefer to surround yourself in *ahem,* things of lesser quality, it only seems appropriate that I refrain from formalities." I fluttered my lashes with the elegance of a butterfly's wing, settling my gaze on the gawking fury of Lady Henrietta. "After all, you wouldn't want to be known as the duke in the company of farmers or servants, would you? I'd imagine you'd be quite embarrassed to admit your title amongst such a crowd."

Duke Ian's face flushed as red as his irritating rose that still remained twisted in my hair. He dropped Lady Henrietta's arm and sulked forward, his voice a low hiss. "Mirabel..."

"Ah, that would be *Duchess* Mirabel to you." I pressed my palm flat in front of his face, only inches from his clenched jaw. "I have not sullied my title amongst those unworthy of my attentions, therefore, I would appreciate if you upheld formalities." I gave him an even glare, my dark eyes cold enough to snap him frozen as I gracefully turned toward the stairway. "Now, if you'll excuse me. I need to find someone who is actually competent of listening to this *rural* duchess's needs."

My chest flared with vicious satisfaction as I flicked my skirts like a flaunting peacock. I didn't have time to train a puppy when there was a beast running about. Since I couldn't rely on my betrothed for help, I would have to find someone else to listen. Perhaps there was a guard in here I could alert...

I fled down the grand staircase, catching my eyes on the elegant spindles twisted with golden vines and ruby roses, no doubt in honor of our realm. The gray marble floors looked similar to a clouded galaxy, dotted with flecks of glittering mica and swirled with milky white stone. Chandeliers dripped with crystals and emerald adorned the floral-painted ceilings, basking the dance floor in a warm glow that made the windowless ballroom feel cozy and intimate. A few of the chattering guests silenced as they watched me descend the stairs, likely curious as to why the bride-to-be wasn't accompanied by her betrothed.

I tried to ignore their gossiping whispers, instead scanning the ballroom for any glimpses of a blue guard uniform. Most of the women had worn red—as was traditional for all but the bride at a betrothal celebration. This should have made it simple to locate at least one blue-clad guard, but nonetheless, I felt as if I was hunting for a black cat in a coal cellar.

*Where have all the guards gone?*

I nibbled the edge of my lip, darting my eyes around the cluster of polished noblemen and ladies a little more chaotically now that I didn't have a higher view. I slid past flouncy ballgowns and weaseled around a few glitzy canes, seeking anyone who would listen if I told them that my bedroom teleported me here. But there was no one... Not a single guard or even a servant rounding with trays of peach cider.

"Your Grace, is everything alright?"

I snapped around a little too frantically, my face hot and flushed as if I'd just completed a morning jog. I wasn't sure who I was expecting to see speaking to me, but I hadn't imagined it to be a stunning young woman in an elegant red gown that flared out at her knees. She had gorgeous skin, close to the color of freshly made caramel, with round eyes in an olive green. She was at least a half foot shorter than me, but her slightly upturned nose and clean-cut cheekbones showed signs of maturity that made it clear she was at least my age, if not older. Her hair was a dark walnut color that framed her slender chin at a shortened length with darling spiral curls. As beautiful as the woman was, there was one feature in particular that drew my eye more than any other.

*She has silver hair...*

Tucked an inch behind her ear, and pinned off with a pearl comb, was a glittering streak of silver intertwined with her dark curls.

*If she's a mage, then perhaps she can help me make sense of what's happened.*

I hastily dipped into a curtsey, barely even noticing the two chaperones who swept up behind her. "I fear that something does trouble me. Miss... Forgive me, to whom do I have the honor of speaking to?" I looked up through my dark lashes, noticing the girl's gentle features twist into soft concern.

"My name is Lady Azura Tressa." She dipped into a flawless curtsey with angles clean enough to out-sparkle the chunky ruby necklace around her throat. Her chaperones followed suit and bowed behind her. The one on her left was tall and slender, with a gold coat that glittered under the candlelight, while the other was his complete opposite, with only simple brown attire and a gaudy pocket watch. "These are my uncles, Lord Illumen and his brother, Lord Tocken. May I be so bold as to ask what troubles you, Your Grace? Is there anything my uncles and I can do to assist?"

My gaze drifted toward the stripe of silver behind the girl's ear, and then again around the ballroom vacant of protective personnel. "Have you noticed that all the guards have suddenly vanished?" I lowered my voice, suddenly concerned that I might alight the entire ballroom with worry if they were to overhear.

Lady Azura's soft eyes tightened for a moment, scrunching her thick lashes and crinkling her brow as she darted her gaze around the room.

"No guards?" Lord Tocken, the uncle with the flamboyant pocket watch, huffed gruffly. His salt and pepper hair was greased back, covering what appeared to be a balding spot on the crown of his head. "That seems rather inconsiderate for the grand duke to neglect assigning any." He frowned as he searched the room, though he looked rather humorous since his stout height made it near-impossible to see over the fluttering crowds.

"Relax, brother." Lord Illumen smacked a hand atop Lord Tocken's shoulder, hard enough to cause him to jolt and send his pocket watch swaying. "Don't go getting offended simply because you don't see anyone. I'm certain they're here somewhere. Perhaps they are in disguise, so they don't cause too much distraction during the celebration. Oh, congratulations by the way, Your Grace." Lord Illumen gave me another bow, this time with a swirling flourish of his hand that caused his glittering coat to catch the light off his sleeve.

*I hadn't considered they were in disguise... But even so, I still needed to find one to alert them about the beast.*

"Do you think you can help me locate one of them?" I asked a little more eagerly than intended. "You see, something happened to me only moments before I entered the ballroom..." I swept in a breath, unsure if this bit of information was necessary or if it would convince them I was mad.

Lady Azura's brows tilted outward, her smooth skin accenting the twinkle of worry in her lovely olive eyes. "Of course, we'll help, Your Grace. Whatever happened, I'm sure it is severe if it has left you this troubled." She gave me a soft nod, and I felt the tension in my chest lighten, knowing that at least one person in this ballroom had possessed the ear to listen. Lady Azura was far more receptive to me than—

"Has something left the duchess troubled?" Like a drip of color escaping from a canvas, Duke Ian slipped out of the blur of vibrant guests to sweep up between Lady Azura and me. His eyes still burned at me with distaste, but his smile was entirely unreadable. "Ah, Lady Azura, so pleased that you and your uncles could make it. I must say, you look as ravishing as a proper Dhurin rose in that gown." His tone warmed a touch as he addressed the young lady, much like a child would when they were looking for a square of chocolate.

"Thank you, Your Grace." Lady Azura curtseyed, but her movements swayed a touch more than they did when she greeted me. "Your betrothed and I were just discussing how it seems odd that there are scarcely any guards present this evening."

Instead of looking around the room like we all had, he snapped his chilling gaze onto me with an accusatory grimace. "Is this what troubles you, duchess? Well surely, if the quantity of guards disturbs you, then you could come to me with your concerns, instead of troubling our esteemed guests." His tone had a touch of a bite at the end of his words, and it took me a moment to recognize that he didn't actually believe I was merely discussing the ballroom's security. He assumed we'd been gossiping about him.

*Of course, because everything in the duke's mind is about him it seems...*

"Your Grace, I beg you to recall that I did attempt to bring up the matter with you, and you were too busy with your *acquaintances* to listen." I narrowed my eyes like a cobra in wait, holding back my lashes in hopes that he might actually offer me aid.

"Well, I can hardly be bothered by such matters when you approach me so brashly," he huffed, tightening his perfect jaw with an unattractive clench. "You are my betrothed. You'll need to learn better than to interrupt me when I'm partaking in social events."

The rose in my hair suddenly felt like it had doubled in size and weight, digging its thorns into my scalp like a piercing rapier trying to skewer me into submission. Any ounce of restraint I'd been nurturing was as far gone as my disappearing suite. "Hold your tongue, *Ian*." I stormed in front of him, closing the few feet of distance with chilling speed, holding myself only inches from his hardened expression. "If you wish to wed me, then you *will* treat me with respect, and you *will* listen to me when I am fearful for the safety of my family and our people. The guards are missing, my parents are locked inside a missing bedroom, your ballroom door is enchanted, and there's a beast wandering the castle. If you don't find those concerns worthy of interrupting your amusements, then I shall hunt down my family on my own and burn your roses on my way out."

Lady Azura pressed a scandalized hand to her full lips, darting her eyes between me, the duke, and her chaperones, who looked equally bewildered. I stepped back from Ian, distancing our proximity so he couldn't feel the fire radiating off my burning skin.

He was the picture of collected rage. His neck was bulging with throbbing veins, his jaw clamped and grinding, and his right eye twitched, yet he smiled. It was a gritted smile, but a smile, nonetheless—the type only a well-rehearsed politician could present in the midst of a spiral of unsettling emotions and humiliation.

"My dear duchess, it would seem that your travels have

made you wary." He exhaled sharply, causing his tension to deflate like a punctured soufflé. "I mean, enchanted doors?" He chuckled, folding his bulky arms with a bounce of his shoulders.

Lady Azura's features furrowed. "Actually, Your Grace, that's not entirely—"

"The duchess is clearly feeling weak from her ailment and lack of rest," the duke interrupted with a commanding lift of his palm. "As you can see, there is a perfectly attentive guard standing right over there; therefore, the duchess is clearly overstrained and allowing her thoughts to cloud." He gestured across the room at a tall guard whose back was turned to us. My eyes bulged as I took in his dark blue uniform, muddied trousers, and the small edge of a scar on the back of his neck. *The beast.* "Wait here, my dear. I shall fetch the guard and have him escort you to your chambers, where you can rescue your *imprisoned* parents." He laughed once more, already making his way through the crowd to greet the wolf in sheep's clothing.

"Ian, wait!" I snagged the edge of his sleeve, desperately trying to yank him back. "That's not a guard, he's the—"

"*Duke* Ian," he snapped, jerking his arm free before smoothing out his coat. His blue eyes burned with a frozen fire stolen straight from the underworld. "Don't make me correct you again, *duchess.*"

I stiffened, unable to voice my frustrations as my throat clamped around itself while the beast turned his scarred eyes in my direction. They were so dark... like a starless sky in a vacant countryside. The duke didn't wait for me to snap out of my paralysis, and instead turned back to the beast, pushing his way through the crowd until he was nearly in front of him. My numbness vanished with a rib-bruising thud of my heart as I turned back to Lady Azura and her uncles.

"Quickly, we must get everyone out of here." I grabbed Lady Azura by the arm, unable to prevent my brittle nails from digging into her caramel skin.

Her chest heaved with shallow breaths. "Why? What's the matter?"

A cry of terror split through the ballroom, shrill enough to shatter the crystals dripping from the chandeliers. I jerked toward the sound and saw that it was Lady Henrietta who had screamed. She must have tried to meet with the duke when she saw him leave me, and now she was only mere feet from where the dead-eyed beast held a wicked dagger to Ian's throat.

Gasps and shrieks echoed around us, and my latch around Lady Azura's arm tightened as I leaned in closer to her shuddering form to whisper, "That's the beast."

# chapter four

*'If you wish to obtain power, you must display power. Without it, you are nothing.'*

I tightened my grip around the squirming nobleman's arm, ensuring that the edge of my blade was gently pricking his skin enough to declare that I meant business. The man's thick biceps made it no mystery that my captive was strong, but his fighting ceased the moment a minor trickle of blood warmed his neck.

*So predictable...*

The guests gawked and swooned in horror as they fled toward the useless doors. I waited patiently as they comedically rushed through the doorways, only to burst out of another on the opposite side of the room. A few of the guests seemed to catch on rather quickly for a dim-witted wellborn, while the others remained less astute and ran back through the doors they'd exited, only to return to where they started. A wicked smile warmed my cold heart as the memories of securing each door with my glistening key fluttered through my mind like a harmonious symphony.

*Welcome to my cage...*

The guests cowered back like frightened animals basking before a raging forest fire, each of their eyes glued to the measly drop of blood on the nobleman's throat.

*'Yes, make them cower. Show them your strength, prove your worth to me.'*

"Well then, now that I've got your attention, let's have

a little chat." I raised my free wrist to my mouth and tugged off one of the golden charm bracelets with my teeth. I then twisted the woven band around my fingers and shoved it against my victim's throat, earning another collective gasp from my audience. The gold glittered to life, both against the nobleman's tense throat and my wrist, connecting our tongues to the same language. "Hello, pet. Happy to hear my melodious voice, are you? Why don't you be a sweet little dear and translate to your friends that escape is useless. Every door in this castle is now under my complete control, and anyone who was outside this ballroom has now been directed outside alongside the guards."

The man's muscles constricted, causing my blade to flinch against his throat. "I am the duke of this province. I will not bow to your threats," he spat, jerking his eyes upward to attempt a glare at me. "Release me at once and your punishment shall at least be swift."

*'Well, won't this be fun.'*

I pulled the blade from his throat and traced it gently up the man's face, barely grazing the skin enough to tickle before I stopped under his right eye. "So, you're a duke, are you?" I whispered with my tedious movements. "Does that mean this is your party? Let me guess... It's an engagement ball for that lovely duchess with the rose in her hair. It would only make sense since she appeared to be occupying the grandest of the guest suites I had explored. She also bears a remarkable resemblance to her brother... the Duke of Omaira, was he?"

Impressively, the man's resolve remained firm and he didn't even flinch at my threat against his bride. "What does it matter if she's a duchess or a slave? It seems to me that your business is with Dhurin, *my* province."

*'A man of business? How useful...'*

The voice in the back of my brain itched at me like an untouchable scratch, forcing me to simply let it play out, no matter how disruptive it became. I leaned my blade closer to the duke's flawless skin, brushing a stray hair from his brow with the glistening edge. "I just think it would be a shame for the groom to have his face bandaged during the ceremony. It's so painful to have your eye clawed by a wolf, you know... I wonder if it would be any less so, coming from a beast? I could certainly go slower to ensure that—"

"Enough!" the duke growled, his face flushed with sweat beading handsomely on his brow. "I'll translate. Just lower your blade."

A smirk twitched at my mouth, pleasing the voice in my head with a rush of adrenaline. I skimmed the blade along the edge of his face, shaving a flurry of stubble from the side of his chin before resting it against his jaw. "Go on then, since you're clearly adept at running your mouth."

He muttered an unsavory word under his breath, then turned to the cowering masses with an unshaken expression. "He's using some sort of cursed object to speak to me. He wants you all to know that the doors are under his control and the guards have been led outside." Shuddering cries and panicked gasps followed, each clinging their gaze to the duke as if he was somehow going to save them with a flip of his perfect hair.

"Well done. At this rate, you might get to keep those pretty teeth of yours." I glazed my eyes around the room, taking in a headcount of the fine hostages I'd acquired. There were at least fifty of them, each more grandly dressed than the next. My gaze snagged on the young duchess for a moment, her vibrant teal dress standing out amongst the sea of red and purple. Her eyes were nearly as dark as mine, but they held a soft warmth to them, much like that of an acorn in a cluster of autumn leaves. The sea-glass-toned silk she wore hugged her gentle curves like a fine sheath held its sword, causing me to wonder if the sharp glare in her eyes was as pointed as it seemed.

"She certainly is a lovely bride..." I cooed in my captive's ear, enjoying the view of his hackles rising. "If you wish for her pretty face to remain, then I suppose it's about time I read you off my list of demands."

A growl rose in the duke's throat, sounding far more like a beast than I ever had. "What do you want? Gold? Jewels?"

"Your province," I whispered, allowing my eyes to dance around the glittering ballroom imagining the changes I would make once it was mine. *I'd certainly get rid of all the ridiculous roses...* "If you want to see your guests make it out of this ballroom alive, then I require for you to hand over your birthright. Don't bother to offer me anything less, for I will only be satisfied when I am named the new duke of Dhurin."

The onlooking crowd darted their eyes from me to their current master, biting their tongue in wait for any translation he would give them. The duke lifted his chin, his eyes cold with a frozen fire. "You're mad," he hissed. His voice sounded too timid to be any way threatening to me. "Dhurin may be my birthright, but the province is still under the control of my parents, the grand duke and duchess. I'm afraid you're only dulling your blade against my meager throat."

My veins tightened, causing my hand to twitch only a fraction of a hair before I regained my thoughts. *Of course... I need to entrap the grand duke, not his useless son.* I bit my tongue until the pain numbed my thoughts, trying to recalculate my misstep before it was noticed.

**'Another mistake? How disappointing...'**

"Shut up," I rasped under my breath, ignoring the odd side-eye from the puzzled duke. Once the voice was silenced, my thoughts collected into a new plan of attack. *You still have hostages... You don't need the grand duke present to make them useful.* "Very well, then. If you can't be useful, then I suppose you'll have to serve as a messenger." I removed the blade from his jaw and smacked my hand on his shoulder, dragging him back to the nearest servant's door with me as the crowd cried out in terror. "Tell your sweet party guests that their grand duke has...

oh, a little over two days to hand over his province to me. For every hour he refuses to abide by my demands, I shall take the life of one of his precious nobles..."

This finally rattled the duke, causing him to snap his head around like a wild mare on a lead. "No! You can't kill them!" He snapped his pearly teeth shut the moment his voice betrayed the privacy of our conversation. While the charm he was touching allowed him to understand my words, the only voice our audience could interpret was the panicked cries of their beloved duke. The squirming infant's eyes went wild, biting his lip as he attempted to rein in the damage he had done. "H-he said that he wants the province, and if he doesn't receive it..." He swore, biting back his voice before he killed anyone prematurely with a swift heart attack.

"Don't worry, dear duke..." I whispered with a fiendish squeeze of his arm. "I'll start with your darling bride. That way she won't have to watch the rest of the suffering unfold."

"You're a beast," he spat, his eyes now fixated on his citizens' horrified expressions.

"If you say so," I growled, feeling a twisted smile radiate from my features as a familiar voice tickled my pulsing brain.

*'Isn't their panic perfectly pleasurable, my boy? Well done.'*

The internal praise caused my sickly smile to flourish as I watched the hysterical captives flutter around in a panic like it was a grand display of theatre. I'd done it. They feared me. They feared the beast who had been cast aside from a foolish pack. And soon, they would be under my control, just like things should have been all along. All that was left was to end a few measly lives and take the first claim to power. First Dhurin's castle; next, the emperor's palace, and then I'll hunt down the golden imp...

*How about it, Father? Are you finally proud of me?*

*'If you have to ask, you'll never know.'*

That was when a scream ended our conversation.

• • • • • • • • • • • • • • • • • • • • • • • • • • • • • • • •

"No! You can't kill them!"

Duke Ian's cry cut off like the final squeal of a slaughtered pig, leaving us all in the ringing silence of his grim exclamation.

*The beast is going to kill us...*

Before I could even shake free from my paralysis, the entire ballroom erupted into hysterics. Ladies burst into sobs, the men kicked at the unlocked doors, and the others scattered like a broken pearl necklace.

"H-he said he wants the province, and if he doesn't receive it..." The duke silenced himself, his darting eyes and the pulsating vein in his forehead already informing us that our captor was prepared for the worst.

I couldn't move. Despite my earlier desire to blacken the duke's eye, I couldn't help but feel suffocated by the view of the blade skimming against his neck. Ian may have been insufferable, but he wasn't weak. Seeing a man with a foolish amount of bravado and muscles that could overpower an ox shriek in fear made me feel just as fragile as the velvety rose petals in my hair.

*What do we do?*

The beast's mismatched eyes snapped to me, freezing my blood solid as a snakelike grin slithered up his face. I could barely hear the foreign drawl of his words atop the fussing crowd, the sound of his cryptic language sending a shuddering chill down my spine.

Ian's attention shot to me, their combined gazes making me realize it was likely *I* was the subject of their concealed conversation.

*Oh, realms, what are they saying? Is Ian telling the beast he wants me dead first?*

"You're a beast." I could scarcely hear Ian, but his body-clenching scowl made it at least obvious that he wasn't on board with whatever the beast had spoken.

My stomach roiled with nearly the same amount of pain that came from ingesting a dinner roll. We were all trapped in a ballroom with the most dangerous criminal in the Ruby Realm... and I had the chance to warn everyone but failed.

I wanted to crumple to the ground, but my bones were locked in place, unrelenting to my mind's wish to run or pound against the doors with the others. I saw the beast; I watched him lock the doors with that bizarre key. If I hadn't wasted my time arguing with Ian, then maybe his neck would be littered with Henrietta's kisses instead of dribbles of blood. I have to do something. I hate him, but he's still my betrothed, and these are still my future citizens.

*But what do I do? I have no weapons, no skills in combat, and I don't wield magic—*

Pain clawed against my scalp, forcing a scream from me as the thick rose stem was yanked relentlessly from my hair. The thorns snagged on my every strand of hair, causing the brittle pieces to snap while the jagged points scratched itchy cuts against my skull.

I don't know if it was truly that painful, or if being paralyzed for so long had caused my voice to build to a grand release, but every eye turned straight onto me and the delicate hand that now held my stolen rose.

"Lady Azura?" I eyed the girl's fixated stare on the lavish rose while rubbing a hand against the shredded patch of my scalp. "What are you—"

"Quiet, I need to focus." She silenced me with a sharp snap of her tongue, her eyes never wavering from the center of the rose as she stared at it like it was a forbidden jewel. The entire ballroom must have heard her hush me, because silence enveloped the grand room, aside from the occasional sniffle or sobbing gasp.

She traced her fingers along the edge of the outstretched petals, caressing it as she swirled her touch in a spiral toward the center of the bloom, then followed it all the way down the stem. My breath caught in my throat like a fragile bubble, afraid to burst and cause even the slightest disruption as I watched the silver section of her hair glitter to life. The small twist of curls sparkled like powdered diamonds, illuminating with a silver glow similar to that of a winter's moon. Her deep olive-green eyes squeezed shut, then reopened with a more vibrant shade, mirroring that of a fresh oak leaf with a ray of sun shining through it. She placed her palm flat over the top of the rose, and in an unmistakable transfer of magic, we all watched as the red petals illuminated with a metallic shimmer, flooding all the way to the point of each thorn.

She squeezed her eyes shut once more and let out a slow breath, reminding me that my lungs had been burning for oxygen ever since I split the room with my scream.

"W-what did you do?" I looked at the rose, now vibrant with the dancing silver glow of her festering magic.

Her features were more relaxed now that she'd accomplished whatever she had with the rose, but her pinched fingers seemed to be venting her panic into the thick rose stem. "Your Grace," Lady Azura called across the room, earning a grim glare from the unamused beast and a furrowed brow from the duke. "I need you to translate to our captor for me."

Ian jolted, but I couldn't be certain if it was from disbelief that she wanted to talk to the beast or repulsion that a young lady was making demands of him in front of his citizens. "What is it?" he asked tartly.

Lady Azura straightened, her short physique suddenly towering over that of the beast with the underfired confidence in her even shoulders and uplifted chin. Out of nowhere, her presence demanded respect, and even I felt my shoulders dip a touch as she stretched out the rose as if it were the crown of Dhurin itself. "I am a caster, gifted with the ability to pass my magic through plants—and, most effectively, flowers."

I narrowed my eyes on the rose, watching the minuscule sparks of silver light dance through the petals like a cluster of fireflies.

*So, she's a caster... Casters are only capable of transferring their magic into living creatures or items. If her magic only works on flowers, then that at least explains why she maimed me for my rose.*

Duke Ian repeated Lady Azura's words to the beast, but he remained so stiff that it was hard to know if he had even bothered to listen at all.

"My gift is protection," Lady Azura continued, her voice growing stronger, commanding the room with each syllable. "I am able to enchant flowers with protection barriers, capable of preventing harm from befalling any being who is within its range." Her tone dropped, a victorious light beaming into her eyes. "A range that's large enough to encompass this whole room." Without even a blink of hesitation, she pulled a long silver hair pin from her curls and held the pointed tip to her palm.

"Azura, hold on a moment!" Her uncle Tocken's voice went unheard as Lady Azura pressed the point into her skin and dragged it across the flesh, deep enough to create a scarring wound.

But nothing appeared.

There was no blood, no wincing from Azura, not even the semblance of a scratch when she pulled the pin away and held it up for the beast to observe. For the briefest moment, his stone walls cracked, exposing the slightest tick of panic through the subtle twinge in his scarred eye and a flex in his bulging biceps. Then tension that had been crackling in my veins simmered, filling my chest with the first spark of relief since I'd seen the beast place a key in my suite's door.

*Azura's magic... That rose... As long as they are kept safe, the beast truly can't harm us.*

"Y-you can't hurt them," Ian stuttered, his eyes bulging at the untouched skin on Azura's hand. He turned toward the beast, matching his steel glare with a smug smile capable of angering a saint. "We may be your captives, but we won't be your victims."

# chapter five

*'Failure... Incompetent... You're just like your brothers...'*

*Enough. Enough! This changes nothing; I haven't failed yet.*

*'But you will. Just like you failed your mother...'*

"Silence!" My deep vibrato rattled the crystals on the chandeliers, causing even the duke in my grasp to jolt from surprise.

My heart thudded against my ribs like a blacksmith's mallet, pounding my bones flat to make room for my raging blood. I locked eyes with the blasted caster, her impermeable stare fueling my rage even further. The rose in her fingers looked like a drop of blood on the pure white canvas that had been my new beginning. All my valuable hostages, reduced to mere nuisances with the existence of a single flower.

The simplest solution would have been to kill the mage and let her magic die with her, but as proven by her uninjured hand, that wasn't an option. If her magic protects living things, then I likely couldn't shred the rose to pieces, either. My plans to use the nobilities' lives as leverage were now in complete shambles as long as that bloom existed.

*But how long can a cut rose exist?*

My thoughts swirled together with the cadence of a crackling hurricane as I eyed the glistening flower with a bloodthirsty glare redder than its own petals. The girl said she was a caster, which would mean her magic could only be applied to living things. How long was the lifespan of a cut rose? Two weeks, max? Maybe a month if the magic prolonged its lifespan?

I growled under my breath, tightening my grip on the duke's arm to relieve some of my stress. A month would be difficult. The enchanted key didn't appear to have limits, but what if its power diluted over time? Or what if the soldiers on the outside managed to break through the walls in that amount of time?

*'How shameful... You can't even execute a proper takeover.'*

"Don't chastise me. This will still work," I hissed, turning my attention to the door I was standing in front of. The duke's confident expression had faded, leaving his eyes squinted and mouth slightly parted as he followed my words. I snapped a challenging glare in his direction, and his mouth clamped shut like a blubbering tuna as I pressed my charm harder against his throat. "Listen here. You tell everyone that they had better take precious care of that rose, because the moment it dies, I will massacre every single soul in this ballroom." The light from his previous victory died like a snuffed lantern, blanching his features with a drain of blood. "You have until the rose wilts to get your dear father to hand over Dhurin to me and save your beloved nobles. Am I clear?"

A lump bobbed in his throat as he swallowed stiffly, giving me a blank nod. "Keep the rose safe, everyone," he calmly projected to the room, not even bothering to face the subjects he was preparing to leave behind in a deathly cage. *Coward...* "I swear to you, I'll do everything in my power to do what's best for our people."

*Best for our people...*

My jaw locked as I clenched my teeth hard enough to chip them. He wasn't promising to save them; he was promising to be a diplomat, and that didn't fare well for my plans.

*Blast it.*

The crowd seemed to pick up on his implications as a grim hush filtered over the room. At the moment, they didn't know if they were standing in a ballroom or an execution chamber. That decision was up to their grand duke.

I latched my fingers around the handle to the servant's door, willing the destination in my mind as I felt the golden key sear hot into my pocket. "Don't forget, your betrothed's life rests in the hands of your family's decision," I whispered to the duke, yanking him in front of the door. "I don't know much about botany, but I wouldn't be too lenient on wasting time if I were you. I don't think the party food will last very long amongst all the guests."

Before the duke could mutter anything else to irritate my already spent nerves, I pulled the charm off his skin and slid it back on my wrist with the second band. With my hand now free, I grabbed the scruff of his neck, earning a disgruntled squawk from him as I yanked the door open, unveiling a blast of daylight and fresh air. I didn't wait for anyone to try to stampede out or in, so I threw the duke through the opening, causing him to stumble face-first into the gravel before I slammed it shut against his shoes. As the smack of the door echoed throughout the room, bitter quiet enveloped the space, leaving only the soft sounds of falling tears and gasping breaths.

*'We'll see how long your ruse upholds.'*

I didn't answer. My gaze fixated on the terrified cluster of people who had begun to huddle around the caster and her rose. Once again, my focus caught on the young duchess, her deep brown eyes drowning me in their bottomless mystery. She looked less afraid now that the rose had shielded them from harm, but her shadowed expression and sunken shoulders made her look bleak, as if she held no hope that her betrothed would save them. My neck twitched along the edge of my scar as I swiveled back around to the same door, willing it to open to any new destination within the castle.

*She had better be wrong.*

I swung the door open and stomped inside, slamming it shut behind me hard enough to rattle the polished cherrywood floors I stood on. I raked my eyes around the room like a skeptical critique, scrutinizing the expensively adorned bedroom like it was a portrait with a piglet's snout in the center.

The rounded suite was filled with lavish furnishings, hand-stitched rugs, and some of the ugliest paintings I'd ever seen. A massive oil painting of a half-bloomed rose, speckled with dots of gray and black that made it look rotted, took up the entire wall behind the four-posted canopy bed. At the far end of the room was a small balcony, separated by two doors framed with stained-glass. Sunlight caught through the jagged images of roses and crowns, creating a disfigured image on the floor made of red, purple, and golden light. Opposing the bed was a mirror, almost as large as the grandiose rose canvas, trimmed in braided gold and dotted with emeralds and pearls.

*This must be the grand duke's suite.*

I'd walked past the door when I locked it earlier, but hadn't bothered to look inside. Just as I had imagined, it looked far too royal... far too familiar.

My brain pulsed against my skull, sending a throb of pain across my forehead and down to my temples as I tried to look away from the jewel-toned light of the stained glass. It hadn't even been a year since I was banished from my kingdom, banished from the Emerald Realm—yet the fineries of a castle still felt like a fading memory. I traced my fingers over the fine silk bed sheets, recalling the nights I had spent in my proper bed, tossing and turning as I fought to quiet the scolding in my mind.

*"Don't ease up."*

Father's dark voided eyes burned in my memory like a searing brand, his voice still colder than the blistering winters of the southern kingdoms.

*"But Father, he's only five. I'm double his age, isn't it unfair of me to—"*

*"Does a king hesitate? You were younger than he was when*

*you won your first duel. Are you saying that Miron is too weak to remain in the castle?"* His sword glittered against the sun's scorching rays, flashing a beam of light into my young brother's blue eyes.

*"No! I'll fight him. See? Neither of us are weak."*

Miron's scream echoed through my mind. My numb heart resisted any sympathy toward the memory as I skirted around the edges of the room in search of anything that could be of assistance. The ornate mirror caught the edge of my vision, but I turned away before I could catch a glimpse of my horrendous scars, the reminders of my failure. The click of the castle floors underneath my boot threatened to stir up more memories, but I pushed them down like a smothered pillow. I needed to think.

My eyes drew to the glass balcony doors and I peered through a section of gold-tinted glass, cut in the shape of a star. Blue dots, made up of Dhurin's royal guard, speckled the grounds below, buzzing around the castle like a swarm of gnats. They flocked in clusters toward the doors, yanking them open, only to find that they led to another exterior exit. I had them stumped, for now... but how long did I have until they found a way around the enchantment?

*'It would seem that rose has made quite the mess of things. Such a shame, that your plan is falling apart. Although, I can't say I'm surprised. You were never one to plan for hiccups. That prideful mind of yours is probably the only unfortunate trait you inherited from me...'*

"Funny, I thought you always said that pride was equivalent to strength. Or was that only before your own got you killed?" I snorted back, my eyes still glued to the disorganized chaos at the base of the turret.

*'The only pride that killed me was yours, son. We could have had all the realms under our fist if you hadn't been such a fool. You could have been a king, but I suppose a grand duke with only one good eye is more suitable for a traitor...'*

I huffed through my teeth, forcing my mind to blur out

the intruding voice so I could deepen my focus. He'd been getting louder ever since I'd failed to take over the beasts, but now it felt like he was hovering right over my blasted shoulder.

*'Admit it, Conan. The only reason I still take residency in your mind is because you know that without me... you're nothing but the beast. A worthless, savage animal, only capable of causing inconveniences.'*

"You're wrong," I spat through gritted teeth, holding back the desire to punch through the glass glittering off the light in front of me. "You're in my head because you're too stubborn to stay dead." My fingers curled into stiff fists, strong enough to shatter the stone walls that closed in around me. "I already killed you; you have no right to haunt my thoughts any longer."

A dark chuckle resonated against the stone, sending a chilling stiffness through my nerves. The sound had echoed—not in my mind, but within the room. "I'm only here, because you still need me here." The voice split through my skull like a bolt of crackling lightning, flooding my body with the trained reaction to buckle down into a kneel. I turned from the window, raking my widened gaze over the room, only to confirm that it was still entirely empty. The foreboding voice of my deceased father lingered in the air with the thickness of a humid jungle. "Face it, son..." I followed the direction of the sound, my eyes locking onto the vivid reflection of the mirror that didn't display a single scar... "I'll always be around, because at your core, you will always be just like me."

Dark eyes, glassy and soulless like polished obsidian, blinked back at me under a stern brow and glistening crown. It had been months since I'd last seen Father, but the image my mind projected onto the glass matched his likeness more than any oil painting ever had. I furrowed my eyes as I stared at the sunken wrinkles of his jowls and the tiny knicks and scars that dotted his forehead and neck.

*Father...*

No matter how hard I stared at the mirror, my reflection was nowhere to be seen. There were no scars, no bloodshot eye, and no way for me to look beyond the man who my mind had become so encompassed with that he now had stolen the image of myself. I looked down at my hands, relieved to see that they were still young and familiar. I didn't actually look like him, but clearly, he was still inside me.

"What are you doing here?" I snarled, causing my lip to curl up the side of my pearly teeth.

"I could ask you the same thing." He retorted coldly, the scrutiny in his eyes just as intense as it had been in life. "How is my son so much of a fool that he requires the advice of the father *he* killed?" His lips curled at the edges with the prideful glow I'd inherited.

"I don't need advice from a dead man." I sneered. I wanted to walk away, but I couldn't tear my eyes from his image. He may have been a stress-induced hallucination or a mere projection of my thoughts, but he was still so real. The man I'd last seen lying cold and dead on the throne room floor, the man who had been proud of me for a single moment before I ended his monstrous reign.

"Is that so...?" he scoffed as he tilted his chin upward the way he always did when he wanted to make someone feel small. "So, you believe you're capable of keeping an entire castle of elite nobility hostage for the lifespan of a bewitched flower?" The belittlement in his tone carved into my bones, etching his disapproval into my ribs like a gleeful torture.

"They can't escape, and the guards can't get in," I breathed hotly, removing the golden key from my pocket to display with a flaunting twirl. "Doesn't matter how long that flower lives. Once it wilts, the grand duke will have no other option but to hand over the province to me."

The ghastly figure *tsked*, his locked jaw and disapproving frown jolting my anger with a surge of frustration. "Relying on another's tools..." He glanced down at the key, his lips twisted like he'd just tasted something foul. "Pathetic."

*Pathetic!? What a hypocrite!*

"Oh, so when you use magic, it's resourceful!?" My throat rattled with the escalation in my voice as I kicked at a flower vase, smashing the painted clay into a million shards. "But when *I* use magic, I'm weak? For the love of the realms, why didn't you materialize in my mirror sooner? I really could have used this outstanding advice of yours when I was being clawed to death by wolves." I jeered a finger at my damaged eye, my chest still burning with hot air on the edge of combusting.

The late king's reflection remained unmoved; his eyes only slightly narrowed like a frustrated predator. "I used the magic of my own citizens; you're using the gifts of an enemy."

I rolled my eyes, tossing the glittering key into the air with a smooth catch. "He's no rival to me." I raised the key to my eyes, inspecting the dancing light within with a disinterested huff. "It was his mistake for lending his tools to a man who actually knows how to use them."

"Only a fool assumes he knows a tool better than its owner," he spat, his grimace deepening with the sink of his frown. "Keeping the nobles locked up will only keep the guards at bay for so long. Hostages are truly only useful when they can shed a little blood."

My muscles clamped around my bones, restricting a new spout of anger from blasting through me. *Even in death I still have to endure his berating...* "What do you recommend then, oh great, powerful, *dead* father? Do you have a way for me to make use of my untouchable hostages? What advice could you possibly have that could be of value to me when I've already outwitted you in our home land? Might I remind you who ended your life?" I lifted my chin, mirroring his challenging glare.

His frown slithered upward into the smallest curl of a grim smile. "You'll be glad you asked." He sneered. "First things first, narrow down the most valuable piece in your game."

# chapter six

Within mere moments of the beast's departure, the entire ballroom broke into pure chaos. Lords and viscounts scoured every corner in search of escape, Lady Henrietta and a few of the other young ladies wailed in the middle of the floor, and a massive huddle of pretty much everyone else orbited around Lady Azura like the rose was their new sun, and her their goddess.

"We're going to die here!" Lady Henrietta sobbed, her colorful eye makeup streaming down her face, making her look like a melting rainbow.

"Quiet, girl!" an older man scolded. The man had dusty brown hair speckled with gray, tucked under a large silk top hat that made him seem more important than he probably was. "Show a little respect for our grand duke! I'm sure he'll reach out to the emperor and get this entire matter sorted out in no time. He wouldn't possibly let us, his most valuable citizens, die by the hands of a vulgar crook."

My gut twisted into stiff knots, tighter than the corset crushing my ribs. *Would the grand duke really give up his entire province for only a handful of citizens? Would the emperor even allow it?* I'd barely even met the grand duke of Dhurin, but if he was anything like his son...

My sympathies shifted toward Henrietta, her hopeless sobs feeling far more validated after recalling her close relationship with Ian.

*Ian would do what was best for his province... But what did that mean for us?*

I didn't want to think about it, and thanks to Azura's talents, I didn't have to right now. We had time. The only thing we had to deal with now was our basic survival. We would deal with the beast if we were still here when the rose finally died.

I scanned the far end of the room where the banquet table stood, flooded with savory hors d'oeuvres, rich desserts, and a sampling of fresh fruits. I approached the satin-clothed table and inspected the array of goods. Small bites of beef wellington, tiny bowls of vegetable and barley soup, and pickled turnips seemed to make up most of the savory foods, while pastries like pistachio croissants, fruit Danishes, and assorted scones completed the dessert tray. Chunky grains of salt and sugar dusted every offering, making each dish glitter under the warm glow of the chandeliers. The punch bowls were nearly filled to the brim with sweetened rosewater and some other fruity concoction that smelled like pears. Just behind the serving table was a small curtain, hiding a water pump and drain, likely used for quick refills or fire emergencies. It looked like a lot, even for an intimate celebration, but the more I inspected the selection, the further I felt my heart sink until it slammed into the soles of my slippers.

*I can't eat it...*

The puffed pastry wrapped around the beef, the barley in the soup which was likely cross-contaminated, and all the baked desserts would serve as the perfect poison for my cursed stomach. Not only that, but all the food was highly perishable. The fresh meats and fruit baked into the goodies would barely last a few days before people risked food poisoning. My stomach growled, as if reacting to the realization that now suffocated me.

*The beast may not be able to harm us, but that didn't mean we couldn't die...*

"Hey! The duchess is trying to hoard all the food!" a prude male accused from somewhere behind me. I spun around to face the man who'd made the claim, but it was impossible to locate the culprit when nearly fifty eyes were locked onto me like starving wolves. My blood crystallized under their ravenous stares as they darted their attention between me and the banquet table, only a breath away from a stampede.

I held up my arms in surrender, showcasing my empty palms while simultaneously trying to signal for them to pause before they trampled me for only a single meal worth of scarfing. "Hold on. I haven't touched anything. I was merely assessing how much we had to ration out." I turned my hands over so they could see the backs before motioning to the spread. The group's collective tension seemed to ease, but their greedy eyes never left the fragrant meats and goodies. "There's a good amount of food, but unfortunately, it doesn't look like it will stay fresh for long. If we're going to be stuck here for a while, then we'll need to create a plan. There's a water pump along the wall, so we shouldn't have any issues staying hydrated, but as for the food, we'll need to be more cautious. I recommend that we—"

"Hold on a moment!" The shrill huff came from none other than Lord Tocken, Azura's stout uncle. He stepped forward, pushing his way through the crowd with a puffed chest that showcased his gaudy pocket watch. "Who said *you* got to be the one to take charge of the rations?" His thick brows scrunched together, forming a unibrow as fluffy and full as a thick brown caterpillar. "Just because you're another province's duchess doesn't mean you're ours yet. If we let you take control, how can we trust that you won't short the rest of us or favor those of higher rank? It seems to me that the best way to go about this is by distributing everything evenly. Then each individual can decide how they'll ration their share."

The crowd remained silent, but a few of the men seemed to nod in agreement with this plan while others looked a little more uneasy. I glanced back over my shoulder, looking at the piping steam still rising from the soups and beef.

"No, that won't work." I shook my head fiercely. "It's best if we keep the food all in one place so we can keep the hot foods together and keep them fresh for as long as possible. We'll also have less risk of attracting mice or insects if we keep it in one place."

"M-mice?" A middle-aged woman with red-painted lips and a black beauty mark under her eye nearly swooned. "They couldn't get in with all the doors locked, could they? Oh, I think I'd rather die at the hands of the beast than share a room with a rat." She shivered stiffly, causing her entire gown to ripple like rings in a pool.

"The beast locked the doors, not the mouse holes." I shrugged. "At least, I don't think he did... Either way, our best bet is to consolidate and ration out one meal at a time. If it's all together, then we'll be able to spot anything that's gone rotten easier, ensuring that no one gets sick."

I may have overexplained a *bit* too much, because suddenly, all of the hungry looks the guests had been giving the food were replaced with skeptical glances, uncertainty lacing their fragile resolve.

Mr. Tocken folded his arms with an uncomfortable twitch in his tight lips. "Very well, but that still leaves the matter of who can be trusted to distribute said meals. I mean no disrespect, duchess, but it is difficult to feel secure with our lives in the hands of a young woman we were intended to meet only today."

*I suppose I can't fault him for that...*

If these people knew the true nature of their young duke, then it was no wonder they were distrustful of a foreign duchess... Luckily for me, I had a surefire way of convincing them that I was the *last* person who would go stuffing their face with the dangerous selection behind me.

"I'm allergic to wheat," I said flatly, my voice calm and level as I shrugged. There was no immediate reaction from the collective mass, but Henrietta's eyes did seem to bulge a touch.

"Everything on this spread, except for the fresh fruit and maybe the pickled turnips, are pretty much toxic to me. I won't say that being the duchess makes me the best candidate for the job, but I will say that my illness makes me the least likely to fall to the temptation of sneaking an extra scone. Believe me, I would much rather starve than endure the backlash of consuming anything I shouldn't."

Despite the increase in hopeful whispers, I still couldn't prevent my gut from twisting into a labyrinth of knots. I was a good choice for monitoring the food supply—in fact I was an excellent choice—because I would be guarding food I couldn't eat... My gaze drifted over toward Azura, noticing the sympathetic part of her lips and glassy stare in my direction. At some point during the chaos, someone had brought her a tall crystal glass filled with water to place the rose in, which she now held clutched to her chest. I blinked at the blood-red petals, imagining the moment the first one would fall as I looked back at our only source of food.

*What will fall first...all the petals, or all the people?*

"It's true." Henrietta's crackling voice, raw from crying, broke through the whispers. "The duke mentioned something about his betrothed having a severe allergy. He said that after tonight's welcoming, every meal would have to be double catered to ensure her health was made a priority." She turned her swollen eyes to me, her cheeks puffy and lash lines rimmed in red. "He complained about it all the time." She laughed weakly with a gentle roll of her eyes.

I let out a soft snort. "I may have only known him for a day, but that definitely sounds like him."

Lord Tocken's knitted brows softened, causing his round eyes to look more like that of a wise owl than a grouchy dwarf. "I apologize for being so distrustful, Your Grace." He dipped down in the slightest touch, his voice loaded with the same sympathy I had seen in his niece's eyes. It was no mystery now that I would be the one to suffer the most from these arrangements.

"There's no need for apology." I smiled softly with a respectful tilt of my head. "We are all in a precarious situation and are simply looking to protect ourselves and our loved ones. I cannot fault you for being cautious."

Lord Illumen stepped forward, joining his brother's side with a far straighter bow that emphasized his tall, lean form. "You are too kind, Your Grace." He smacked a hand on his brother's shoulder, causing the pocket watch to fall from its clip and forcing Lord Tocken to bumble awkwardly to catch it. "Please, how can we help you preserve the food we currently have?"

Without hesitation, I started instructing the brothers, along with a few other volunteers, to group the hot foods together and surround them in the metal trays and covers. Lord Illumen gathered a few stray candles from light fixtures and helped position their flames around the edges of the metal, creating a warming box to keep the food temperature in a safer zone. As for the fruits and bread, a few of the older women set to work, wrapping each of the baked goods in linen napkins to preserve their freshness, while another helped me separate the fruit and pickled turnips from the items that were unsafe for me to touch. Once the food was stored as well as it could be, I washed my hands with the water pump to ensure I hadn't left any wheat particles stuck to my skin.

We counted the rows of bundled pastries and the tiny bowls of soup, calculating the number of meals required per day with how long the food would remain safe to eat. As I added up the last of the pickled turnips in my head, I felt an uneasy lump stick in my throat like a chunk of charcoal.

*Two days...*

With fifty-two guests trapped in the ballroom and only bite-size snacks and desserts available, it shouldn't have been surprising that the rations would only last so long. But even so, two days was barely even enough time for the grand duke to talk over the hostage situation with his advisors, let alone make the decision to exchange Dhurin for our lives.

I bit the inside of my cheek, gnawing at the soft skin until my gaze landed on Lady Azura. She had seated herself in the middle of the ballroom floor with her red skirts billowed out like an extension of the crimson rose in her lap. The unyielding confidence she had displayed earlier was now dormant, buried behind her dimmed green gaze that remained fixated on the thick bloom. I hiked up my heavy teal skirt and gingerly approached her shrouded form. Her attention was so absorbed by the rose that she didn't even notice I had joined her until my skirts bloomed beside hers with an inelegant squat.

"How is the food supply looking?" she asked quietly as her thumb skimmed the edge of the crystal glass. The glittering magic of the flower reflected off the iridescent crystal, creating a kaleidoscope of rainbows and dazzling shapes in the flower's water. Her expression was muted, but I could see the slight tense in her wrists as her gaze briefly darted toward the stored food.

*I suppose there's no use in hiding the predicament... They'll all find out in two days, anyway.*

"It... could be better." I sighed, my stomach growling practically on cue. "We got everything packaged as well as we can, but there's only so much to go around." The lump in my throat stiffened, stifling my voice as if admitting our dilemma aloud had truly made it real. We only had two days... Two days to find another source of food. I took in a heavy breath, thick with the taste of the enchanted rose's fragrance. "If the beast doesn't provide us with any other meals, then we may need to go look for some ourselves."

Azura's faded gaze snapped to life, her pupils dilating like a spreading droplet of ink. "Go look? But how? No one can leave the ballroom without the risk of being slaughtered by the beast, not to mention the doors don't lead anywhere but back here."

*Do they still lead back to the ballroom...?*

My thoughts buzzed louder than a nest of wasps, each one stinging at my brain to warn me against the dangerous line of thought. "I'm not so sure that's still the case anymore..." My gaze lifted over Azura's head, eyeing the unmarked servants' door that our captor had escaped from. "Think about it. He planned to use his hostages as leverage against the grand duke, but now that we're untouchable, his plans are at a stand-still until the rose dies." I gestured at the bloom, Azura's confused eyes flicking between it and me. "How far does your magic's protection stretch? To the ends of this ballroom, you said?"

She startled back half an inch, one of her thin brows arching like a perfect rainbow. "Uh, yes, from what I can tell, but its radius will likely shrink as the rose's life force weakens."

I nodded as I chewed the edge of my lip, my focus now shifted back to the door. "So, if your magic can only protect us in here... Then wouldn't it make sense for the beast to leave the other doors open to the rest of the castle? It would be a clever tactic, really—to let us all grow desperate enough for food that we leave the safety of the rose in search of additional provisions." I rose to my feet, my interests now fully piqued by the latched door.

"Your Grace, I don't think it's wise to..." Azura's timid voice faded into my mind as another growl from my stomach interrupted.

*He wouldn't expect us to go exploring so soon after threatening us. If I can get out now...*

I crossed the room in a mindless daze, my attention only consumed by whatever existed on the other side of the door. When I reached it, my fingers laced around the door's polished brass handle, and for the first time, I noticed it was warm and slightly aglow from the infusion of magic.

"Your Grace! Wait a moment!" Azura's voice echoed off the marble floors, followed by the patter of her slippers across the stone. "Don't open that!"

For the briefest moment, I hesitated to ensure I was still prioritizing my brain over my stomach, but even after the momentary pause, my hand refused to loosen from the handle.

*If I don't look behind this door, then we'll never know the boundaries of our cage.*

I yanked the door open, half expecting to see a view from the ballroom's balcony or the shielded corner of the other servants' entrance. But when I peered down the hallway, I saw... a hallway! Thick carpets embroidered with golden leaves and silver doves ran down the passage, accenting the silk tapestries and gold-framed art pieces. A sparse spread of doors dotted the walls, each with a simple frame made of gabled hickory and simple carvings of more doves. It was definitely still within the bounds of the castle, but it wasn't the ballroom. I eyed the other doors with greedy fascination, wondering if they too had been enchanted to lead somewhere new...

Like the kitchen, perhaps?

My foot moved forward on its own, making it halfway onto the thick carpet before a firm hand grabbed my shoulder and pulled me back hard enough to nearly dislocate it.

"What are you doing!? Have you lost your mind!?" Lord Tocken's round face was set with a sunken frown that opposed the bulging panic in his widened eyes. Directly behind him was Azura, Lord Illumen, and pretty much everyone else in the ballroom, all looking as pale as a snow lily.

I stepped aside from the door, ensuring they could all see the open hallway. "Look, we can leave the ballroom. This might be our only chance to collect supplies that will help us survive long enough for the grand duke to get us out of this castle."

Everyone peered down the hallway, but no one looked nearly half as happy about it as I did. Actually, they all looked terrified, as if the scarred beast would jump out of one of the doors at any moment and shred them with his dagger.

"Your Grace..." Azura stepped forward with a nervous quiver in her voice, the rose clutched tightly to her chest. "You said so yourself, the beast is likely trying to lure us out so he can make good on his threats. If you leave the ballroom, the rose can't protect you from harm."

My legs tensed, itching to dart down the hallway and collect as much as I could before the beast caught my scent. "Then why don't we bring the rose and all of us go?" I implored, earning a few sharp breaths and nervous chatters from the older women in the back. "If we stick together, then even if he finds us, the beast won't be able to hurt us."

"You mean, *when* he finds us," Lord Tocken huffed as he crossed his arms over his rounded belly. "The beast has complete control over the castle; he's likely created a labyrinth intended to lead us all into a far less comfortable dungeon or worse. If we leave this room, we risk being trapped all over again with *zero* rations and water access."

Lord Illumen stepped forward, his slender and angular features somehow appearing softer than his round-faced brother's. "I'm afraid my brother is right." He placed a hand on the door, causing my heart to stiffen with anxiety as he paused before pushing it closed. "If the beast caught us, there would be nothing stopping him from luring us all into a cellar or even attempting to split us apart from the rose with his control over the doors."

No one even attempted to argue with him, and as he slowly creaked the door shut, the squeaky hinges harmonized with the collective breath of relief the hostages gave. My chest burned with building pressure as I watched our one hope at long-lasting survival disappear inch by inch.

*Why is it that, even now, people still believe they know what's best for me?*

The bubbling frustration burst from my core, and I

shoved my slipper in front of the door, catching it before it could shut. Lord Illumen jolted, but didn't remove his hand from the door as I met his flickering amber eyes. "Then I'll go alone," I said firmly, my voice strong and unyielding. "Let me scout the castle and see what I can bring back. I won't be immune to the beast if he finds me, but I would hope he's smart enough to let the grand duke's future daughter-in-law live longer than one day."

Silence followed the lingering echo of my voice as it bounced around the dismal ballroom.

"Mirabel," a small voice squeaked. It almost sounded like a child, but when I followed the sound, I saw that it was Lady Henrietta who had broken the quiet. Her pretty face and rose lips had paled, her sunny yellow dress now washed out her once glowing skin. Her makeup-smeared eyes had developed dark shadows from her past hour of sobbing. "Please don't go... At least, not while we still have some food to keep us going. I... We don't want to see anyone die..."

For the first time since this entire hostage situation had begun, I truly felt the collective fear of everyone here sink onto me like my dress had suddenly been soaked, causing the heavy satin to weigh me down to the floor.

*What am I doing...? I am acting like... well, me.*

But nobody needed independent, wannabe-hero Mirabel right now. They need Duchess Mirabel Jada Brantley, the stable and dependable young lady, who would soothe their fears with a meal plan and calculated ration distributions.

With painful reluctance, I slid my foot out from the door, allowing Lord Illumen to close it with a *click* that sounded more like the snap of my thread of hope. My stomach growled in resentment, sending a flush of pain through my head as my eyes caught on the slim pickings of bananas and pickled turnips for me to safely consume.

I swallowed back the grievous sigh that bobbed in my throat and forced on my practiced '*I have everything under control'* smile. "You're right. I'm being too brash," I said smoothly, taking note of the easing shoulders and relaxing expressions. "Why don't we just take this matter one day at a time, and plan from there? I'm sure the grand duke will get us out of this situation before we even know it."

# chapter seven

*How long can one puny flower possibly live?*

My scarred eye blurred as my blood swelled throughout its injured vessels. I switched to my good eye, peering through the slim crack in the ballroom's side door to spy on my menagerie of pets. The protective rose sat in the dead center of the ballroom atop the painted crest of the Dhurin province, circled by six people with the caster at the center. It almost looked like the starting pose for a ballet, with them all evenly spaced around the single bloom.

One of the older men turned in my direction and I tightened the opening, leaving only a sliver left to peep through.

*'Never get caught, son. Getting caught is getting sloppy, and only dead men are sloppy.'*

"So, is that why you're dead, then?" I huffed hotly, widening the crack another half inch as the man turned his attention to an older woman with a limp feather sticking out from the top of her deflated bun.

It had only been a day since I'd left my captives to stew in their confinement, but even so, they were already starting to look a little worse for the wear. Even though the cut rose still looked perfectly healthy, most of the wanderers didn't stray too far from the center of the room. The men had all discarded their top hats and fitted suit jackets in one corner, while a pile of heeled slippers and chunky jewelry rested in another. The cloths from the serving tables lay strewn across the room, along with a few tapestries and decorative draperies, likely having been used as makeshift bedding. However, one curtain still remained intact—the one that sectioned off the water pump and drain from the rest of the ballroom. A disgusted grimace wrinkled my nose as I realized the drain and water source were likely being used in lieu of a chamber pot. I tore my eyes from the curtain, reminding myself why I was spying on my herd to begin with.

*"Narrow down the most valuable piece in your game..."*

Father's words echoed through my head louder than the screech of an untuned fiddle. My head pounded from his stress-inducing criticisms, cracking my defenses far enough that I was willing to follow his advice if it brought me a moment of quiet. I raked my gaze over the collection of captives, quickly ticking off the shriveled-up debutants and crotchety old men as the least useful. I fixated my attention on the young caster, her bright red dress as vivid as fresh blood.

*She is certainly useful... but is she the most valuable?*

The girl remained latched to the rose, flanked by a few other young women who appeared to be engaging her in mindless conversation. She was the sole reason any of them felt safe within the ballroom walls... On top of that she clearly possessed some level of rank, and she had not one, but two, chaperones, who likely cared for her in some regard. She may indeed prove to be the piece I'm looking for. But then there was the other candidate...

I caught a glimpse of the duchess's teal skirts, their wrinkled fabrics rippling with her steps like a shallow sea. She was impossible to miss with how much she stood out. Her dark skin, elongated figure, and undeterred posture caused her to stand out as vividly as a swan amongst geese. Her status alone made her the most valuable in terms of rank. She was the heir to her own province, as well as the betrothed to Dhurin's pathetic duke. Though I couldn't understand her language during our first encounter, I could tell she wasn't as dimwitted as the typical noble. It had barely taken her a moment to realize that

I wasn't a real guard, despite this not being her home territory. She might have recognized my features from the wanted posters, or even from her brother's stories of our encounters, but even so... She had done what most nobility couldn't and looked past the uniform to inspect the man beneath. Perhaps her value stemmed deeper than her title...

For the next few minutes, I kept a close eye on the young duchess. She paced around the ballroom with the serenity of a duchess who already commanded the castle, checking on each of the hostages with a gentle smile. Or... not checking on them, but giving them something. The minuscule amount of visibility I had made it nearly impossible to notice that the girl had been handing each person she interacted with a small bundle of food. One by one, she distributed the rations, then returned to the hoarded pile of food and selected a single banana for herself.

*Interesting... So, she's been placed in charge of the food supply.*

Once the duchess had seated herself with her meager meal, the strength on her expression numbed and her delicate features sharpened into a far more furrowed thought. There wasn't a coin I wouldn't pay to get a glimpse into what was inside that head of hers. In the blink of an eye, she went from appearing as a compassionate, almost mothering provider, to a deathly strategic general. It was then that I reminded myself that this girl was more than just the duke's betrothed; she was a future grand duchess by birth. There was little doubt in my mind that she had studied more than just the etiquette and skills necessary to snare an advantageous marriage. She was clever enough to get herself placed in charge of handling the food, and in a situation like this, she had essentially gotten a room full of strangers to entrust her with their lives.

*She's resourceful, well-bred, and intelligent... Which makes her dangerous to me, but valuable all the same.*

With my question satisfied, I pulled away from the door,

slowly stepping back into the shadows as I closed the slim crack of light. It was nearly sealed when a sudden pair of dark brown eyes snagged me harder than a fisherman's hook.

*The duchess.*

She saw me. It was as if she had been expecting me to be at the doors all along, just waiting for the moment I returned to their prison. I don't know why, but I stiffened, my blood converting to lead as I froze dead in my tracks. It was my scarred eye that had stopped in front of the door's crack, my skewered vision barely able to track the widening of her indescribable eyes. The women in my homeland held no comparison to the raw, foreign beauty this girl held. Her black hair had been pulled tight into a lavish updo when we first collided and embellished with that realm-forsaken rose. But now her curls had fallen, wound loosely into a thick braid that rested on her slender shoulder. She was clearly startled to have spotted me, but her face didn't depict much fear, but more... intrigue?

She continued to stare into my scarred eye for a silent moment before she shifted, as if ready to run straight toward me or warn the others of my spying. I instantly came to my senses and slammed the door shut, cutting off our eye contact and willing the other side of the door to lead back into the ballroom. I'll keep a few doors open to the castle in case one of the flock strays, allowing me to go hunting, but right now, I wasn't ready to deal with the duchess as I still hadn't quite gotten a full read on her.

"Sloppy." The mirror sneered behind me, the voice inside holding a sharp resonance, as if it was actually echoing off the glass. "Truly, is there anything you can do competently?"

I rolled my neck with a slow huff through my nostrils before pivoting around to lock eyes with my father's reflection. "I can kill a king," I said stiffly, walking straight past his disapproving scowl to peer out the balcony doors. The guards were still lingering around the castle walls, but now in a far more orderly fashion than their initial frenzy. A few tents had been implanted in the gardens, likely acting as makeshift war rooms since theirs had been overtaken.

"If all you can kill are kings, then why did you ever believe you could overthrow a grand duke?" The mirror's abrasive voice grinded against my skin with the rigidness of a bladed washboard. "You slayed me, but where has it gotten you? Trapped in a grand prison with a flower serving as the ward?" He scoffed, his biting laugh nipped at my scars like the wolf's teeth that had left them there. "You're truly an imbecile. How did a man as great as I end up with a spawn like you?"

My fist swung out from my body, slamming into the wall hard enough to punch through whatever artwork had been hanging there, sending it clattering to the floor beneath my frozen fist. "Shut up!" My breath hitched in my throat, burning hot with the fanned flame of years of pent-up words. "I am everything you raised me to be! If I'm any less than your idea of perfection, then it's only because that's how you raised me." I turned away from the doors to face the mirror's glass, my hand swelling from a fresh bruise, but the adrenaline and anger piping through my blood numbed any pain. "Never once did I disobey, rarely did I argue, and even still, you act as if I was just as traitorous as my brothers." I stood eye to eye with him, letting every ounce of my hatred pour out into my searing gaze.

*It doesn't matter if I'm perfect; I'll never be good enough for him...*

The thought urged me to feel empowered, to embrace the fact that I could overcome my father's expectations and cut him loose from my mind for good. But when I looked into his voided eyes, I felt no release from his choking grasp...

He was smiling... A cold twisted grin that could only be produced from a man who possessed the chilling blood of a demon. My muscles tightened, as if anticipating a strike to the face or a blow to the gut that had often followed that look when

I was a child.

"Oh, Conan... We both know you've disobeyed me in the past." His eyes sparked a sickly gray, much like an alchemist's poison puffing up a toxic cloud. My breaths suddenly felt constricted, slowing and growing shallow as the buried memory he was alluding to faded impermissibly into my brain—the memory I would do anything to drown in the darkest depths of the realm's seas. Father's smile twitched upward in pleasure as he caught some sign of my discomfort. "Never forget what happens when you ignore my lessons, boy. We both know what happens when you do. Your poor mother—"

"Enough," I snapped under a clipped breath. My heart pounded in my chest, causing my entire torso to feel like it was being compressed by a crushing force. The pressure didn't stop at my chest—my legs, throat, head, all of it felt like I was a thousand leagues under the sea, drowning with my mother's image circulating endlessly through my constricted mind.

*It is all my fault.*

*I failed her. She's dead.*

*Father's dead.*

*I didn't listen. Why didn't I listen!?*

*Why are they dead!? How could I have killed him!?*

*I need him! He made me strong. He would have made me king.*

*And now...*

I destroyed everything. Anything my hands could find, I shredded, pounded, and kicked until it crumbled in my hands. The pressure my body was applying to my heart was strong enough to form it into a diamond. I squeezed the shredded stuffing of a cushion that lingered in my palms, finally feeling my heart rate lessen. I slowed my breaths, trying to tame the tangled mass of thoughts clawing at my brain until it finally permitted me to take back control of my tongue. I returned to the mirror, my eyes as glassy and unreflective as the surface in front of me.

"What do you suggest I do, then?" I asked bluntly, my voice monotone and absent of any turmoil that still circulated in my veins.

If I could have seen myself in the mirror, my expression would have been vacant, empty of every touch of my soul. It was how I always looked when I disposed of the nipping emotions that Father found wasteful of brain function.

His smile never faded, the dark shadows above his hooded eyes giving him an appearance I could only equate to a ravenous ghoul. "Did you locate them? The most valuable piece?"

I nodded wordlessly, my head bobbing as mechanically as a marionette. "Yes, the duchess. She's powerful, intelligent, and most importantly, has gained the trust of every hostage." I didn't hear the words that fell off my tongue, though I knew they were there. My entire mind was fixated on pushing away the echoes of my mother's sobs, entangled with Father's sharp words.

Father nodded, his face teasing a pleased look, but not fully there—an expression I was well-familiar with. "Good, then that's the captive you'll need to kill."

For a moment, my barriers cracked, invading my emotionless calm with a slurry of questions and spiraling sensations. "Kill her? But why?" I asked a little more bluntly than intended, earning a scowl from the mirror. "I mean, it seems she's the only one smart enough to ration their supplies and keep them all alive. Killing her would be like infecting the rest of the hostages with a slow-moving poison, and leveraging the hostages is the only way I can claim the province."

"It doesn't matter what happens to the other hostages," Father interjected, his tone short with his impatient temper. "All you need is one important corpse to drag outside through your enchanted doors. You made the foolish mistake of letting knowledge of the rose's protection make it outside the castle when you sent your messenger. You've given your enemy the advantage of time, so to correct this mishandling, you'll need to take it away..." His chin lifted, showcasing his thick beard and sinister smile hidden beneath it. "If the girl has the favor of the hostages, then they'll fall apart once she's gone. The rose can't protect them from their own failure to survive. With such a powerful piece proven killed, the people outside the walls will panic, and the grand duke will have no other choice but to prioritize rescue to avoid being despised for all eternity as the man who let so many of his beloved citizens die at his hands."

He finished with a smug lift of his thick brow, his face radiating with pride from his apparent full-proof plan. My thoughts clamored into each other like a crash of rhinos, each overlaying atop the other in an endless mountain. Killing the duchess made zero sense... She was likely the only hostage worth saving from the grand duke's point of view, and without her guidance, the other brainless hostages would fall over, dead. Nonetheless... I wanted to see where this was going. Whether I followed through on it or not still remained to be seen.

"How am I meant to kill her if she's hiding in the ballroom? Do you suggest I attempt to take the rose by force?"

His eyes flared, his upper body jolting forward with enough momentum to make me wonder if he was going to break through the glass. "No. Under no circumstance should you touch that rose." His voice was strong and commanding, with an urgency that, if I hadn't known my father, I might have imagined was fearful.

"Why not?" I asked stiffly, wondering why I hadn't considered the idea in the first place. "They have no weapons. Sure, I can't harm them, but they can't harm me, either. It shouldn't be difficult to push through them and remove the flower from that caster's spindly little fingers." I smirked at the idea, imagining the satisfaction of swiping their worshipped bloom right out from under them.

"Only do so if you wish to join me in the afterlife," he said grimly, his tightened jaw and stiffened neck showcasing no trace of jest.

I frowned. "Afterlife? I didn't think anyone around the blasted flower could die?"

Father rolled his eyes, a rigid growl rising in his throat. "You truly are an imbecile... Magic flows differently here than it does in the homeland. Interfering with a mage's spell can cause the power to reverse on the intruder, much like the human body's attack on a virus."

I furrowed my brow, my gaze drifting ominously to the pair of gold charms on my wrist.

*Is that true? Could rebelling against a magic's intent cause such backlash?*

"Fine. If tampering with the rose could backfire, then how do *you* recommend I lure the duchess away?" I folded my arms against my chest, trying to stifle the uncertainty that festered inside me.

*Is killing the duchess really the right move? Or is there another reason Father wants her dead? Although, it isn't as if a dead hallucination can have ulterior motives... can it?*

"For that, you'll need to be a bit patient," he continued, his ghastly smile returning. "You said she was taking charge of the food, correct? Wait long enough for them to get hungry... and then leave only one door unlocked. No prey can resist the bait for long..."

# chapter eight

My spine screamed at me as I rolled over on the solid marble floors, earning a cry of protest from my neck and shoulders as I tried to settle on my side. The thin satin tablecloths I'd swiped from the banquet tables did little to cushion my tender bones from the unforgiving ballroom floor, and only barely acted as a blanket. It was nearly impossible to tell what time of day it was since there were no exterior windows in the intimate ballroom.

I curled my spine upward with the resistance of dried out taffy. I regretted the movement the instant I was upright, feeling my stomach roil and cramp from the movement. Everyone else was still asleep, so it must have been early, or even still night—it was hard to tell after how many times I'd gotten up to be ill. Piles of other table linens, wool tapestries, and other odd fabrics swaddled everyone in a massive bundle in the center of the ballroom, much like a pack of dogs keeping warm. I shifted my position to sit up further, earning another wince from my raw gut.

*How much longer can we survive like this?*

It had been four days since we'd been confined to the ballroom, but the nauseating discomfort of the last night made it feel like it had been years. We'd managed to stretch our rations further than expected, but by now, our food supply was practically non-existent, compiled of only two questionable bowls of soup and three soft brown bananas. Just looking at the fruit made me want to spill the non-existent contents of my stomach again. After three days of eating nothing but bananas,

I had grown sick enough of the taste that even a sour pickled turnip sounded like an angelic treat.

*Oh, how wrong I was...*

The turnip had tasted fine, but it was only a mere hour later that I had realized it hadn't been safe for me to consume. Somewhere along the lines of its preparation, it must have come into contact with wheat, because I had been enduring the satanic torture of the turnip's wrath all night long. At first, I had hoped that maybe the rose would protect me from the allergen's attack on my system, but sadly, internal ailments didn't qualify as 'physical harm' to the magic's unwritten rules. My head pounded from dehydration as I stumbled over to the water pump to replenish my empty glass.

The sight of the pitiful pile of food twisted my abused stomach even further, causing a wave of fear and even anger to seep into my weak limbs.

*I should have explored the castle when I had the chance...*

Despite being well on our way to starvation, the other hostages' stances hadn't changed on venturing out of the ballroom. The stress of our situation was appearing the take a toll on even the most collected members of our group, causing tension to rise quicker when controversial topics were discussed.

I couldn't claim to be much different. I'm not sure if it was the lack of food, the confinement, or the constant reminder that there was a psychotic monster peeping in on us from time to time, but each morning I had woken up feeling more and more aggravated. The beast was lucky I hadn't seen him since I caught him spying through the door, though the next time I saw him I might fancy adding another scar to his pretty face.

I gulped down my glass of water, feeling my stomach swell with the liquid in an uncomfortable sloshing manner. I'd loosened the ties on my corset the first night of my imprisonment, but it still felt too tight with even its gentle squeeze. My slippers rested somewhere in the far corner, piled with the other ladies' shoes, allowing the coolness of the marble floor to seep in my bare feet. The once lively ballroom, filled with light and music, had grown cold and dismal. The candles that had flickered amongst the crystal chandeliers had long since burnt out, leaving only the wall sconces and candelabras to illuminate the massive space. The tall ceilings disappeared into the cloaked shadows, making it feel as if we were camping under a starless sky. Well... a starless sky with chandeliers dangling in the center.

Someone shifted in the sleepy pile of ragged bedding, and I glanced over to see Azura roll over, her face only mere inches away from the rose. The pain in my stomach dulled in comparison to the creeping anxiety that tunneled into my mind as I gaped at the wilting bloom. The stem's healthy green shade was now fading, and the tips of the petals were darkening to the color of dried blood. The weight of the massive bloom had caused the stem to bend, allowing the wide flower to tilt unsteadily. My heart wrenched as I watched a petal fall from the rose, lilting easily through the air until it settled atop the tiny pile of its fallen counterparts.

*The rose is already dying... which means the magic is as well.*

The harsh growl of my stomach nearly shook me as it rudely reminded me that we had bigger problems than the lifespan of our shield. We were starving, only barely, but we weren't necessarily preparing to harvest any crops from a crack in the marble anytime soon. We had no food, and no way of knowing whether the grand duke was planning a rescue. My frustration bubbled inside me, threatening to squeal like a narrow-spouted kettle as I looked over to the servants' door.

*I've sat still long enough; now it's time to take action.*

I raked my gaze over the sleeping captives one final time, ensuring no one had roused awake before I crept over to the door. My toes barely skimmed the floor, softer than the brush of wind, as I stopped in front of the simple door. My fingers laced around the cool brass handle, and my heart jumped to my palm, throbbing hotly against the brass.

*Just be quick and quiet.*

I steadied my breaths as I slowly pulled the door open, reminding myself that a swift end from the beast was still preferable to starvation. When I had the door cracked open, I felt my roiling stomach drop with a breath snatching fall.

The hallway was gone.

I blinked my dazed eyes, scanning the doorway for any tricks of light or sleep-deprived hallucinations as I stared at my own back from atop the ballroom's balcony entrance. My throat tightened, cutting off my gasp as I clicked the door shut and opened it a second time, only to see the same exact view.

*No... Am I too late? Has the beast truly trapped us for good?*

Panic threaded through my muscles, fueling my exhausted limbs with adrenaline as I hurried to a second servants' door, and then another, and then the front entrance. Each time, I practically threw the door open, feeling my heart constrict tighter every time it led back to the ballroom. I trudged up the balcony steps, no longer mindful of my noise level as my breaths came out in shallow wheezes.

*If we're trapped in here... then that's it. This ballroom is officially our coffin.*

My heart hammered against my ribs, causing my movements to stutter as I stopped in front of the grand balcony doors. I placed a shaking hand on the handle, once again feeling the throbbing of my pulse against the cool brass.

*Please...*

The wish lingered on my tongue, but I was too afraid to speak it aloud, fearing that if the beast could hear what I wanted, he would strip away that hope as well. My lungs stiffened with paralysis; my entire body frozen in wait as only my arm managed to pull against the heavy door.

*Please... lead somewhere. Anywhere.*

Like an angelic light gracing heaven itself, a stunning hallway completely different from the first one appeared through the doorway. I nearly choked on a sob as I stared misty-eyed at the embellished walls and wooden floors.

*Yes!*

A new rush of hope filtered through me with powerful endorphins, practically curing me from the lingering pain in my stomach. I placed one foot through the door, only pausing for a moment to consider that this was likely a trap set by the beast meant to lure me into his claws. He could try to kill me, but I wasn't going to go down easily after all the torture he'd put us through.

*Let's see who's scarier, a murderous beast or a hungry woman.*

Without further hesitation, I crossed the threshold and instantly felt renewed. The anger that had been gnawing at my mind and the intense cabin fever lifted from my shoulders, making me feel lighter than air. I hardly knew anything about the castle's layout, and even if I did, there was no knowing where each door would lead now. But even so, I was determined... and I was hungry.

The hallway may have looked as gorgeous as a historic palace to me, but in reality, it was rather plain. Only a few art pieces lined the simple gray halls, and the polished floors didn't possess any of the unique patterns or mosaics the others I'd encountered had.

*This must be a servants' hall.*

I bunched up my wrinkled skirts and darted down the hall as silently as I could, checking the corners with held breath before I made any quick turns. My eyes dilated with excitement as I peered around the wall and saw the glorious light of day stream through a small arched window at the end of the next hall. The sight of real sunlight made me throw all caution to the wind as I half-ran, half-stumbled over to the window to press my palms and nose against the cool, diamond-paned glass.

I slammed my hands against the glass so quickly that I didn't even notice the lopsided nail poking out from the frame. My skin grazed the sharp metal tip, causing me to wince and pull back to inspect the spreading blood from the center of my palm.

*Looks like I'm outside of the rose's protection now.*

I squeezed my fingers against the shallow wound, then turned my attention back out the window. The first thing I noticed was the height. At least five stories separated me from the sweet grounds of freedom. I hadn't realized I was panting until it was interrupted by my own gasp as I noticed the scattered tents that now surrounded the castle's perimeter. It was difficult to make out much from such a distance, but I could definitely see patrols of blue-coated men circling the castle's expansive walls and turrets.

*It's the grand duke's forces... They're looking for a way inside.*

An indescribable rush of hope enveloped me in a soothing embrace. The grand duke was trying to find a way inside... He really did care about his citizens—well, at least his wealthy, influential ones. Even so, seeing the forces below meant we weren't as alone in this mess as we felt.

*We just have to stay alive for as long as we can.*

With my cramping stomach reminding me of my original mission, I pulled away from the glass while still lingering an extra second to soak in a final ray of sun. My heart pattered in my chest as rhythmic as a toddler playing a xylophone. Each door I passed gripped my attention, but the fear of the beast waiting on the other side urged me to keep moving until I finally reached the end of the hall. A lone oak door, likely meant to lead to a stairwell, blocked the end of the hall. The door could easily be my gate to heaven, leading me straight to the kitchen or even a parlor with leftover tea cookies, or it could just as easily be my gate to hell...

*Guess I won't know by only staring at it...*

Never in my life had I put so much anticipation behind just opening doors, but it couldn't necessarily be helped. This door had a high-pitched *creak* to it, clearly in need of some oiling. I peeked through the crack in the door, darting my gaze around in search of any clue as to my portal's destination before I committed to entering. The first realization I made was that it wasn't the kitchen. In fact, it almost looked like a bedroom... if a bedroom had been scheduled for demolition by a pack of coyotes.

A thick, luxurious carpet rolled down the expansive floor, littered with shrapnel from broken vases, cracked canvas frames, and the stuffing from various cushions. A few candle sticks and lamps remained upright, but none were lit, casting the room in eerie shadows that blurred the far corners from my vision. It was so quiet...

I creaked the door open another inch, feeling my curiosity draw me with an indiscernible pull. Despite the damage, the room was beautifully built, with vaulted ceilings, twisted gold wall sconces, and a dazzling pair of stained-glass doors that led out to...

*A balcony!*

A gasp rushed through my lungs as I stepped into the ravaged bedroom. Perhaps the balcony wasn't as high as the other window I'd seen. Maybe I could get the attention of the guard below and jump to safety. Oh! But I'll need to go back and get the others first. I'll just check through the doors first and see if...

My heels clicked to a halt in the dead center of the room and my rock-solid remorse anchored my feet to the floor.

*The doors... They may be glass, but they're still doors. The beast likely already locked them, too.*

I pressed my hands to my forehead as I drew out a frustrated groan. My fingers dug into my oily hair, greasy and slick from four days without a proper wash and sleeping on waxed floors. I trailed my tense fingers through my scalp and entangled them in my fraying braid as I tilted my head back to breathe out a quiet whine.

"Why... Why trap the girl who was already in a cage?"

I tilted my neck back up, my fingers still twisted in the top of my braid as I met my haggard reflection in an elaborately framed mirror. It had been days since I'd last seen my reflection in anything other than a silver spoon, and I had to say... I think I preferred the spoon. My flawless skin my home province always gushed over was pale from malnourishment, with dark shadows filling in under my eyes. My face had thinned a bit on the edges, and my frazzled hair and lopsided dress did little to emphasize the beauty that had gotten me invited here in the first place. The mirror's braided gold frame, which glittered with pearls and rubies, encompassed my ragged reflection like an elegant cage, barring me in like a pretty little portrait.

*If this is how the duke first saw me, would he have ever requested my hand to begin with?*

The question didn't linger in my mind for long, because out of the corner of my eye, something glittered off the bottom of the mirror as vibrantly as a fallen piece of sun. I followed the glint and saw it was coming from just in front of my feet, where a tipped over nightstand rested. I crouched to inspect the glint and instantly felt my stomach plummet out of my body.

It was a woven bracelet... with a sparkling gold charm twinkling in the center.

*Isn't this what the beast used to communicate with Ian?*

My hands trembled, but I couldn't stop myself from reaching for the discarded band. The round gold charm was no bigger than a glass bead, but the dancing light of magic within made it more vibrant than the clearest diamond. I pressed the charm against my palm, feeling an odd surge of warmth spark through me as I rose unsteadily to my feet, my eyes still directed on the bracelet.

"If this is in here, then that means the beast..."

"Was here first."

# chapter nine

*It would seem Father's trap worked... and what a pretty mouse I'd caught.*

The duchess spun around; her warm brown eyes went as wide as a harvest moon, glowing with an equal amount of intensity and intrigue. The shock that twitched her soft features did little to distract from her undeniable beauty. Her startle caused her smooth cheeks to gloss in a nervous blush and pressed ruby lips to swell.

*Realms, she is stunning...*

I quickly shook off my distraction with a stiffening of my shoulders, ensuring that I eyed my prey with the commanding presence of a proper captor. Luring her out had been successful, but now that she was here, what was my next move?

*Father has been right so far...*

A large bite tore from my pride, leaving my dignity wounded as a brief flicker of the late king's image flashed behind the duchess's petrified form in the mirror.

**'Now's your chance.'** His slithering voice crept into my ear, sending a chilling ripple down my unmoving spine. **'Kill her... Her corpse will be the perfect motivation for the grand duke.'**

I didn't answer him; my gaze remained latched onto the surprisingly brave woman who had yet to scream or run. She was definitely afraid... yet she didn't cower. It was just like the moment I first saw her in the hallway. She had been startled then too, but she didn't run from me. She didn't run from the marred beast...

It would be so simple to kill her, it could even be painless, and her beauty would simply freeze, as if she had merely fallen into a peaceful slumber. But killing her still seemed so... foolish. Why should I get rid of my strongest bartering piece so early in the game?

"I-it's Conan, right?" Her stammered voice nearly caused me to jump. I'm not sure if my shock came from not anticipating her to speak, or the fact that she had actually used my name. I'd heard her voice before in her native tongue, but now that the talisman had translated it, I could hear a sharpness hiding behind her melodic tone. "Or do you prefer 'the beast' instead?" Her voice steadied with each word as her almond eyes swept smoothly between our two bracelets. It was as if she was testing the water, seeing how much man was actually buried inside the monster she'd already seen.

*'Don't answer her.'* My head pounded with the aggression of a bucking stallion. *'Kill her before she makes a run for it.'*

"Call me whatever you see fit." I took a looming step forward, ignoring the picking voice as I tested the waters myself. The girl was tall, but still no match for my towering build. I stopped a foot away from her, tucking my chin to my chest in order to look down at the unmoving duchess. "Now, what are you doing outside the ballroom?"

She didn't wince, but I could see her throat bob with a gentle swallow, her steel gaze shielding the true spiral of emotions that lay behind them. "Who said we couldn't leave?" she said pointedly, her voice pitching a touch at the end despite her impressive display of bravery.

*'What are you doing!? Kill the brat!'*

"Quiet," I hushed, my teeth gritted in a tense clench. This time the duchess did flinch, but it looked more offended than fearful.

"Why? You asked me a question?" Out of nowhere, a spark flared her voice, cutting through the lingering terror as if it had merely been a curtain veiling something far more vicious. "If you lured me here to kill me, then the least you can do is be polite about it." She balled her fists, snapping them to her sides like a toy soldier as she glared.

I couldn't help but arch my scarred brow, still keeping my dominating posture solid. "You may be a duchess, but this is my castle now," I growled, tilting my head to flaunt my less appealing side as I narrowed my bloodshot eye on her. Her feet shifted uncomfortably, but impressively, her stone façade didn't even twitch. Maybe killing her wouldn't be such a bad idea after all... Stubborn hostages were often more troublesome than they were worth. I slid my dagger from my belt, flicking the light in her direction with only the shrinking of her pupils to alert me she had even noticed it at all. "My castle, my rules."

She crinkled her delicate nose, a surprisingly attractive scowl souring her face. "I do believe that until the province is signed over to your beastliness, the castle is indeed *not* yours. Currently, you're just an uninvited guest with impeccably terrible party manners, and I, for one, don't appreciate being growled at after I so generously delivered myself into your death trap." She folded her slender arms with a heated huff, all fear fully dissolved into headstrong irritation. It was as if she had accepted that walking into this room sealed her death, but her running mouth wasn't going to let her last words be in vain. "If you're going to kill me, then get it over with already. I'm too hungry to put up a proper fight, so don't worry about me running off. Although, I can't promise I won't attempt to kick you between the legs or punch you in the nose before I go down. I've had a long night, and honestly, I could use a little stress relief before the end." She flicked her eyes between the two potential points of injury as if calculating which she would be the most likely to hit when I lunged for an attack.

Never in my life had I felt at such a loss for words...

For a brief moment, all I could do was study her, trying to

determine if the confinement had diluted her brain capacity or if she truly was this blunt. Either way, she had me puzzled. Was this the standard way for duchesses to conduct themselves? Or was this one broken? My thoughts scrambled, debating between putting the odd creature out of her misery or keeping her around like a quirky three-legged dog. Although, she was more like a panther than a poodle... It didn't feel doubtful that her bite would live up to her bark.

Her long dark lashes flicked like a butterfly's wings as she darted her eyes between my blade and tangled expression. "Hmm, so you're *not* going to kill me, then?" Her full lips quirked, her eyes still locked on my nose in case the punch was still necessary.

"I'm still mulling it over," I clipped, my throat tightening as I watched her cheeks suck in a touch.

"Ah." She bit her lip with a gentle nod of her head. Loose pieces of her black curls tumbled in front of her face, framing her uncertainty more vividly than any of the hideous canvases that were in the room. "Well, don't let me rush you." She rolled her eyes sassily before fixating them back on my blade. "But if you do decide to kill me... You should know that your hostages are out of food."

My blade dipped as my muscles loosened to make room for the sheer bewilderment that funneled through my veins. This girl was facing down the tip of a monster's dagger... yet she still bothered to prioritize those ridiculous captives. Truly, they wouldn't last a day without her, considering she possessed every brain cell in that ballroom.

"That hardly seems like my problem." I sneered, my breath hot and flustered against my lips.

"Actually, it *is* your problem," she jeered back, once again unleashing the veiled panther scratching beneath her pretty surface. "Did it ever occur to you that the grand duke won't hand over the province unless he can see the captives *alive* first? If we all die, then it won't be any better than you trying to purchase land with fool's gold. Kill me for intruding if you must, but don't be such a hothead that you let the others die simply because you're too stubborn to give them a blasted sandwich!" Anger fumed off her like a steaming pork cutlet, flushing her neck with a red that could shame the bewitched rose.

"And is that why you left the ballroom? For a *blasted sandwich*?" I scoffed, folding my arms as I tried to pinpoint the source of her frustration. Was she truly just hungry? Or was the ballroom more aggravating than a suite with a back-talking mirror?

She placed her hands firmly on her curved hips, swishing her skirts like a smooth breeze as she tightened her glare. "Yes," she huffed, then paused to bite her lower lip in unspoken thought. "Although... As Duchess Mirabel of Omaira, I feel I'm permitted to request perhaps a blasted fruit salad instead..." She removed her hands from her hips with a taut shrug. "That is, if you're taking orders. Or are you still working out whether to kill me?"

I knitted my brows, my head throbbing with the intruding presence of the king.

*What an odd woman... An odd duchess...*

For the first time since this entire takeover, my thoughts began to flow clearly, like a muddied pond suddenly filtered through a thousand sieves. This woman was a duchess... One who was intended to inherit her own province. My mind flashed back to my time in Omaira, recalling all the political information dumped on me by the beast's previous leader. Mirabel Jada Brantley... The woman who was gifted her brother's birthright.

*'Are you done babbling with the woodworm? Or are you ready to finally inherit a province?'* Father's voice screeched in my brain like a squealing teapot, and a wicked smile curled my plotting expression.

*Oh, I'll inherit a province, Father. In fact, I'll inherit two.*

"Congratulations, Duchess Mirabel, was it?" I flashed her my pearly smile, thankful I couldn't see how hideous my scars made it look in the mirror.

"Mira," she snipped, her almond eyes squinting with suspicion. "I don't usually require the *common folk* to use my title." Her ruby lips smirked a touch at the edge, causing my charming smile to grind.

"How thoughtful of you to ditch the formalities, dear Mira." My smile turned crooked, and for the first time since our initial meeting, her fortress of unyielding bravery crumbled just a touch. Her suspicion turned anxious, causing her fingers to entangle themselves in her wrinkled skirt.

"*Dear?* Realms, you either want something or you actually want two punches before you take my life." Her tone hardened, rebuilding the cracks in her walls as she released the bunched fabric.

"Actually, I've decided to let you live." I folded my arms behind my back, slowly stepping away from the puzzled duchess without letting my smile fade. "That is, if you're willing to bargain for your life... and the lives of the hostages."

Her eyes dilated, then instantly narrowed, nearly slitting like the eyes of the panther that growled within. "What kind of bargain...?" Her voice was sharp, clinging to each word as if she needed to use them to fight another round.

I huffed out a quiet chuckle. "Why, it's simple, my *dear.* I'm looking for a province, and it just so happens that you're in line to inherit one." Her jaw dropped like a broken marionette, but her eyes remained tight and flared. I smirked, removing my arms from behind my back to hold them out more welcomingly. "I swear to let you walk out of this castle alive, and even provide daily meals for the other hostages... if you agree to marry me."

# *chapter ten*

"Marry you!?" My voice came out part-gag and part-squawk, probably similar to the splitting scream of a peacock. "Do you truly believe that after all the suffering you have inflicted upon me, my family, and all the starving captives in that ballroom, that I would ever let you marry into my title!?" His smug grin caused his dark ebony eyes to alight like a distant nebula, swirling with mystery and an irritating amount of the unknown. I clenched my jaw with enough pressure to crack a diamond. "Let me tell you something, *beast*." I took a hazardous step forward, closing the distance between us with the tension of dogs in a cage match. "I've already met my life's quota of one despicable betrothed, so I'm afraid you've missed your window. That, and I'd rather swallow glass."

His twisted smile parted into a low chuckle. "Well, you did say you were hungry. Shall I fetch you a plate? I must say, some of the red-and-purple-stained windows do look rather delectable." His infuriatingly perfect smile tilted as he cocked his head to the side, causing his dark hair to fall over his brow and cover half of his red-veined eye. With most of his scars concealed, it was easy to see how handsome he must have been. It was no wonder he was so overly-confident. He was probably used to getting everything he wanted with a face like that.

"If I eat it, then will you feed the hostages?" I snarked with a challenging tilt of my hips.

"I believe the proposed bargain was that they only get fed when you marry me." he retorted, his voice lilting between a serious captor and a teasing flirt.

"Are you sure I can't eat the glass instead?" I scrunched up my nose as I made a show of looking him up and down. "It can't be as painful as the pickled turnips."

The teasing light left his eyes as I slowly picked at the thin layer of his patience. "Enough bartering. The deal remains as it is." His shoulders stiffened, revealing a tensed vein in the side of his muscular neck. "I won't kill you, but the choice of whether you live is still yours. So, what will it be? Starvation or matrimony?" He tilted his chin upward, as if his gaze needed more height to tower over my shorter stature.

Anger burned in the forefront of my chest, searing a hole to burst out at any moment. I had never truly wanted to marry Ian, but I was willing to do so for the sake of my citizens. But to marry the beast... It would still be the *noble* thing to do since it would provide for the captives, yet it was so much worse... This time, my choice was being manipulated. If I didn't sacrifice myself for the greater good, then how could I ever declare myself a duchess? My blood turned to pure fire.

*How dare he... How dare this man treat me like a convenient tool, assuming I will simply bend to his threats out of a good-natured heart.*

I stormed up to him, my face twisted in searing hatred and disgust as I raised my palm and slapped him straight across his beastly face. The slap echoed against the stone walls, but not even a groan or gasp of air escaped the silent beast. It was as if being struck on the cheek was no different from accepting my hand for a shake. However, his coy smile was wiped away, leaving a muted expression with his serious eyes now hollow and his lips pressed into a fine line.

Not even an ounce of my anger felt relieved as I steamed in front of his unbothered expression. "I'm a woman, not a contract." My vocal cords rattled together with the grittiness of crunching gravel, my flaring eyes skewering him in place. "If you want my province, then you had better rethink your reluctance on killing me, because no number of manipulative bargains or twisted schemes will ever convince me to wed a *beast*."

I leaned forward, hissing his title an inch from his nose before I pivoted to vanish back out the door I'd entered. Heat erupted from my chest, filling my toes and burning at the pads of my fingers as I yanked the suite's door open, slamming it hard against the already damaged walls.

I stormed through the door as it swung shut behind me, not even noticing that it hadn't directed me back to the original hallway until I was in the middle of an unfamiliar room. My heart pounded with the force of a stampeding elephant, running off a dangerous mixture of fear-induced adrenaline and fury.

*I ran straight into the beast's trap, but instead of killing me... he proposed?*

My thoughts swirled like an electrified tornado, jolting me from every angle as I spun around the room to take in my new surroundings. It was another bedroom, but this one looked to be unoccupied. Seeing that the beast hadn't directed me to a dungeon or cellar caused a slight knot of tension to loosen around my pulsating heart. I pressed a gentle hand to the center of my chest to quiet the hammering organ, but nearly jumped when I felt the bracelet shift in my palm.

I pulled my hand away to inspect the glittering gold charm that adorned the woven band. I must have twisted the band around my fingers when I was stressed and forgot I was still holding it.

*Well, at least now if I see him peeking in on the ballroom again, I can curse at him in a language he'll understand.*

I slipped the bracelet around my wrist as I inspected the new room with a curious eye. It was just as nice as the suite I had initially been given upon my arrival, only smaller. A large four-posted bed with a satin canopy rested against the far wall, opposed by a tall wardrobe, cherry-wood vanity, and a small settee. My stomach rumbled alongside a fierce cramp, practically dragging my ailing body to the thick mattress.

With a puff of cushions and thick blankets, I fell face-first onto the burgundy coverlet, breathing in the fresh scent of clean linens and a lingering rose spray. After a few moments of letting my body sink into the snuggly mattress, I rolled onto my back and stared up at the canopy as if it were the most richly designed painting in the Ruby Realm.

*What do I tell the others when I get back? Should I go back?*

I pressed my palms against my eyes, ignoring the sting from the freshly-clotted cut on my right hand. They were likely already panicking about me being gone, and if I told them I ran straight into the beast, they would definitely demand I never leave again.

*But what would they say about the beast's bargain?*

My stomach interrupted my thoughts with a painful growl that caused my head to split. I pressed my thumbs into my temples as I sat up from the pillowy mattress, then scanned the room once more. If I felt this bad, then it was likely the others were in a similar state. I couldn't just abandon them when I had an opportunity to bring back something useful. This wasn't the kitchen, but there were still pillows, blankets, and a few other useful trinkets.

My limbs moved as stiffly as rusted gears as I forced my aching body to approach the tall wardrobe. I pulled open the carved doors and found a small collection of more simplistic dresses, some clean stockings, and a wool cloak. I snagged a pale blue dress from the rack and wasted no time changing into it, casting aside the heavy satin gown with as much delight as a snake shedding its irritating skin. The soft cotton hugged my waist and flared out at my hips flatteringly, with a pleated skirt embroidered with white blossoms. The short sleeves puffed subtly at the shoulders, and the skirt stopped a few inches above my ankles. It was probably a touch too small for me, and intended for a younger lady, but it wasn't made of yards of bulky satin, so I was going to flaunt it like it was stitched from diamond thread.

I hoisted as many of the other dresses I could from the rack, along with the cloak and stockings, then tossed them onto the massive bed. I dug through the drawers and found a small wind-up clock with a bent hand, as well as two old candies wrapped in cellophane. The clock joined the pile of clothes on the bed, and I popped one of the candies into my mouth, instantly puckering from the tart lemon flavor. The candy coated my stomach, easing some of the cramps as I shoved the bed pillows to the center of the bed and wrapped the entire bundle up in the blankets like a giant sack.

The makeshift blanket bag was comedically large and heavier than a medium tugboat, but nonetheless I dragged the supplies off the bed and yanked it to the door. The task was far more laborious with a half-starved body, causing me to grow dizzy and short-breathed just from dragging it a mere five feet. After pausing to catch my breath, I placed my hand on the doorknob with a bitten lip, curious as to whether the door would lead me back to the ballroom, or the beast's lair... or perhaps somewhere else entirely.

Either way, I'd already picked the room clean of anything useful, so sticking around wasn't really an option. Feeling far too cranky for any further hesitation, I pulled the door open and was instantly greeted with the grand entrance to the ballroom's balcony. Part of me felt relieved when I saw I didn't need to drag my haul any farther than a few inches, while the other part dimmed at seeing the same four barring walls.

"Your Grace!" Azura spotted me first, gasping like it was the first time she'd breathed air in weeks as she jeered a finger in my direction. The rest of the eyes followed her outstretched hand, flooding the previously quiet space with stampeding feet and relieved gasps.

Before anyone could make it to the top of the stairs, I

tugged my bulging blanket bundle through the door and closed it behind me before anyone could argue about it being open. Lady Henrietta was the fastest, practically tackling me in a hug. When she pulled away, her eyes were round and glassy with unshed tears.

"Your Grace, you're alive!" she choked, her fragile features scrunching up like a dried tulip. "W-we t-thought the beast had stolen you away in our sleep and k-k-kill—" She couldn't finish, her sobs bursting through as the rest of the hostages encircled me. They stared at me like I was an apparition, their faces pale with uneasy disbelief.

Azura slipped through the crowd, her wrinkled red dress catching the light of the nearest candle like a fluttering cardinal. "Mira... Where did you... H-how did you...?" Her olive-green eyes had shifted to a charcoal gray under the heavy shadows of her unspoken terror and the low lighting.

"I'm alright," I announced, ensuring that even the few who hadn't been brave enough to step away from the rose and run up the stairs had heard me. I put on my most dignified smile, flooding it with reassurances I didn't feel as my stomach once again ground within me. "I left on my own accord to search for food and supplies. While I was unable to locate the kitchen, I did run into the beast and—"

"The beast!?" Lord Tocken nearly pushed his niece over as he shoved to the front of the crowd, his round face tight from the pressure of his deep frown. "What were you thinking!? You're meant to be our grand duchess, yet you go and do something as reckless as running straight into the beast's trap!?"

Lord Illumen placed a hand on his brother's shoulder. "Jarold, calm yourself. As you said, this is our future grand duchess, not our niece; you shouldn't be so outspoken in your opinions."

Lord Tocken swatted his brother's hand away, swiping his furrowed glare from me to him. "It doesn't matter if she's Azura or the emperor's daughter! She's put us all in danger by proving to the beast that his tricks can work."

"Uncle!" Azura snapped, stepping in front of the two men with her hawk-like stare skewering Lord Tocken. "That's enough. We haven't even heard the full story yet, so there's certainly no need to jump to conclusions."

My heart jolted with a twinge of anxiety as the focus of the squabbling trio turned to me. The truth of the matter was that I *had* fallen into the beast's trap, and he *did* seem to be considering laying more. Well, not so much traps, as unagreeable bargains. I pressed my tongue against the back of my teeth as I collected my thoughts in an attempt to phrase my castle explorations in the most appealing way possible.

"I found his other bracelet," I said a little too quickly as I held up my glittering wrist. Soft whispers murmured on all sides of me as the other hostages took in the sight of the magical charm. "We were able to communicate, well... to some extent. I wouldn't necessarily call him a friendly conversationalist."

This seemed to snatch everyone's attention, their whispers instantly quieting. Henrietta's thick lashes fluttered curiously. "W-what did you talk about?" She looked like a school-girl awaiting to hear whether the boy she was pining for liked her back.

"Uh... not much." I scratched at the side of my neck as our lengthy conversation about whether he was going to kill me lilted through my mind. "I told him we were low on food and that his hostages would be useless if we were... you know, not *useful* hostages."

"And what did he say?" Lord Tocken folded his thick arms a touch below his dangling pocket watch, his full brow knitted tighter than a woolen sock.

I moved my scratching hand from my neck to my chin as I debated the wisdom in sharing the beast's absurd bargain with them. "Well, he didn't kill me when I asked for food." I shrugged nonchalantly, switching my attention to the wadded-up blanket beside me. "But he did lead me into a spare bedroom where I managed to grab some extra comforts and some spare clothes for a few ladies."

As if I'd just told them I'd delivered a steaming plate of smoked turkey legs, every eye widened, larger than burning stars, as they turned their attention to the bundle. To my relief, the mysterious collection of cushions, stockings, and trinkets tore everyone's interest away from my conversation with the beast long enough for me to take a few steps out of their cluster. As I moved down the staircase to the open center of the ballroom, echoes of ladies squabbling over the clean dresses filtered through the stuffy air. It took me a moment to realize that Azura and her uncles had followed behind me, their shoes clicking off the marble floors like out of sync shadows.

My chest tightened with the realization that I hadn't entirely escaped sharing the full story after all. With a forced smile, I spun around to face the trio. "Did you not want to look through the supplies I gathered?" I questioned a little more hopeful than I had meant to. "There's a lovely clock you might be interested in seeing, Lord Tocken."

His forehead crinkled with a sour frown. "Your Grace, I don't need another clock," he said tartly. "What I need is to know what the beast plans to do about our accommodations." His voice was stern, but a slight squeak in his words gave a clear window into the fear he was harboring.

Azura's caramel skin paled, her eyes dimming as she looked between her uncles and me with twiddling thumbs. "The rose is getting weaker, but I'm sure I can make it last a few weeks. I'm just worried we won't even need that much time before..."

*Before we starve...*

A painful cramp twisted through my abdomen as another fierce growl erupted in my stomach. Lord Tocken was right to be so worried. The beast seemed to have little care on whether we survived, despite the fact that we were his only leverage. I chewed my lip, almost enjoying the feeling of touching my teeth to something that wasn't another banana.

*I can't keep the beast's deal from them... Not when it doesn't only affect me...*

"The beast doesn't intend to feed us," I said grimly, keeping my voice low and soft before it had a chance to echo off the stone floors.

The blood drained from their faces, and Lord Illumen nearly stumbled backward. "N-not at all? But if we die, then—"

"He knows," I clipped, my breath hot from the returning frustration of the beast's insufferable pride. "He simply doesn't care... mostly because he thinks he can get something out of us by withholding meals... or more specifically, get something out of *me*." I tilted my head back, unable to bite back the groan as I laced my fingers around the back of my neck.

Azura sucked in a sharp breath. "Oh, my realms... you're the duchess. Did he ask you to—"

"Yes," I hissed, once again cutting them off in a less than ladylike manner. "He wants a province, and apparently any province will do." I huffed a stray hair from my eyes, watching the two lord's expressions twist into understanding and slight disgust. "If I marry the beast, he'll let everyone eat."

No one spoke for a long, uncomfortable moment, leaving the space as awkward as someone proposing in the midst of a funeral. The lords snuck each other a few unspoken glances, and Azura's face burned with a red blush as she furrowed her green eyes in deep thought. I simply rocked back on my heels, itching to get a glimpse into their hungry thoughts.

"No, no, you can't possibly let him marry into your province," Lord Tocken finally declared, his words tittering like a flustered old woman. "Better for us all to starve than to let an entire province go hungry when he salts their fields and burns their villages."

Lord Illumen cocked his head. "Now hold on a moment, let's not go that far..." His eyes drifted to the ceiling, still clearly swaying in thought. "Imagine if the duchess *did* marry the beast. Marriages can be annulled, can they not?"

*Annulled?* My stomach knotted at the thought of marrying the beast, only to send him packing the moment we were set free. Something tells me he wouldn't be the type of ex-husband to leave quietly...

"Don't be ludicrous," Lord Tocken huffed. "Marrying the beast is only a short-term solution with a set of long-term consequences. She's not marrying him and that's final."

My veins crackled, sparking my earlier frustration into a churning anger toward the stout lord who felt inclined to dictate my prospective marriages.

*He isn't wrong, though. Marrying the beast will only make things worse for the realm, but even so...*

"I'll take care of it myself," I said tartly, lifting my chin to shield the rising flames in my eyes.

Both men appeared instantly taken aback, Lord Tocken's mouth opening and closing like a suffocating fish. "Your Grace... with all due respect, I don't think it's wise for you—"

"Actually, there was no respect due, because I don't require foreign lords to validate my decisions." My tone was ice, but I kept my expression as smooth and polished as the marble beneath our feet. "Tomorrow, I shall return to the beast to negotiate for our meals. Then I shall decide for *myself* whether joining him in matrimony will be the best decision for Omaira and the imprisoned citizens of Dhurin."

Azura stretched out a weak hand, her eyes wide with fear. "But, Mira... What if he tries to kill you?"

*Well, he already tried...*

I gave my shoulders a soft shrug and rolled my eyes as I

completely abandoned all etiquette. "I'll die either way, but if my choices are starvation, slashed by a beast, or matrimony, then I suppose with a wedding there will at least be something to eat."

# chapter eleven

"You're being a fool." The mirror sneered behind my back.

"Shut up!" I snapped, my brain crackling with a hundred sparks from his verbal jabs. "Don't you have anything better to do than insult me?" My blood curdled in my clenched fists, itching to shatter the stained-glass doors I was peering through.

More troops had gathered below the towering balcony, along with what appeared to be heavy-duty tools and even some machinery... They were no longer setting up camps for diplomatic discussions involving the transfer of a province's ownership; they were now preparing to break down walls.

*Obviously, they don't fear me enough.*

"If it's true then it's not an insult; it's an observation," the king's insufferable ghost chided behind me, the growl in his tone building like a rising storm. "The fact that it tampers with your temper only proves it's true. You were always too stubborn to admit when you—"

"I said, be quiet!" I twisted my shoulders around to spear him with my fuming scowl. I could feel the intense red heat seeping into my skin like the veined paths of a rock volcano, threatening to crack and split into a raging inferno. "Don't you dare speak to me like you know me. The only parts of me you truly know are the ones you crafted, and I doubt even *you* can comprehend the damages you so lovingly caused my mental state." The image in the mirror flickered for the briefest moment, but I couldn't tell if it was his presence fading or if my mind was confirming my psychotic state.

"Your little 'breakdown' is all your own doing." He snorted with a roll of his voided eyes. My muscles clenched, burrowing my nails into my palms until a warm dab of blood dampened my fingertip. His brows furrowed as stiffly as his stone heart. "Need I remind you? Your sanity cracked *after* you thrusted a sword through my heart!" His deep voice escalated with a rising vibrato, causing my fury-blurred eyes to wonder if I had seen the mirror rattle from the noise. "You're the problem, son."

*Son.*

My anger was eclipsed by the numbing pain of that jabbing syllable. I was this monster's child, and even once his heir, but I was never his son... Sons didn't have to kill their fathers to ensure they didn't do it first.

"I'm not the problem." I kicked the stubby leg of the bedpost, which instantly snapped as easily as a twig, causing the bed to slant with a crash onto the floor. "You are. You're the one who groomed my addiction for power. You're the one who sparked a war in our homeland. And you're the one who is clouding my mind so densely that I can't even manage a proper takeover!" My chest heaved and burned as the rest of the magma bubbled out of my spewing lips. I looked up at my father's image in the hopes of seeing any glimpse of humanity slotted inside his dark eyes, but his expression was blank. Robbing me of any satisfaction I might have seen behind the cold, hard glass.

"You can't accomplish anything, because you can't obey." His tone was rigid, scratching at my skull and peeling it into tiny irreparable shreds.

"I did obey!" My voice cracked as I grabbed the nearest stool and hurled it into the writing desk with a shower of splinters. "For years, I did nothing but obey! And when the time came, I took control..." I staggered forward, my hands trembling so aggressively I had to squeeze them back into fists. "You trained me to be the most powerful man in the room... so I killed you. But even in death, you're still here, always occupying my mind to remind me that I'm not what *you* consider strong."

He didn't blink, his thick wrinkles barely twitching around his stern frown, making him look more like a haunted portrait than a hallucinated image. "If you were *strong* then that measly duchess would be dead already." His eyes narrowed so quickly that I had to blink to ensure they hadn't slitted vertically like a proper serpent. "If you were strong, your mother would still be alive."

The cobweb-coated scar around my heart split open with a vicious crack. A collection of decade-old pain, anger, and numbness spread through my veins like a rapid infection, fighting against the defenses shielding my mind.

"Leave her out of this!" I growled through a blinding throb of pain in my skull. My hands shot to my ears, pressing against them as if I could prevent his words from creeping into my possessed mind. I needed to distract myself, needed to tear my thoughts away from the shredding pain of those memories. "The duchess only lives because she's most useful alive," I hissed through my teeth as a touch of the pressure released from my skull. "Killing her this soon would only be wasteful."

The king snorted. "*Wasteful.*" His scathing glare branded me with a hot sear across my scars. "Wasteful is to let this castle slip through your fingers the same way you did our homeland." His voice was biting, so much so that I almost didn't catch the crack of a knock against the master bedroom's door. *A knock?* "The girl can't be counted on—no pawn can. If you truly wish to regain your power, then you must do what's necessary instead of continuing your streak of weakness."

My head felt foggy, like a thick mist of toxic vapors had seeped into my blood and clouded my irises. Another knock rapped at the door and I moved forward, stumbling over the broken leg of the stool I threw earlier. "I'm not weak." I tried to sound intimidating, but my voice came out more a mumble, allowing the fog to infect even my tongue.

"You're feeble," the mirror spat. Each flick of his tongue burned against my scarred flesh, sticking his verbal lashes to me like a hot wax seal. "A worthless mongrel, fit to don the name *beast.*" I stopped in front of the door, my heart swelling with the rapidness of my rising blood pressure.

*He's wrong...*

"I'm not a beast." My voice came out gravelly, lined with a fresh bloodthirst that swirled into my gaze as I looked down at the brass doorknob. "I'm a king."

"Then prove it." The voice faded behind me, but the sharpness of his words still grazed me. "Kill the girl and take what's yours."

My fingers clenched around the doorknob with a throbbing fist. Father didn't think I could do it. He didn't think I had what it took to be powerful, to be a ruler. He was wrong, and I needed to prove it. Once I did, maybe then he'd finally release his claws from me and vanish from my mind for good. I just have to kill the duchess... Kill her and use her corpse as a final warning to the grand duke.

*Then the province will be mine, and Father will be gone.*

I twisted the door handle with an unnecessary amount of force, swinging the door into the wall with a room quaking smack. My shoulders rose and fell with a hot intake of air, my teeth bared and gritted with a bloodthirsty rage as I stared down at the startled young duchess whose knocking fist hovered where the door had once stood.

I lowered my red-glassed gaze onto her, barely even seeing her doll-like beauty through the screeching desire to end the torture saturating my mind. She didn't look up at me, her autumnal-brown eyes fixated on the wrecked room behind me. Compared to my daunting height, she looked so small... Much like a fragile field mouse unaware of the preying lion who's shadow she lurked in.

*All I have to do is—*

"Oh good, you're awake." Her tart voice interrupted my thoughts, jarring me as she pushed past my towering form as if I were a dainty silk curtain. Despite initially being taken aback by the state of the room, she waltzed straight into the suite as if she'd done it a thousand times. The red drained from my vision, replaced with an open-mouthed gawk as the woman casually dusted broken glass off a bench and seated herself with a graceful fold of her hands upon her lap. "We need to talk."

The door swung shut behind me, actually causing me to jump. *Does this woman not possess the ability to channel caution? Or is she just plain clueless?* I straightened my spine with a ragged clearing of my throat, composing myself as I shifted my gaze in her direction.

"I see no reason for us to do so," I said starkly, my finger grazing the edge of my dagger as I slowly crept forward. *I'll make it quick. One fatal blow right in the view of Father's ridiculous mirror.* "You already made it perfectly clear that you have no interest in aligning with me, so I'm afraid—"

"Excuse me, but I don't recall ever giving you a formal answer." She held up a dainty hand, cutting me off as if I were a child asking for an extra biscuit. My voice silenced, too baffled to respond. "You cannot expect a lady to make such an important decision in a matter of seconds, especially when she's being pressured by a brooding and obnoxiously egotistical captor." She crossed her long legs, fluttering the light blue skirt around her ankles. "So, I've come to discuss the terms of the bargain with you, hopefully in a far less heated manner."

Every ounce of bloodlust dissolved from my rigid muscles as I focused all my mental efforts on trying to wrap my brain around this strange woman's words.

*She... is considering my bargain?*

My fingers dropped from the edge of my blade as I forced my expression not to give away the utter bafflement that was bubbling beneath my skin. If she was truly considering my offer, then killing her would be a grave mistake... at least for now.

I tilted my head, jeering out my chin a touch with a suspicious incline of my brow. "Are you saying that you'll agree to marry me...?" I folded my arms loosely in front of me, my head spinning with the fresh idea.

"Oh realms, no!" She actually laughed, rocking back on the bench before grabbing the edges to pull herself back forward.

I wrinkled my forehead and huffed as a new flash of irritation tugged at my nerves. "Then you're not here to bargain."

"Of course, I am," she said promptly with a stiff cross of her arms. Her sweet nose crinkled with an offended frown, accentuating the vivid expressiveness of her eyes. "I have more to offer than just my title, you know."

"The title is all I—"

"Oh, hush." She batted a hand at me, once again snatching my tongue as I gaped at her in disbelief. "You don't know what you want. At least that's what people always tell me, so I figure it must be true enough for me to tell you, too." She huffed a quiet sneer under her breath, small enough that I didn't believe it was geared toward me, but someone else entirely. "Anyway, I did a lot of thinking last night while I was squirming in bed with a shriveled stomach, and I think I've devised a solution that would be beneficial for the both of us. I'll tell you about it, but you have to promise not to get all huffy with me like last time."

I nearly threw another stool.

*Me? Huffy!?*

I took a heavy step forward, my eyes furrowed with a teeth-bared frown. "Come again, *duchess!?*" I growled, my temper officially snapping after all the switching between murdering and not murdering. "You haven't let me finish a single sentence since you barged in here! What makes you think I want to listen to some ridiculous plan of yours, when I could just as easily kill you where you sit?" My fingers twitched for the dagger, but I didn't grab it yet. I couldn't kill her without at least unraveling her wild mind first.

"We've already been over this. You won't kill me." She rolled her eyes, her tone completely assured in her safety. "And I'm not going to tell you if you can't keep your temper under control. I have dealt with enough impatient men for the last few days, and I'm not putting up with it any longer." Her warm eyes brimmed with ice, more serious than a swearing nun.

I felt the urge to tear out my hair one strand at a time, fighting the urge to snatch her by her delicate throat and dangle her, feet-first, off the balcony. But as much as I wanted to watch her confidence crack, I couldn't fight the desire to know what she *thought* she had to offer. The never-ending itch for power my father had instilled in me urged me to learn more, to learn what could be mine...

"What?" I clipped through clenched teeth. "What deal do you *think* you can offer me?" My hands balled into steel fists, channeling my shaking anger as best as I could.

A small, sweet smile spanned the duchess's lips, causing my tremors to halt long enough to notice that her eyes sparkled with the tiniest flecks of gold when cast in the right light. She smoothed out her skirts, then laced her fingers back into a proper fold. "I would like for you to provide me, and all the other hostages, daily meals for the duration of our confinement." She paused, and her sweet, ladylike smile shifted back into her serious and unmoving stare. She slipped one of her hands from her lap, raising it up so the golden bracelet twinkled around her wrist in the light. "And in exchange, I'll teach you how to communicate without this."

My fists unraveled as I stared blankly at the simple charm that had acted as both my bridge to freedom and my shackle, preventing me from taking full control. "You'll teach me your language?" I questioned faintly, trying to hide the interest that festered in my mind.

She nodded firmly. "Yes." She lowered her wrist, placing it back in her lap as she looked up at me with hollow eyes. For the first time since her bold entrance, I noticed just how weary she looked. She hadn't looked wonderful yesterday, but today she truly looked weak. It was surprising that she had commanded so much authority when she was struggling to stand. "Give us access to the kitchens. With each meal you let us prepare, I promise to teach you as much about our language as I can until the meal is complete. The more often you feed us, the more you'll learn. I know it's not as advantageous as inheriting a whole province, but we both know you can't rule without at least being able to communicate with your advisors. And this..." She pointed at the bracelet again with a disdainful look. "We both know where it came from, and I, for one, wouldn't barter that its power is infinite."

I followed her gaze to the bracelet, feeling my chest tighten as roughly as a rusted screw. She was right. I couldn't rule this land without at least knowing the basics of the language.

*Blast it...*

I swallowed a lump in my throat, pricklier than a sea urchin. My thoughts swirled to try to deduce another solution to this outcome, but no matter how my mind spun it, there was no other better option. The duchess was right... She had something that I needed, and never in my life had it been more painful to admit that.

"You can have access to the dining room," I bartered, my voice firm and unwavering. For a moment her eyes widened, softening her features with the surprise that I had even partially agreed. "The kitchen has too many tools and potential weapons. I don't need anyone getting brave and swiping a cleaver from the cupboard."

Her thin brow arched and her full lips pursed curiously. "So, are you going to host us then?" she inquired thoughtfully.

"Host? What are you, parasites?" I scoffed. "No, I'll only bring a few items from the kitchen to make a meal. You all can handle the preparation yourself."

She nodded, a quiet thought frozen on her slightly parted lips as if there was still something troubling her about this arrangement. "Very well, then," she finally said, raising from the bench a bit more woozily than I had expected. "I think we have a deal. You let us eat, and I'll teach you how to communicate without sounding like an *actual* beast."

She crossed the room to extend her hand to me, and for a moment, I only glared at it, still feeling my aggravation stir. The mirror was barely in the corner of my vision, so I could tell that my father's ghost was absent from it, but somehow, I could still hear him screaming at me from beyond the glass. His voice tore into me, berating me for striking a deal with the duchess he had requested to see dead on the floor.

*You told me not to rely on other's gifts...* I glanced down at the charm glittering on the duchess's wrist, feeling the one on my own chafe against my skin as I wrapped my massive hand around her petite, smooth one. *This way, I won't have to.*

"Deal," I grumbled as she gave my hand a gentle shake. "The doors will lead to the dining room at six. Don't be late."

# chapter twelve

When I stepped out of the beast's tattered room, I found myself stepping into a lavish art gallery. Tall ceilings stretched up to curved cedar beams, painted with dark woodsy colors and embellished with gold etchings of leaves and flowers. Long windows, stretching almost two-stories' tall, lined the walls in between paintings, looking almost more stunning than the artwork itself. I stepped froward into the massive gallery, my steps echoing as if I had entered a cave. The stained-glass that filled each window seemed to depict moments of history in the Ruby Realm, with five windows lining the far wall, one for each province.

*Perhaps I should bring the beast here to learn some of our history as well as our language...*

My neck stiffened at the thought of trying to teach the stubborn man anything aside from a few manners. It was Azura's rose that had given me the idea to offer lessons to the beast. All the hostages had become so dependent on the flower that they'd lost the ability to think beyond its restrictions. They'd confined themselves to a bubble, allowing their lives to be dictated by its limitations out of fear of what will happen if they stepped away.

The beast was the same way.

I lifted the glittering charm into the warm orange light from the stained-glass's glow. It sparkled hypnotically in the jewel-toned silhouette of the realm's capital, Shainee. Rolling desert hills framed the lush oasis that housed the glass interpretation of the empire's royal palace. Shainee was the first province established, existing longer than our history books could date, which was the primary reason why it became our capital. In the corner of the glass mural was a small basket with charmed snakes dancing out of the top, alongside a winged lizard with a beady, purple-glass eye.

*The basilisks.*

Just how Omaira formerly had to deal with the beasts, and Dhurin had been plagued by the griffins, each of the other provinces had dealt with their fair share of monsters over the centuries. Although it wasn't until the last few decades that the mythical groups started removing themselves from the shadows and making their presence known as more than just mere myths.

I wrapped my arms around my torso, suddenly feeling chilled in the empty gallery. I passed by the other windows, taking in the abstract landscapes that actually soothed my cabin fever. The next window must have represented Dhurin, as made obvious by the flourishing gardens flooded with thick roses and fully bloomed dahlias. The castle in the glass mirrored its exterior almost perfectly, with the only abnormality being a stone griffin perched at the head of the elongated front gate.

The next window contained the rolling green forests of Isleen, the province in the upper east that contained most of our coal and oil mines. A small cave marked the corner of the glass, with an ominous black wing and tail poking out from the entrance to symbolize the province's dragons. The second to last window appeared to be for the lower eastern province of Sonal. Unlike Omaira's cold oceans and black pebble beaches, Sonal was a tropical paradise with white sands and warm turquoise waters. The sea-green glass twinkled like real water in the sun, making me long for a cleansing dip in its pure waves. At least, until I spotted the monstrous cameo in this window as well—a massive sea beast, larger than a whale, with a jagged tail and pointed teeth. The leviathans had always been the most elusive of the five criminal groups, always appearing to be an old wives' tale right up until an entire ship went missing overnight.

I moved onward, stopping in front of the final window with a sullen breath as I looked up at the familiar image of my beautiful province. Homesickness tore through me as I admired the likeness of the glass castle gleaming in the sunlight. The dense forests and black pebble shores were coated in a thick line of clouded white glass, creating a perfect resemblance of our lengthy winters. My heart snared at the thought of ever seeing snow again, ever feeling its icy sting as I brushed it off my shoulders on a blustery day. My longing eyes snagged on the ugly patch of brown lurking beneath the trees. A bulky creature, with golden eyes, sharp talons, and long fangs, marred the beautiful landscape with its mere existence.

*The Beasts.*

The sorrow in my heart twisted like a straining ratchet, tensing my core with my undeniable hatred toward the monster and his pack. My brother had smoked out the Beasts' leader only a few months ago, leaving us to believe that Omaira was finally free of their control on the province's underbelly. But that was before we knew one got away... one remaining monster who had fled his pack to infect another province with his dirty tricks.

*And now I was going to teach him the alphabet.*

I kicked at the floor as I stormed away from the image, no longer feeling nostalgic for my homeland. All my life, I had wanted to do nothing more than protect my province and the rest of the realm. Even when my ailment blocked my first desired path, I was content with choosing another, but now... Now, I was trapped. Trapped with an enemy of my home that I had no choice other than to help.

My skirts flicked with audible snaps of the fabric from the haste in my step. I went straight for the nearest exit and swung the door open, not caring about the magical gamble of where it might lead. The inflamed blood in my cheeks cooled the second I passed into the new space, practically causing my anger to leave itself at the threshold. A tall aviary, with a glass ceiling and an indoor garden sucked my breath from my lungs.

Birds fluttered around every corner as wistfully as a blurry dream. Their chirping and melodic songs saturated my mind in the flap of a wing, numbing my anger with the tune of their sirenic melodies. Sun cascaded through the glass ceiling and washed the room in a natural glow that felt almost healing for my frail mind.

Birds of every color, shape, and size flapped around me in a kaleidoscope of movement, inspecting me with curious chirps.

"My realms... I never knew the grand duke had pets." I looked around the massive space, nibbling my lip nervously. "Are you all hungry, too? I doubt the beast has been taking the time to feed you."

As if answering my question, a small daffodil- yellow parakeet fluttered in front of my eyes and dashed to the corner of the room. The bird perched itself atop a torn sack of bird-seed and pecked at the spilled contents with a contented whistle.

"Ah, I see," I cooed at the creature with a soft smile, making my way over to the torn bag. "It would seem I'm not the only resourceful creature in this castle."

The parakeet didn't startle when I picked up the bag, but instead, hopped back a few steps so I had room to drag it. One by one, I sought out the ceramic bird feeders and filled them with seed, earning joyous songs of gratitude from the stunning creatures. After filling their feeders, I left the torn bag in the center of the room, then tore open a second one I found stashed in the corner. That way, if I was unable to find this room again, the birds could still feed themselves for a while. Before stepping away, I picked out a few sunflower seeds to crack and munch on, my fragile nails splitting as I picked them apart. In the back of the aviary, a small spring bubbled up from a pump in the wall, filling a bird bath that likely doubled as their water source. I fished out the stray feathers that polluted the clear water and tossed them into the untrimmed bushes.

"There," I stated proudly as I wiped my soggy hands on my skirt. "Now your cage is far more suitable than mine." My satisfaction dimmed as I felt the heaviness of my words pull on me like a closing curtain.

*Perhaps my cage was the same as theirs after all...*

Even if the beast set us free, and my marriage with Ian went forward, I would be no different from these beautiful birds. A wild creature, trapped beneath a false sky, only allowed to fly in the confides of finery. But what else should I expect? Like these birds, I was bred to be beautiful, effortlessly graceful, and destined for a gilded cage. But unlike them, I was also born with an ailment that left my wings clipped.

*Perhaps they were still better off than me after all...*

Unshed tears choked at my throat, but I swallowed them back in a painful lump. This wasn't a new revelation, so there was no need to cry about it anymore. I made one more round around the aviary, taking in the warm sunshine and beautiful singing for a few moments longer before turning back to the enchanted doors. This might be the only time I have actually flown freer than those around me, so I needed to make the most of my knowledge and ensure the others are taken care of.

I pushed open the nearest door and felt my heart drop as it opened up to the dim ballroom. I had been hoping it would take at least a few more doors to find my way back, not realizing how badly I'd wanted to avoid the dismal space until I was back inside it. The room reeked of candle smoke, rotten food, and unbathed hostages. My empty stomach jolted, urging me to step back into the clean, airy aviary, but I still allowed the door to close.

*They need food, and now I can tell them where to get it.*

"Look! Mira's back!" Henrietta pointed at me from her spot on the floor where she and nearly every other hostage sat around the rose.

Unlike the last time I had returned from the dangers of the beast's labyrinth, no one even bothered to approach me. They acknowledged that I was here, and some even looked up to give me a relieved smile, but none seemed interested enough to move from their spots around the enchanted flower.

*At least they don't seem as panicked as before...*

"How's everyone doing?" I skirted up behind Azura, who was seated in a puddle of her red skirts. A few of the girls had swapped into the simpler dresses I had scavenged from the bedroom, but it appeared Azura and some others had stuck to their wrinkled ballgowns.

"Oh, wonderful. We're absolutely phenomenal. Can you not tell by our smiling faces?" Lord Tocken turned his face up to me to flash his impressively hideous scowl.

I tucked my skirt over my knees and crouched on the floor to join them. Once on their level, I caught sight of what they'd all been staring at.

*The rose...*

Another cluster of dark red petals sat beneath the wilting bloom like a pool of drained blood, sucking the life from our only shield. If you didn't pay attention to the falling petals, the bloom still looked rather healthy, aside from its bending stem and slightly darkened petal tips. It was a dismal sight, but I still would have thought it would install more hope than sorrow at this point.

Azura leaned in beside me, cupping her hand over my ear as she side-eyed her distracted uncle. "Things have been a little tense since you left," she whispered, then pulled away with a shrug. "I'm guessing the hunger is starting to get to everyone." Her stomach growled to confirm, followed by the distant rumblings of a few other captives.

I smiled softly. "Well then, I suppose I have some

good news for you all." I raised my voice, drawing in their attention like a dinner bell. "The beast and I have struck a deal." A collection of gasps and tight whispers interjected my announcement, and from the corner of my eye, I could see Lord Tocken's round face flush beet-red. "He has agreed to feed us," I added quickly, before Lord Tocken could spew another fuss about me conversing with our captor. The room went quiet, all eyes filled with a heart-wrenching hope for a bite of food. "I agreed to teach him our language so he no longer has to rely on magic to communicate with us or anyone else in the realm, and in exchange, he has agreed to invite us to the dining room where he will provide regular meals—"

"The dining room!?" Madam Ophelia, an older woman with oily black hair, peppered in white, stood promptly from the floor. "We cannot possibly meet him there. That just sounds like a scheme to lure us away from the rose!" She jeered her untrimmed nail at the flower, her cheeks as flushed as its fallen petals.

I rose to my feet with her. "Madam, it should be perfectly safe." I held my hands outward, calming her like I would a yappy poodle. "We made a deal. Why would he bother to harm us when he knows I'll only teach him if he upholds his end of it?"

Lord Illumen jumped to his feet alongside us. "Was that in your deal? Did he swear not to harm us if we left the ballroom?" He folded his lanky arms, his typically cool demeanor buried under the group's shared tension.

I pressed my tongue against my teeth, fighting the urge to bite my lip. "Not exactly..." I admitted softly. "He didn't promise not to hurt anyone, but I also don't think he would try anything when he seemed so eager to learn our language."

"Don't be naïve." Lord Tocken waddled awkwardly to his feet, rising from the floor with the grace of a beached whale. "He's a *beast*, a lowly criminal with a thirst for power, not knowledge. He's only twisting your mind to make you think he wants to learn, when in truth, he wants to trick you into dragging us away from our only source of protection!"

*Ah, so now I am too naïve.*

The tips of my ears burned like the wicks of the smoking candles, fuming with my rage toward the old geezer. *I'm many things, but naïve isn't one of them...* After all the times I'd seen the beast, never once did he show more humanity than when he reacted to my offer to teach him our language. He was isolated, and he wanted that to change. Why would he risk his only opportunity to free himself from the bonds of his language when this might be the only opportunity he had?

"Then bring the rose," I said rigidly through gritted teeth. "It can be the centerpiece at the table. That way, you can all come eat and not have to worry about him carrying out any surprise attacks." Honestly, I was starting to care less whether some of these people found their way to food. I'd gone through all this effort to lead them to water, and now that they were here, they were too skeptical to even drink.

"Move the rose!? Are you mad?" Sir Eric of Western Manor waved his hands protectively over the flower, as if he had expected me to snatch it straight from its glass. "What if that's what the beast wants? Perhaps he thinks he can swipe the rose from us if we bring it to a space we can't protect as easily."

*Protect? Is that what they were doing all huddled around it?*

"I think the beast would have already taken the rose if he could," I snarked with an unmuffled snort. My patience for these people was starting to wear thinner than my splitting nails. "Why would moving it into the dining room be any less safe than keeping it here?"

I eyed the fragile bloom, but my gaze was cut off by Lord Tocken as he rudely stepped between it and me. "Because it was the *beast's* idea to move it."

I swallowed a rigid gulp of air and jeered my face into his, only an inch from his round nose. "No, it was *my* idea to move the rose," I defended with quaking fists.

*What is this lord's problem? Doesn't he want to eat?*

"Your idea or the beast's, it's all the same," he retorted, his voice steely and sharp. "It's clear that neither of you possess the mental skills to think scenarios through fully. Moving the rose is not an option that can be agreed upon, and that's final."

"Final!?" My voice boomed against the walls, vibrating against my flared cheeks in sync with the tremble of my rage. "Are you saying that you speak for everyone? No one here wants to risk visiting the dining room, even if it means getting fed?"

I darted my gaze around the other hostages, searching for one, just one, supportive face. But there were none... Not even Henrietta or Azura moved to stand with me. They all veered their gazes away, fixating their eyes on the rose that had stolen their very spirits.

"I'm sorry, Mira..." Azura whispered from the floor. "We just can't risk it. I mean, your brother dealt with him head-on. You, of all people, should know how dangerous he can be."

I whipped my head away from Lord Tocken's smug grin, snapping my betrayed gaze to the caster. "He may be dangerous, but he's still human," I hissed, feeling my blood curdle in my veins. "He wants this; he would have killed me if he didn't."

"Again..." Lord Tocken sighed with a *tsk*, pressing his hands against his wrinkled forehead. "You only think you know what he wants. You're too clueless to understand that he's only playing you."

My heart rattled in my chest like a growling panther, clawing at my rib cage for a chance to remove his tongue for good. "Even if I didn't know what he wanted, I know what *I* want." I turned from the crowd, leaving them to worship their precious flower as I stormed back toward the doors. "And I want dinner."

# chapter thirteen

After ditching the ballroom, my mind began to clear from the group's toxicity. The doors had led to another random hallway, with burgundy rugs patterned with geometric lines and shapes. There were other doors I could have ventured through, but I decided to remain in the narrow hall, pacing until I could have sworn I saw some of the patterns fade under my scuffing heels. A small grandfather clock stood proudly at the end of the hall, acting as the only element that kept me sane while I wasted the hours before dinner.

The clock's melodic ticking synced with the rhythm of my beating heart, slowing its furious pounds to a slow, even pace. I stretched out across the thick carpet, laying all the way back until I was staring up at the ticking hands from the floor. My whole body felt as weak as a newborn kitten. Having lived the privileged life of a duchess prevented me from ever enduring the suffering of an empty stomach, and now I was more grateful for that upbringing than I had ever been.

As the agreed upon dinner hour drew near, I considered finding my way back to the ballroom to give the others one last opportunity to seek out a fresh meal. However, the mere thought of peeling my spine from the floor caused gravity to shove me down another inch.

*If they wanted to come, they would have done so.*

My nerves twinged like a twisting pinch, riling up the frustration I had allowed to go dormant. I was still irritated at how they had been so overly cautious and judgmental, but my anger didn't sit as heavily as it did now that I'd had the chance to clear my head. There was something about being in the ballroom that simply shredded my patience. Maybe it was the low lighting, its unhygienic state, or the fact that everyone there expected me to act like a proper duchess. Either way, the fact that an empty hallway was more pleasant than a ballroom as large as some villages was truly telling at this point.

When the clock hands read one minute until six, I made the agonizing effort to scrape my fragile form off the plush carpet. My stomach growled and cramped, as if it was shriveling to the size of a dried plum. With one hand placed gingerly over my aching abdomen, I laced my fingers around the closest door handle, watching the clock for the moment it struck six.

As I waited through the painfully long final seconds, all the doubts from the other captives wove into my mind like a knitted net. My mind flashed with images of the beast spiking the food with poison or snagging a dinner knife and slashing toward me in a flash of silver. The clock struck six, and the elegant ringing of its chimes filled the silent hall like the bell tower in a cemetery.

*Don't let them get in your head... If he wanted to kill me, he would have already done so, right?*

My jabbering stomach acted as the last needed incentive for me to push open the door. As I pushed against the door, I felt it grow heavier as the standard cedar wood opened into a ten-foot-tall frame. My gaze first absorbed the lighting —brilliant gold chandeliers, bronze wall sconces cast in the shape of open-winged owls, and jewel-encrusted candle sticks forced me to blink until my vision adjusted. More stained-glass windows lined the wall, each making up a section of the Dhurin crest of arms. Below the center of the chandelier sat a table, longer than most commoners' houses. The dark walnut wood was left mostly bare, with only a red table runner with gold trim stretching down the center. Atop the plain wood was a disorganized spread of porcelain plates, dulled silverware, and crystal glasses sitting in front of most of the cushioned dining chairs. And at the head of it all, was him...

The lone beast stood as straight and rigid as a marble statue, his scarred eye following me like a haunted portrait. He was waiting at the head of the table with his arms crossed stiffly behind his back. A spread of silver dome-covered platters —which I could only dream contained food—were sprawled out in front of him. My mouth salivated as the lingering smell of charred beef drifted to my nose like an intoxicating perfume. Even if he had truly lured me here to kill me, I officially had no issues allowing him to do so as long as I received a single bite of whatever he brought.

"I told you not to be late." His cold voice drifted across the expansive room, causing my wrist to warm where the charm activated to translate his voice.

My brows knit together, and I stepped further into the room to get a better look at his expression under the light of the chandelier. "I'm not late; you said six o'clock." His dark eyes tightened around the rims, though no other emotion reflected in his cold expression.

"I did, so why are the others not here yet?" His low voice snapped like the crack of a whip, betraying his impatience.

The spike in his tone wasted no time yanking on my nerves. I popped my hands on my hips and glared at him like the impatient child he was mirroring. "There's no need to get so brash. They simply aren't coming."

His jaw shifted in a tight grit. "Not coming?" He barked, the resonance of his tantrum reverberating off the expansive windows. "Why not? Didn't you tell them I was providing dinner?"

I removed my hands from my waist to fold them crossly as I leaned on my back leg. *Why is he being so fussy about the rest of them staying in the ballroom? Did he truly have something nefarious planned for us?* "Of course, I told them," I huffed tartly. "But none of them wanted to risk leaving the ballroom because *you* enjoy throwing around death threats like rice at a wedding!"

He ran a hand through his dark locks with an aggravated growl as he darted his gaze at the table spread. He looked irritated, but not in a 'I wanted to murder all my dinner guests' sort of way. He almost looked... flustered?

"What's the matter?" I walked around the edge of the table, attempting to get a better look at the hidden plates while still being cautious of my proximity to him. "Feeling disappointed that you can't poison us all in a single meal?" He snapped his onyx gaze to me with his lips curled in a partial snarl. I raised my hands in defense as I paused at the edge of the table's corner, greedily scanning over the covered trays. "Relax, I won't tattle. Just give me the meal with the highest dosage so I can perish the moment I'm feeling blissfully full."

For a brief moment, I thought he was going to gape at me, but he snapped his jaw shut before I could fully notice his smooth lips part. "Don't be absurd." He scowled, turning away from me with what looked like a pout as he snatched the top off one of the silver trays. A neat pile of sandwiches, stuffed with the charred beef I had smelled earlier, wilted lettuce, and even sliced tomato, gleamed at me like a fallen star. "Why would I poison the food when it took so blasted long to prepare!?" He slammed the lid down atop an empty spot on the table, folding his arms with a tight-lipped frown. "All that effort, and not a single noble to grovel with gratitude."

I tore my eyes from the tantalizing sandwiches to stare at him in surprise. *He went through all this effort, just to gain their gratitude?* I suppose it wasn't terribly hard to believe when you saw the realm through his prideful eyes. He intended to make this province his own, so it only made sense that he would try to win over the highest-ranking nobility. Or at least, leave a better impression than only trapping them in a ballroom to rot.

*Although he didn't have to go to the trouble of actually*

*cooking anything... Maybe there was a touch of humanity in there, after all.*

"Well, I'm here. So, that's still one noble you might get some groveling out of." I quirked him a bemused smile, testing to see if the human inside would crack through. If it was there, my smile didn't unveil it.

"You, grovel?" He snorted, his eyes rolling unevenly as his scarred one only made it half-way. "I've already spent enough irritating time with you to learn that stubbornness well exceeds your gratitude."

I had to bite my tongue to choke back a laugh. He'd only known me for less than a week and had already picked up on more of my true personality than even my own subjects. I suppose stress really brought out my true colors, and this man was currently the embodiment of my stress. Although, right now, he had food, and that certainly had me in a forgiving mood.

"You never know..." I said ominously, drifting my eyes from the wheat-infected sandwiches to the other covered trays. "Depending on whatever is hiding on those other platters... you might have me kissing your boots." I gave him a teasing giggle to showcase that I wasn't serious... even though I sort of was. If he had brought even a single cashew that wasn't contaminated with wheat, I might even forgive him for leaving me with only pickled turnips and bananas for the last four days. But not really... I still wanted to kick him in the unmentionables for that, but a proper meal would certainly convince me to kick a little less hard.

He cocked his head at me, kind of like the way a big dog would inspect a yapping Pomeranian. "Are the sandwiches I made not properly suited for your refined tastes?" he asked bitterly.

I looked back down at the mouth-watering meat poking from the toxic chunks of bread, longing for a taste. I swallowed back a sigh— and maybe even a few tears—as I returned my attention to the beast. "I'm starving. I would probably eat paste if you put enough salt on it." I gave him a look that was just serious enough to make him visibly uncomfortable, which was far more satisfying than it should have been. "Now why don't you show me what's on the other platters before I start seasoning your fingers as an appetizer." I tilted my head toward the platters with an urging raise of my brows.

He rolled his eyes and grumbled a few unsavory words under his breath, but still reached over to pull the lids off the platters. The silver-domed lids flashed before my eyes like the unveiling of the world's most priceless jewels. My heart pounded, and I had to swallow back my drool before it dribbled down my lip as he unveiled...

Bananas.

My mouth dried, turning my tongue into a slab of sandstone as it fell flat. The second tray had a few apples and a handful of nuts, but it was accompanied by stale crackers that were intertwined with pretty much everything. Which meant the only safe things I could consume on this dinner table were maybe a few shelled nuts and more bananas...

Suddenly, eating paste and salt didn't sound so far-fetched.

"I only had time to prepare the sandwiches," the beast said gruffly, likely reading the disappointment on my face like it was a flaunted pamphlet. "Everything else I just scrounged from the pantries." His voice turned cold, matching the judgment in his eyes. "Since all my guests were too rude to even take part in my efforts, perhaps tomorrow I'll feed you like true prisoners. Bread and water would be far simpler to prepare."

"No!" I couldn't stop the words from popping off my lips. I sucked in a breath as if I could retrieve my outburst, but the beast had already heard me. *If he only gave us bread... I'd be tortured to death.* Not knowing what else to do, I reached in front of him and snatched a banana from the tray. My hand brushed his arm for a moment, sending an odd shiver rippling through my skin. Ignoring the strange sensation, I peeled the banana and took a massive bite. "See? I'm completely grateful," I mumbled through my pudgy cheeks. His stone facade couldn't mask the utter bewilderment that now stained his dark eyes and chiseled jaw that hung slightly open. I swallowed the mouthful in a half-chewed clump, unable to taste the fruit for longer than necessary. "Thank you for holding up your part of the bargain. Is that what you wanted to hear? Because you could have just asked for a thank you instead of threatening me again. Didn't your parents ever teach you how to play nice with the other kids?"

He didn't answer, his shocked expression morphing back into his unfazed stare. I watched him curiously for a moment and wondered if I'd said something to offend him. *Was it the part where I threatened to eat his hand?* My stomach growled, both protesting the bland banana and begging for more. I popped another bite into my mouth, then dragged the closest chair to the edge of his. He seemed taken aback as I plopped onto the chair right beside his unused one, his eyes searching me as if I were some elaborate maze he couldn't quite find his way out of.

"Well, you fed me," I mumbled around my chewing. "Did you still want to learn our language? Or is my witty banter enough payment for your kind services?"

His shoulders jolted at the mention of our language, like he had forgotten that was the reason he had bothered to throw those trays together in the first place. "If your banter is going to accompany our every meal, I might need to rethink this agreement," he scoffed, lowering himself onto the seat next to me.

"You should have thought of that before," I said snidely, making no effort to maintain my table manners as I reached in front of him for the nearest water pitcher. His eyes followed my hand, as if they were locked in some sort of trance. I poured the water into my glass to the brim, then took a slow sip while peeking up at him from the cup.

*He is so... foreign. But not just because of his nationality; it is as if his entire mind has been pushed a thousand miles away from this room. Curious...*

"How do you plan to teach me?" His question was soft and mumbled, almost enough that I would have missed it entirely if I hadn't been staring at him.

I nearly choked on my sip of water, fearing he had caught my fascinated glare. "I was thinking we start with the alphabet," I rasped unattractively as I wiped a droplet of water from my lip. "Did you bring anything to write with? I can write out the Rubian alphabet and you can write out yours, then we can compare for similarities and use that as a starting point."

His gaze lingered on me for a moment, long enough that I wondered if I'd smeared banana on my face. But after a few quiet seconds, he reached into the pocket of his trousers. One at a time, he tossed out folded pieces of parchment and a pair of graphite pencils, letting them slide haphazardly across the table.

I stuffed another bite of banana into my mouth before I gagged, then swiped up a piece of parchment and a pencil to get to work. He did the same, though a little more reluctantly. It was probably belittling for him to become the student of an unrefined excuse for a duchess, which personally, only made the experience all the more tolerable for me.

"There." He slid his parchment over to me with a short clip of his brooding voice.

I placed the parchment beside mine, comparing the letter shapes and order to search for any similarities. His handwriting was surprisingly light-handed, which caused many of the markings to appear thin and faded. "Can you tell me which ones are vowels?" I questioned with an uptilt of my eyes and found myself nearly gasping as I realized how close he had gotten. The beast was halfway hung over my shoulder with his focus glued on the two alphabets. He was so close that his warm breath tickled my ear, sending spiraling shivers down my neck and back like a cluster of butterflies. My cheeks flushed, and I lowered my gaze to the papers, trying to ignore his soft breath and close proximity.

"I already underlined them," he said shortly, jeering a finger toward the small lines he had scratched under a few of the letters.

I squinted until I could make out the faded marks. "Oh, I thought those were part of the lettering. It was a little hard to see with your handwriting."

He leaned back in his chair, finally giving my body a chance to relax since he wasn't so close. "Your job is to teach me your ridiculous language, not to scrutinize to my penmanship."

I took in a tight breath through my teeth as my fingers tapped impatiently on the edge of the table. *Does he always have to be so... disagreeable?* "I wasn't scrutinizing anything," I huffed, pressing my palm flat against the table. "If you want to learn our *ridiculous* language, then I'm going to need you to be a little less prickly." I couldn't control the sass in my voice, my eyes teeming with as much dislike as a feuding alley cat.

His chair legs squealed with a piercing scrape, and he shoved himself back from the table. "Prickly? Is that how duchesses refer to their hosts in this realm?" His huff reverberated with a low growl as his dark eyes narrowed in offense. "My, I shall be certain to add that to my new vocabulary. How do you say it in Rubian again?"

I hooked my ankles together with a numbing pressure, meeting his glare with a look more tense than a debutant's corset. "It sounds like this, 'I'm a halfwit.' Just make sure you put the extra emphasis on the end when you practice in the mirror." I could feel the anger boiling off him, but promptly ignored it as I turned my attention to the first vowel he'd underlined. "Here, this one looks similar to ours. We pronounce it as 'ee,' like in eagle or eat. What sound does it make in your language?"

He didn't answer, instead keeping his jaw locked tight as he continued to glower from my insult. I tapped my pencil against the table with a patient purse of my lips, waiting for his resolve to break until he finally rolled his eyes.

"'Eh' like in entity or existence," he grumbled.

I nodded, pressing the pencil to the edge of my lips as I looked between the two lists.

"That's not too far off from our pronunciation, so perhaps these languages are closer than we assumed." I scratched out a simple word on the parchment, starting with the letter we'd just gone over. "Try reading this word aloud, but use the Rubian pronunciation."

He fixated his eyes on the paper and slowly formed his lips into the shape of a word. "Eh- eeiis."

His voice faded, releasing a puff of air. "This is ridiculous," he jeered a hand at the paper. "I can't possibly pronounce it like that; it's absurd."

I scrunched my brow together, looking down at the Rubian spelling of the word 'easy.' "Absurd? It's our language. That's just how it sounds," I countered. My ears burned as his aggravating frown deepened, like the grave he was digging for himself. I pressed my palm to my forehead, trying to collect myself with a long breath. "Look, I know it seems silly, but I know you can do it. All you have to—"

"Of course, it's silly!" he interrupted, his injured eye pulsating from the inflamed veins. "I held up my end of the bargain, but now you're taking revenge by teaching me gibberish."

My veins throbbed, burning with a level of heat that was reserved only for this irritating man. "For the love of the realms, this isn't revenge! Would you stop acting like a child?" I snapped while digging my nails deep enough into the wood table to indent crescent shapes into it.

His eyes narrowed, growing beady and predatory. "How dare you refer to me as such. Is this how you show your gratitude toward a captor who went through the effort of preparing you a proper meal?" His tone sharpened, filling with offense I couldn't possibly validate.

"I'll refer to you however I please!" I pushed up out of my seat, my heart drumming against my ribs like a ramming boar. "I may be your captive, but I am not your subordinate. You agreed to let *me* teach *you*; therefore, I demand the same respect that you would have given any of your other tutors!"

His rage snuffed out like a smothered candle in the blink of an eye. All of a sudden his eyes went wide and glassy, as if something I'd said had been the incantation of a spell that had flashed him out of his senses. He lowered his head, his eyes shadowed like a hollow skull.

A dark chuckle billowed out of him, entangled with a sadistic growl. A chill washed over me, and the heat cooled in my cheeks. "My father was my primary tutor," he said coldly as a twisted darkness swirled in his eyes. "You don't want me to treat you like I did him."

A hard lump built up in my throat, and my legs shook with uneasiness as an eerie quiet followed his unsettling words. Fear scratched at the back of my throat, but I swallowed it with the dense lump, allowing my curiosity to take root.

*What happened between him and his father...?*

"Fine, then," I clipped, my breath huffy and shallow. "Treat me however you please; just know that the moment you cross my lines, I'll leave. So, it's in your hands how much you learn during each meal." I stepped back from the table, our eyes locked in a silent duel until I looked down to pick up the untouched tray of sandwiches. "Tonight's lesson is complete. Study those letters and see if you can craft an apology out of them by tomorrow."

Then, with sandwiches in hand, a banana in my stomach,

and unfiltered fury in my heart, I stormed out of the dining room. "But don't worry, I won't hold my breath."

# chapter fourteen

"What an utter waste of time!" I burst through the doors of the master suite with my fist clamped around the duchess's ridiculous excuse for a lesson. I tossed the crinkled papers atop the lop-sided bed, watching them flutter atop the shredded blankets like the feathers of an obnoxious parrot. "Can you believe she had the gall to insult me!? And after all that blasted effort I put into crafting them a decent meal!" I threw a fist at the nearest dresser, cracking the wood with a shower of splinters.

The mirror flickered in the corner of my vision, unveiling the unsympathetic scowl of my ghostly father. "Didn't I tell you? The girl is better off dead." His voice hissed like a flaring cobra, his beady eyes completing the resemblance perfectly.

I ran my hands through my hair, tilting my head back with a part-yell, part-groan. "She'll be just as useless dead as she is alive." My chest tightened oddly as my tone grew defensive. "She's a stubborn prude, but I still need to learn their blasted language!"

I kicked at a pile of broken ceramic from a shattered vase, the clattering sound acting as a necessary white noise for my clouded brain.

"You only have yourself to blame," the mirror retorted coldly, his stern chin lifting with a superior glare. "Why did you bother to make the hostages a meal in the first place? Has your madness truly driven you to such levels of boredom?"

I clenched my muscles, whirling around on the mirror to respond, but I remained mute when no answer came to my tongue. Or no answer I was willing to admit to my father. In truth, I had intended to shock the duchess in the same way she had baffled me. Surprise her with the fact that I could turn into a charming host with only the flip of a script. It was a manipulative tactic that had worked rather well for me in the past, though typically benefitted from having a crowd to comment on my actions. Frankly, it was a waste of my skills, but I wanted to prove to her that she didn't have me as figured out as she thought. That there was still enough uncertainty about me that she wouldn't feel as if she held any power over me. Realms, did that backfire...

"I'll need at least a morsel of the nobility's trust once I overtake their province," I answered smoothly. "I can't necessarily expect to build a court out of commoners, can I?"

His brows furrowed with a narrowing of his pupils, the look of his internal lie detector. "You're getting soft." His words dripped with venom, eyeing me down like I was a pathetic stray with a broken leg. "These people are mere roaches. Any crumbs you feed them will only attract more until you're swallowed in an infestation of worthless beggars."

I stepped away from the mirror before I smashed it, catching my eyes on the crumbled-up alphabets I'd left on the bed. "I'm not soft," I snipped, snatching the papers and holding the duchess's foreign scribbles up to the light. "I'm getting wise, and you simply hate to see me thinking through outcomes you were too narrow-minded to see." I scanned my eyes over the infuriatingly complicated letters, biting my tongue so he couldn't notice my struggle.

*If I'd killed Mira, I might have been offered the province, but I still wouldn't be able to understand a single document. They could sign me over a graveyard, and I wouldn't know the difference between it and the ownership papers to Dhurin.*

"Only a child believes his motives are wiser than his elders," Father grumbled. His captious words were finally starting to numb on my ears, hitting my nerves less than Mira's had.

*"Would you stop acting like a child?"*

Her voice rang through my head like a chiming clock locked inside my skull. I wasn't a child; I was a king, and soon-to-be a grand duke. I didn't need her scolding. Not when I was a well-educated monarch capable of learning a measly alphabet on my own.

I held the parchment closer to my face with a new intensity, waiting for the letters to untangle from their jumble and jump out at me from the page.

*"I know it seems silly, but I know you can do it..."*

I growled, causing my teeth to vibrate as her false encouragement seeped into my mind. She didn't actually think I could do it; she didn't think I could do this without her—just like someone else I knew...

"Don't waste your energy." The king sneered, causing the hairs on the back of my neck to rise like the hackles of a true beast. "You've already proven yourself to be unteachable. All this time, and you've still never learned, even after what happened to your precious mother..."

My veins clamped, and I dug my nails into the parchment until it was a fraction from tearing. "You don't get to call her precious," I hissed, turning my attention back to the paper, still just as lost as before.

*Blast it. How did she say that letter was pronounced again?*

I slammed my fists to my side, wrinkling the parchment further as I stormed back toward the door with the golden key burning in my pocket.

"Where do you think you're going?" the mirror echoed, his eerie tone already implying that he knew the answer.

"To prove to this putrid realm that I'm more than capable of learning the alphabet."

• • • • • • • • • • • • • • • • • • • • • • • • • • • • • • • • • • • • • • •

It was difficult to push open the ballroom door while balancing a tray of sandwiches, especially when their tantalizing smell had me intoxicated. The savory smell of the charred meat had me practically melting into a puddle on the ballroom floor. I wanted nothing more than to take a hearty bite of the beast's handiwork, but I had no doubt that if I did, I would have truly wished the beast had poisoned it.

As expected, the group was clustered around the rose, exactly where I had left them. Their attention was so glued to the petals, it was almost as if they feared another would fall if they looked away.

Madam Ophelia was the first to notice me, barely catching sight of me from the edge of her sleepy eyes. Her thick black hair flicked over her shoulder as she snapped her neck to the side to do a double take, widening her pupils at the sight of the sandwich platter in my arms. "Oh, thank the realms! You've found food!" She scrambled from her spot on the floor, tripping over the others before they had the opportunity to process what was happening.

Before I could get trampled under the stampede of half-starved hostages, I set the tray on the floor and stepped back a good four feet. One by one, the tantalizing sandwiches were snatched from the tray, causing my banana-filled stomach to groan in mourning. They were lucky I had even bothered to grab the tray at all. A big part of me wanted to make them regret making me attend the dinner by myself, but in the moment, I couldn't stop myself from doing the right thing. Although, watching them devour the mouth-watering sandwiches right in front of me was making me regret my choice...

"Mira, you're really a lifesaver!" Henrietta mumbled through a mouthful of bread and meat. Her crumb-coated lips were actually rather tame compared to some of the other nobles, who had foregone all sense of decorum.

"I didn't do much." I resisted the urge to scowl, my envious heart feeling slighted as I watched them all enjoy the meal only I had bothered to attend. "I simply went to the dining room."

Azura scampered over, a half-eaten sandwich in her hand. "So, you went after all?" She pressed a dainty hand to her lips with a weary glance at her sandwich with a gulp. "What happened? Did he..."

"Irritate me? Yes, exceptionally so, but otherwise, he was just as harmless as I'd imagined." I couldn't hide the aggravation that seeped from my locked teeth as my gaze drifted accusingly toward the gawking crowd. "All we did was dine, and I taught him a few of our letters. No foul play involved."

Lord Tocken huffed across the room, his fat fingers digging through his sandwich as if inspecting it for glass shards or a droplet of poison. "*Hmph*, not yet." He returned the top piece of bread to his sandwich, seemingly satisfied with its contents. "He likely didn't think we'd be wise enough to avoid his dinner invitation, so he played nice in the hopes that we'd all join him for the next meal. He's tricky, but not very clever."

*Not clever? Says the man who's sleeping on a curtain.*

My blood pressure rose like a primed geyser, ready to burst through my veins at any moment. "He wasn't being tricky," I spat. "You were all just being cowards. I know that he's our captor, and a rather messed-up individual, but he's not a murderous lunatic!" My cheeks were inflamed with the hot frustration that always seem to follow me whenever I entered this room.

"Don't be such a child." Sir Eric sneered. His beard was littered with crumbs as he licked his fingers clean. "Tocken's right. The beast is only trying to lure you into a false sense of security."

"That's right," Lord Illumen chimed in from his cross-legged spot on the floor. "You can't trust a vile man like him. He's not called the beast because of his fluffy warm heart."

My hands balled into fists, and I squeezed them as tightly as I could in an attempt to vent out some of my spewing frustration. "I never said that I trusted him, just that—"

"You trusted his bargain?" Madam Ophelia snorted with an insinuating glare. "It's the same thing, little duchess. The others are right; you shouldn't be so careless around wild animals."

Hot breath puffed out of my lungs. "He's not a... and I don't —" My voice stammered in staccato huffs of fire. I grabbed my braid and yanked it with an unsightly groan. Why was I even trying to defend the beast, anyway? He was the entire reason I was trapped with these imbeciles in the first place.

*Although, admittedly, he was slightly more tolerable than they were... as surprising as that was.*

"Mira..." In the midst of my hair-pulling, Azura had crept up beside me. Her olive-green eyes were shining again, likely from the first proper meal she'd had in days. "Why don't you and I take a little walk around the edges of the ballroom?" Before I could answer, she tugged on my arm, guiding me away from the fussy hostages before my frustration funneled into my fists.

"What?" I sneered, glancing back at the ungrateful crowd with a curled lip. "Not afraid to step away from your all-powerful rose?"

Azura squeezed my arm, keeping her lips sealed until we were out of earshot of the others. "I'm not too worried about it," she said coolly, under a hushed breath. Something about her words felt ominous, like an eerie fog leeching into a meadow.

"You're not?" I quirked a brow as we stopped at the far end of the ballroom, half-hidden behind a tall marble pillar.

She flicked a glance over her shoulder to ensure the others were occupied, then leaned forward. Her dark hair fell partially over her eyes like a mysterious curtain. "I think you're right," she whispered. "It doesn't make sense for the beast to kill us when he needs something from us. He can't run the province without knowing the language, or even read any documents that would claim the province as his. I personally believe you're perfectly safe to wander the castle at this point."

Shock froze my tongue as I stared at her with widening eyes. "Wait a moment... If that's how you truly feel, then why were you so insistent that I didn't visit the dining room earlier?" My head swam with memories of her pleading eyes, begging me not to risk my life by waltzing into the beast's trap.

She tilted her head in the direction of the others, her eyes flicking toward her uncles. "Isn't it obvious? My uncles have been watching me like a hawk ever since we got trapped here. If I showed even an ounce of interest in leaving the ballroom, they'd probably tie me to these pillars. That, and the others all seem to believe that if I leave the rose, its power will fade."

My throat tightened. "Will it?"

She flashed me a catlike smile. "No," she snorted. "My magic stands on its own, though I have been reinforcing it every day to try to prolong its lifespan, so I suppose there is *some* use to keeping me close."

I nodded and chewed my lip. The fury that had been stirring in my chest earlier was seeming to settle now that I'd realized I had an ally. "Alright, so what do you think I should do? Do you think I should I keep visiting the beast?"

"I do," she assured. "Especially if you can keep bringing us back meals like you did today. I know it's a lot to ask, but we really need you, Mira. They won't admit it, so let me do it for them." She took my hand in her small, fragile grasp, squeezing my hand hard enough that I could feel her heart beating in it. "Please, keep teaching the beast. Don't let us starve just because my uncles and the others are too stubborn to see you're helping us, not endangering us."

Her quiet words were all the validation I needed. I hadn't planned to stop seeing the beast, especially since I'd barely gotten a banana out of our last meal. But hearing Azura believe in me was enough for me to swallow my pride.

*They need food, and I am the only one willing to go out and get it.*

I squeezed her hand back, letting out an easing breath. "You can count on me, Azura. I'm not your duchess yet, which means I don't have to listen to the advice of any of these foreign geezers."

She stifled a giggle and released my hand with a relieved sparkle, turning her eyes a beautiful jade color. "Thank you, Mira." She smiled sweetly. "You might want to try sneaking out when no one is paying attention though, otherwise you might have a small riot on your hands."

*She's not wrong there.*

I glanced back at the distracted group, then turned my eyes to the nearest door. "Well then, I suppose I'd better slip out while I can."

Azura blinked at me, her long lashes creating a tiny breeze. "Wait, right now? But you just got back. Will the beast even be ready to see you?"

I stepped around her, my sights fixated on the door. "Who said I was going to look for the beast? There's still plenty of the castle left for me to explore." I approached the door with a fresh eagerness in my steps, my fatigue only slightly diminished after the tiny meal entered my blood. "Don't worry. I'll be back in time for dinner tomorrow."

Azura's mouth remained open, as if there were a litany of concerns trapped on her tongue that she couldn't quite formulate. I creaked the door open and stepped into the mystery room before she could try to talk me out of leaving. I couldn't wait to get out of the ballroom again, and I was willing to take any excuse I could to distance myself from the rosy-eyed morons.

The room opened into an overwhelmingly large space, disorienting me briefly as I clicked the door closed behind me. It easily could have been as large as the ballroom, but it was difficult to tell since every square foot was crammed with bursting bookshelves.

*A library?*

The scent of cedar and ink flooded my senses as I digested the sheer amount of knowledge I was staring at. Shelves, brimming with multicolored spines and dusty book jackets, lined every wall, giving the vast space a cozy atmosphere. Warm lanterns gleamed atop scattered tables, surrounded by plush armchairs and scattered papers leftover from the last visitors. The few windows that were left uncovered were framed in thick, wine-colored drapes. I wondered how blissfully peaceful the room would feel if all the drapes were closed. With all the books insulating the walls and sounds, this might have easily been the most peaceful room in the entire castle.

*And the most useful.*

My attention turned to the endless rows of books, feeling a sudden spike of inspiration. There were easily thousands of books in here, and there had to be something I could use to make teaching the beast easier... Then perhaps we could avoid another disaster like tonight.

I started skimming the spines one by one, searching for children's literature or basic spelling. I moved toward the more youthful stories when I had reached the end of the shelf. I darted around the bookshelf and rounded a corner in front of the next one when I collide into something solid and tall. The air was knocked out of my lungs with a jarring gasp, sending me stumbling back a few feet as the daze cleared from my eyes. Standing in the center of the shelves, with a book tucked under his arm, was none other than the dark-eyed beast.

My heart jolted as I felt a flush tinge my cheeks from crashing straight into his strong chest. His expression was just as startled as mine, but he masked it far smoother than I ever could.

"What are you doing here?"

# chapter fifteen

"Why do you need to know?" I gave the towering beast an unwavering glare, trying to hide the fact that my heart was still hammering after our collision. "I thought we already established that you never stated I couldn't leave the ballroom?"

His jaw went rigid, the sharp curves of his bone structure broken up by the jagged scar. "And I thought we already determined that this is *my* castle, and I make the rules."

I raised a skeptical brow. "No, you waved a knife around and said 'finders' keepers.' All you own is an impressive ego and a nasty temper."

He lifted his chin, flexing the ego I'd just mentioned. "Well, I'm a beast, aren't I? Aren't we supposed to be nasty?" He snarled his lips as if trying to mimic the monstrous creature.

"I also thought beasts were meant to be intimidating?" I fired back. It was just my luck that I would be transported into the only room in the castle the beast had decided to go for an evening stroll in.

He pressed his lips together to smother a scowl, but not before I could feel the satisfaction of knowing I'd knocked him down a peg. My eyes flicked to the book tucked under his arm and my curiosity bit at me. "So, what brings a nasty beast to a library at this hour? Looking for some good picture books?"

A soft groan rumbled in his throat. "So nosey, yet you have the audacity to think I ask too much..." He rolled his eyes, untucking the book from his arm to flash me the cover. "If you must know, I was looking to further my studies of your

147

language. It shouldn't be too difficult to pick up on it if I study these texts." His tone warmed with a self-imposed pride as he brushed his fingers across the top of the pages.

*He thinks he can teach himself?*

I inspected the book cover he was flaunting, first noticing the decorative scroll on the front with the title written in flowery calligraphy. *"Poems for the Swooning Heart?"* I read aloud, "Goodness, I never expected you to be such a romantic." I pressed a hand to my lips, stifling a snorting laugh.

His pupils dilated in sync with the crimson flush that shot up his neck as he snapped the front of the book around to inspect. "What!? That's preposterous. The cover clearly shows a diplomatic scroll on the front; it certainly must contain valuable insights into politics or trade." He flipped open the book with a determined clench on the pages, skimming over the words as if the word *sword* or *negotiation* would jump out at him in his language.

*So stubborn...*

I placed my hand over the top of his book, slowly lowering it until his darting eyes separated from the page. "Don't you know you're not supposed to judge a book by its cover?" I smirked, unable to force away the humor of watching the ferocious beast desperately try to read a book of love poems.

He snapped the book closed, nearly catching my finger in it with a snort. "That saying only exists to make the weak feel better about their measly states in life." He frowned, stuffing the love poems back on the closest shelf. "If you can't command power by entering a room, then you don't deserve to stand in it in the first place."

My smirk faded with a crinkle of my nose as his contagious frown overtook me. "That sounds like an arrogant way to live your life, and an unfulfilling one at that." I turned my attention back toward the bookshelf, skimming the spines for something more helpful. "Imagine all the wonderful people you would miss out on meeting if you snubbed every person you judged by their exterior."

I could feel his gaze brush over me. It was an odd sensation, like being brushed against by a black cat that could either be a sweet interaction or a modem of bad luck. "Why does it matter if I never know what I missed?" he asked coldly, his voice distanced and bleak.

My finger froze on the spine I was scanning as the rest of my body seemed to force me into a pause. *Does he truly feel that way?* His words soaked into me like a heavy marinade, saturating my mind with the first touches of sympathy. I didn't know much about this man other than the trouble he had constantly stirred up in our realm, but in this frozen moment, I couldn't help but wonder how he'd spiraled so far from the rest of humanity. Was he truly just content living a life with no further purpose than what he had already set out to do?

Memories of lying in bed with writhing pain flicked through my mind, reminding me of the day I was informed of my unfathomable allergy. That was the day my life had been stripped away from me. All my goals and dreams to work for the emperor were shattered all because my health was too unstable to leave my gilded cage behind. I suppose I might never understand him, because unlike the wild beast, I was destined to remain in captivity.

"It doesn't change the fact that you still missed it," I said softly, my throat suddenly growing tight as the painful memories seeped back into my heart. "But if living in the dark is what fulfills you, then don't let me stand in your way. I'm only the tutor." My eyes caught on the narrow spine of a children's book as I swallowed back my lingering thoughts. "Ah! Perfect!" I tugged the book from the shelf and turned back to the beast with an accomplished grin, but when I looked at him, he wasn't sharing in my excitement.

His dark eyes had softened somehow, glistening with

the puzzled curiosity of a skittish cat. His chiseled jaw wasn't clenched for once, and his frown had eased into an unassuming spread of his pressed lips. Without a scowl or threatening glower on his face, he almost looked... handsome. I mean, he still had scars that traced his face like the tracks of a carriage with a tipsy driver. But even with his reddened eye and disfigured skin, I felt as if I could finally see a glimpse of the man beneath the beast.

"What is that one called?" His smooth voice cut through my thoughts, surprising me with the mellowness of his tone. For a moment, I spaced out, uncertain of what he was referring to until he motioned to the book dangling from my fingers. "It's not another love story, is it?"

I snapped out of my daze and flipped the book around to remind myself what I had actually pulled from the shelf. "Sorry to disappoint you, but no; this is a children's story about a rabbit and a wolf."

His frown turned askew, as if he'd just been fed something bitter. "A children's story? How am I meant to learn anything from something so juvenile?" He directed his sour grin toward the whimsical picture of the fluffy gray rabbit and the fierce wolf adorning the front of the book.

I sighed, already sensing the pattern between this disagreement and the one at dinner. "Listen, this arrangement is only going to work if you let me help you, and I *can* help you. I just need more than five minutes of an opportunity to prove it. You want to learn Rubian, don't you?" I lifted my brow and tilted the book at him daringly.

He averted his eyes from me, his gaze drifting to anywhere that wasn't the book. "Yes..." his breath hissed, his gaze finally meeting mine with a clenched pout, "but must we use something so... degrading?" A low groan rose from his throat as he finally looked at the book, staring at it like it was a plate of boiled liver.

*Ah, so the beast can feel shame, after all.*

"Yes." A smug grin tugged at the edge of my lip, and I stretched out the book to him, smacking it against his iron chest. He didn't even flinch, not breaking eye contact with the book as he took it in his fingers with the apprehension one would have when handed a piece of molded cheese. "Like it or not, you're going to have to start from square one if you ever want to progress. So, pick a table and let's go learn what happened to the fluffy bunny and the scary wolf."

He flashed me a dirty look, and I returned it with an unapologetic smirk.

*Point, Mira.*

With only a few muttered grumbles, he sulked over to the nearest table and pulled up a red velvet armchair. I slipped into the seat next to him and scooched my chair close enough that I could vaguely make out the words, but not quite as close as we had been at dinner.

"Can you see from there?" he inquired with a tilt of his head. For some reason, I had expected him to occupy the velvet chair with a rigid posture, but instead, he eased into the cushioned back like he'd been sitting in it his entire life. "I may be less than pleased with your choice in teaching materials, but I'm not going to stab you for it. If I have to find out what happens to the blasted fluffy bunny, then so do you." Without warning, he placed a strong hand on the arm of my chair and dragged it over with a single yank.

My heart skipped a beat at the unexpected jerk, then continued to pound impermissibly as my chair cozied right up next to his. He was at least a head taller than me when we were seated, forcing me to gaze up at him through my lashes. His hand lingered on the arm of my chair for a moment, and I remained stiff in the center of it. "Thank you," I said dumbly, unsure of what else to say in such a situation. Perhaps 'That was unnecessary,' or 'Get your hand off my chair' would have been better, but my hammering heart made it difficult to process my thoughts. I cleared my throat. "So, why don't we start with the title? Can you try to sound out these words?"

He turned his head toward me with a slow, irritated spin. "The Rabbit and the Wolf," he said stiffly, not even looking at the cover as he did so. "You already told me the title."

"No..." I wagged a finger at him. "I told you what it was about, but I never told you the title. You'll have to read that part for yourself." I moved my finger back toward the cover, pausing just below the first letter. "Start with this one. Can you sound it out for me?"

He grumbled quietly, but this time, he actually studied the cover. I watched his eyes squint and soften as he fought to decipher the simple letter, like it was an encrypted code. A few times he opened his mouth to try to pronounce it, but each time, his voice was swallowed back by a look of uncertainty.

*Why won't he even try?*

I watched as the frustration grew on his face, his cheeks flaring with a burning red, and his knuckles clenching the top of the table. I wanted to urge him to stop fooling around and just say something, but I knew that egging him on would only shorten his temper faster. There had to be a reason why he wasn't even making a first attempt...

*Could it be...?*

"You know..." I cut through the quiet, keeping my voice soft and gentle so I wouldn't rile up his emotions. "It doesn't have to be perfect on the first try." Immediately, his attention flicked off the cover, his burning eyes digging into me as if searching for an insult that wasn't there. I shrugged. "Failure is a part of learning. If you make a mistake, then we try again, and it's alright if you need to ask for help. That's why I'm here."

The intensity in his expression softened. His brows relaxed, scrunched eyes loosened, and even his tightened lips parted ever-so-slightly, donning a look of true disbelief. "You can't possibly mean that," he said with a confounded breath. "You're a duchess. Surely you know the consequences of failure."

I blinked at him. *Consequences of failure?*

"You mean... like having to work a little harder to succeed?" I shifted in my seat to look up at him easier and noticed my heart flared again when I reminded myself of our close proximity.

"No," he sputtered, looking slightly taken-aback. "I'm referring to weakness. Only the weak endure failures and asking for help is just as good as admitting defeat." He shifted back into his chair, and I noticed a coldness seep into his dark eyes.

My beating heart ceased, freezing as I felt the infection of his cold reality. It was no wonder he was always so cross—he believed power equaled perfection. He was power-crazed and by the look of those scars, he was far from perfect. He was trapped reaching for a goal that was unattainable to him.

"Who taught you that?" I asked quietly.

The coldness in his eyes solidified into pure ice, once again like he had been overtaken by a spell. "My father," he said starkly. His entire body tensed, turning his relaxed posture into the image of a man who could easily have been mistaken for stone. "He didn't settle for anything less than perfection, and he didn't accept failures as sons."

"Sons?" I questioned with wide eyes. "You have brothers?"

His eyes went glassy, mirroring the grimness of his body language. "*Had.*"

An icy chill swept up my spine and caused each hair to stand up straight along my neck and arms. Dozens of questions clawed at my brain. *His father, his brothers, his mysterious past.* I don't know why, but I wanted to know more. Something within compelled me to unravel the beast and see if I could get to the bottom of why he had become so... beastly. But this wasn't the time for that, and my prodding wasn't going to accomplish what we were both here to do.

"Well, I'm not your father." I inched the book closer to him, offering him the slimmest glimpse of an encouraging smile. "I have essentially failed at everything I ever aspired for my life. So, I promise you, I won't judge if you make a few mistakes, too."

He said nothing for a moment, as if he was lost in an internal battle, trying to determine if I was being truthful or crafting an elaborate trick. But gradually, his stiffened shoulders dropped and the invisible walls trapping him in his perfect form seemed to crumble alongside a long exhale. He shifted in his chair, once again allowing his body to sink into the cushion as if he needed it to cradle him after the efforts of his internal war.

He turned his eyes toward the cover. "A-ah, d-drave..." He stopped and sighed, squeezing his eyes shut, as if he could hide from his own humiliation.

"You're close." I smiled sweetly. "The first two words are 'A Brave.' It looks like our languages aren't as different as we thought." He opened his good eye, keeping the other one shut as he inspected the title with the true pronunciation now in his mind. "Do you want to try to pronounce the last word?"

He opened his mouth again, preparing to answer my question on command, but halting with a puff of air. "I... can't," he admitted softly, and to my surprise, a light flush burned his cheeks. "I might need some... some..."

"Help?" I finished, a cheeky smile threatening to spread along my lips.

He sighed. "Yes..."

I stifled a giggled, leaning slightly over him to reach the book easier. My heart still drummed when I brushed against him, but the sense of panic didn't seem to follow me like before. It was hard to feel threatened by a blushing beast. "I would be happy to."

# chapter sixteen

A large yawn parted Mira's lips as she sleepily batted her ebony lashes. "I think that's a good place to stop for tonight." She closed the book on the leprechaun fairy, adding it to the growing stack of stories we'd successfully stumbled through. She turned her sleepy eyes to me, glossy and sparkling like brown tourmaline.

It had been hours since the sun set in the library, leaving only the light of the table lantern to illuminate our books and cast us in a warm glow. "Very well, then." I pushed my chair from the table with a reluctant strain of my comfortable body. It had been a while since I'd felt that at ease during a study session. I almost didn't want to stop while we were making so much progress, but the sunken shadows forming under the duchess's eyes and excessive yawning told me I was going to have to wait. "We will pick up again tomorrow, after dinner."

Her gaze jumped to me with a scrunch of her dainty features. "Dinner? Does that mean I've proven myself useful enough to be worthy of another meal?" Her tone lilted playfully as she poked me in the ribs with her elbow.

Her charming tease tempted me into twitching a smile, but I tucked the reaction away. I was still her captor; therefore, it was important I didn't betray any emotions that could make me appear malleable. "For now," I said ominously, earning a taut frown from her deep red lips.

She sighed dramatically with a tall stretch of her arms. "There's truly no pleasing you, is there?" she tutted, scooching her chair out from the table. "Though, I suppose I can only expect so much from a ruthless jailer who reads bedtime stories about bunnies and baby fairies." She flicked me a smug smile that rounded the edges of her cheeks like a sweet cherub.

Heat spiked through my blood, but I pushed it down with a roll of my eyes. "There was a story about a dragon, as well," I snorted callously.

"Ah, you mean the one who learned to love?" She placed a hand over her heart, fluttering her lashes like a swooning debutant.

I tensed, wrinkling my brow tighter than worn leather. It wasn't my fault that all the books in the library were about frilly lessons on friendship and love. We never even had children's books in my home kingdom, except for the few Mother had hidden in her suite...

"If you're awake enough to chastise me, then perhaps I should select another book for us to go over?" I gestured toward the insurmountable number of books with a devilish smile. "I have no qualms about working until sunrise."

Her playful smile dropped faster than a crashing chandelier. "That's quite alright, unless you don't mind working around a puddle of drool when I pass out on the desk." She rubbed one of her tired eyes. "Funnily enough, a single banana doesn't provide enough energy for such late evenings, so you'll have to pardon me as I bid you goodnight." She turned away from the table to start heading to the door, and I noticed a slight sway in her walk.

An odd tension compressed around my chest, irritating my windpipe as it shallowed my breaths. The sway in her steps was more prominent than it had been the other day, and her eyes looked hollow and woozy. *She looked so... weak.*

**'As she should.'**

I nearly jolted as the intruding voice cracked through my skull. It had been a while since he'd clawed around inside my head... I guess I hadn't noticed it until now, but perhaps part of the reason I'd been so relaxed during our study session was because the voice had gone dormant. *Was it because this was the first time I'd had a real conversation in a while?* Aside from speaking with the beasts, griffins, and various people I was threatening, I hadn't truly had the chance to simply talk with someone since I'd been banished from my realm. Maybe that's why I'd been going so mad...

*'That, and you're a broken man without me. Never forget that.'* Father's reptilian voice snaked into my ears, tickling my brain with a spine-tingling chill.

I didn't answer him, and instead, refocused my attention on Mira to see if interacting with her truly affected his presence in my mind. "Will you return to the ballroom?" I inquired, my eyes following the unsteadiness of her steps.

She paused in front of the door, her slender back facing me as she balanced unevenly on her feet. "I suppose I should." Her voice was heavy, thickened with a drifting sigh. "They might go mad if I keep disappearing unnoticed."

My muscles stiffened at the mention of the other hostages. Unlike Mira, they had been nothing but nuisances who didn't possess any sense of self-preservation. *Why does she care so much about them? Is it a political play to protect her future role as their duchess...?*

*Or is that just who she is...?*

As I was lost in thought, I nearly missed seeing Mira's hand drift sleepily toward the doorknob. She looked dizzy, her eyelids drooping and widening as her head rocked back and forth on her shoulders. *Could she even make it until dinner tomorrow? What would happen if she collapsed on the ballroom steps?*

"Wait!" The word burst out of my mouth before I even realized what I was doing. My blood crystalized in my veins as life suddenly popped into her eyes as she flicked them over her shoulder. Her gaze pinned me in place, rendering me speechless as I fought to untwist my tongue. "I-I..." My voice choked as her big, curious eyes somehow made my thoughts even more disoriented.

*For the love of the realms! What are you doing? Say something!*

I cleared my throat, scrounging up my dignity before I truly made a fool of myself. "I meant to invite you... to breakfast, I mean," I added a little too hastily with a hard bite of my cheek.

Her dark pupils grew as wide as a prized black pearl, and she turned her body away from the door to face me. "Breakfast? But I thought our bargain only extended to dinners?" She blinked at me dazedly, like she wasn't certain I'd really offered her more food, or if she was witnessing a sleep-deprived hallucination.

I straightened my posture to a commanding stance, attempting to recover from my unsightly blunder. "As I said, my castle, my rules." I lifted a daring brow. "Care to argue with me this time?" Her lips parted and shut like a blubbing fish, but ultimately, she remained silent. A victorious smirk twinged at my lips. "Good. We'll see if any of the others are courageous enough to join me at the table. If not, then they'll just have to wait to get leftovers at dinner again." A sense of victory washed through my blood, almost as strong as how I felt when I won duals against my brothers.

*There... This way she won't be fainting on me by the time I'm ready for another lesson. That's why I couldn't hold my tongue earlier... A tutor is useless if they can't keep their head up during sessions.*

She stared at me for a moment, her pretty face vacant and full of wonder. "If that's what you wish..." Her voice sounded puzzled, but soft, like she was analyzing a purring lion. "I shall see you in the morning for breakfast, then." She turned back toward the door, but kept her gaze fixated on me even while she touched the handle, as if she was too fascinated to look away.

I'd never been looked at like that before... Most people who stared at me did so because they were too terrified to blink. So, it was strange feeling the eyes of someone who actually wanted to see me.

*Does she want to see me...? Or is she only gawking at the beast?*

She stepped through the door, and I watched as her slender form disappeared into the dim ballroom. I didn't look away until the door clicked shut, feeling just as drawn to watching her as she had seemed to me. The moment my view of her was cut off, a sick sensation squeezed at my stomach, followed by a compression in my chest.

*Am I growing ill?*

I touched a hand to my forehead in search of a fever, then breathed a sigh of relief when I didn't sense anything amiss.

*Must be in my head...*

I approached the same door Mira had exited through, willing its destination as the key burned in my pocket. I pulled the door open and stepped into the tattered master suite, finally noticing the volume of clutter after having stepped away from it for so long.

*Realms... maybe I am a beast after all.*

Starlight drifted through the stained-glass doors, causing the colored shadows to appear distorted and thin across the scattered remains of the broken furniture. I peered through the glass to glance outside, noticing the piles of rubble pulled away from where soldiers had begun digging through one of the walls. Fortunately for me, even if they bypassed a wall, they would still be met with more doors. While my time was still limited, it was not in danger... yet.

I stepped away from the glass, taking in the shadowed space with a fresh perspective. The room felt so much gloomier now in comparison to the cozy library, but the warm sensation of self-pride pushed away any cold from the eerie space.

I had done it. I had successfully taken the first steps to becoming a true member of this realm. After I had a solid grip on the language, I could be free from relying on monsters like the Golden King. Maybe I could even be free from the monster inside my head...

"Well? Have you killed her yet?" The mirror's oily voice seeped through my cheerful state like black ink on a white rose. "Or are you still a failure?"

*Failure...*

There was that word again—the word that had prodded me for countless years, pricking me in the spine every time I got too close to it.

*"You know... It doesn't have to be perfect on the first try. Failure is a part of learning."*

Mira's gentle words crept into my head like the cooing of a mourning dove. Her way of thinking may have been juvenile and lacking in logic, but admittedly, it was far more desirable. Maybe that was because it was similar to my mother's way of thinking...

I turned toward the mirror, and my cold expression met the dead-eyed reflection. "Even if I am a failure, then at least I learned something from the attempt." I kicked a pile of shredded cushions aside, approaching the scowling mirror.

He didn't reply for a moment, gaping at me in disbelief before bursting into laughter. "D-did the little girl tell you that?" He rolled his head back with a cackle that could shame a hyena.

My teeth ground against each other, straining my head from the pressure. "She's not a *little girl*," I growled with a fierce snarl of my lip. "She's a duchess, and a rather clever one at that. Not everyone can keep an entire ballroom full of bumbling idiots alive."

His laugh tamed, morphing into a scrutinizing grin.

"You've been swayed by the temptress, haven't you?" he snorted. "And here I thought you were better than your brothers."

My eyes widened as blood coursed through my veins like crackling fire. "It's nothing like that!" I barked. "She's simply not as dimwitted as the other nobles and not as ruthless as you. She's like... like..."

"Like your mother."

The room went silent as a thick cloud passed in front of the glass door, shrouding the room in darkness. A soft silver glow nestled in the edges of the mirror, forcing my eyes to draw to it no matter how badly I wanted to look away. The ice in his breath froze me to my core, stiffening me as the realization of his statement burrowed down into my soul like a nest of vipers.

"No..." My voice was quiet, suffocated by the intensity of his too-real image. "T-this is nothing like that. You're dead now. And even if it was the same... there's nothing you can do." Despite what I said, the words felt flat and meaningless. I knew he was dead; I had killed him.

So then why did I still fear what he could do?

"It's exactly the same," he said coldly. His eyes were rimmed in a steely gray, gripping me with the strength of an iron shackle. "You remember perfectly well what happened the last time you chose to be soft-hearted. This girl's lessons are no different from the lies your mother used to feed you. If you follow her path... maybe the same fate that befell your mother will befall this land's duchess..."

My heart jolted like it had been speared with lightning, siezing all my muscles with a nauseating quake. "No!" I shouted, slamming my fist into the wall a mere inch from the mirror's frame. "You're dead! Don't pretend like you have control over anything other than that blasted mirror." I raised my eyes to meet his relentless stare, my heart pounding like it was going to burst into a rage of fire. "I killed you. You can't hurt anyone else."

A vile grin spread across his lips, and he leaned forward, practically pressing his forehead against the invisible barricade that kept him trapped. "But I can hurt *you*."

# *chapter seventeen*

For two weeks, my daily lessons and meals with Mira continued. Every morning she joined me for breakfast, where we then proceeded to the library for a lesson, and then she would return to the ballroom. It had become an odd routine of sorts, but one that was beneficial for the both of us, and helped keep me distracted from the fact that there still hadn't been any word from the grand duke. Mira and the hostages received daily meals, and I was becoming more prolific in Rubian by the day.

*Everything would be splendid, if it wasn't for the raging military outside and the psychotic king inside my head.*

I paced around the dining room with a morbid headache drilling into my skull as my father's words pulsated through my mind. There was no sense in trying to sleep with his voice always ringing in my ears, so I spent the entire night in the kitchen. I'd never cooked much until now, aside from over a campfire while I was traveling alone. So, my efforts were mostly for distracting myself while trying to craft something for breakfast that even Mira wouldn't turn her nose at.

The scent of hot potato cakes filled the dining hall like a savory fog. A fruit salad sat beside it, made up of bruised apples, overripe oranges, and extra bananas, since Mira seemed to like them so much. There was truly no reason for me to put so much effort into a single meal. But, like before, there was a chance the other hostages would attend, and I did need to improve their impression of me if I was going to rule.

*I wonder what Mira will do after I become this province's grand duke? Will she simply return home? Or will her family still want to forge an alliance with Dhurin...?*

My thoughts were interrupted by the *creak* of the far door, causing my face to flush in surprise. I hastily straightened and pretended to be distracted by the sunrise to hide the rush of blood in my cheeks.

*Why did I have to start thinking about those sorts of things at a time like this...*

"Good morning." Mira's lilting voice mirrored that of a nightingale's song. I'd come to appreciate her company in an odd way, mostly because speaking to her gave me a sense of sanity that didn't come from speaking to my mirror.

I turned from the window to face her, expecting to see her tender smile gracing her like an angelic swan. But when I looked at her, there was no smile, no sweetness, and no morning glow. A frown, deeper than an ocean chasm, stained her expression, accompanied by sunken eyes loaded with loathing and fists tight enough to crush stone. She thundered across the room, only halting when the scent of the potato cakes seemed to smack her like a stone wall. Her eyes widened and her nostrils flared, wiping the anger from her features as smoothly as a fresh coat of paint.

"Good morning," I said. My tone was low and cautious, unsure if her soured mood was from something I'd done. "Will it just be you joining me?"

The hypnotic hunger vanished from her glassy expression, switching back into her stony scowl. "Yes." She threw her arms up in the air. "As usual, the others are being insufferable! Lord Tocken actually had the gall to tell me a proper duchess wouldn't be so irresponsible and careless. Me? Careless!? After all the effort I've gone through to feed their whining mouths!? Ugh!" She smacked down into a chair, slouching so far that her eyes almost didn't meet the edge of the table.

It was interesting to see this side of her. She'd definitely lost her temper at points with me during our previous conversations, but her feathers were far more ruffled this time than they had ever been with me. Or at least, from what she'd shown me... I suppose this may only be the first time she's comfortable expressing her true feelings around me. That, or the hostages were truly that unbearable.

"You're not careless," I grunted, crossing the room with a plate of potato cakes and fruit. "They're blind if they believe that." I set the plate in front of where Mira was slumped, and her nose twitched like a hungry rabbit's at the scent of the salty meal.

Her eyes drifted to me, like she was waiting for the 'but...' "You don't believe I'm being foolish?" She slid up in her chair and darted her eyes greedily over the plate of food. Her stomach growled, louder than a behemoth, as she inspected the potato cake with narrowed eyes. "You know, for risking being so close to the bloodthirsty beast?"

I returned to my chair as she took her first bite of the greasy cake. "I don't think you're foolish..." Memories of my conversations with the mirror crept into my skull with the skittering of a thousand spider legs, drumming up the headache that had only started to fade. She looked up from her fork, her soft brows wrinkled. "But I do think it's still a risk... visiting me."

Mira may be useful to me now, but that didn't mean she wouldn't pose a problem later. I would like to believe that I could think through my problems rationally at this stage in my life, but the screech of my father's voice had offset any assurances I had of myself. How easy would it be for him to convince me to kill Mira off another day?

*Would I allow him to make it easy?*

"Why?" she asked quietly. She pressed her fork to the table with a gentle *clatter*, turning her full focus onto me. "Why is it a risk for me to share a meal with you?" Her eyes surveyed me as she folded her fingers together and rested her chin atop them.

*Because I'm your captor. Because I nearly murdered your*

*betrothed. Because I'm attempting to overtake your future province.*

"I nearly killed you." My voice echoed around the room like the ambiance of a catacomb. I felt the urge to look away from her, but I kept my gaze locked. She needed to know just how dangerous I could be if she was going to stay close. "When you first found me in the master suite, I was mere moments from ending your life." A fresh strain tugged at the end of my voice, almost as if it was painful to admit out loud.

*But why is it painful?*

"I know," she said calmly, with not even a touch of fear cracking behind her deep brown eyes. "We had a whole debate about it, remember? But in the end, you didn't kill me. Are you saying that you're still considering killing me now?" Her confidence swayed a touch with a tense in her shoulders, but she didn't look away.

"No," I said firmly, surprised by how easily the word came to my lips. "Not while you still have more to teach me."

Her tension softened, revealing the slightest smile as she picked up her fork. "Then there's truly no risk in me dining with you, especially considering how much you have left to learn." She took a massive bite of the potato cake and her eyes nearly rolled back in her head from bliss.

For a while, neither of us spoke. We ate and drank, and cast each other side-glances, but the conversation still lingered like an irritating loose end.

*How...? How is she able to be so calm while she's literally sharing a table with her captor? Is it only because I said I wouldn't kill her? Or...*

"Mira." I caught her eyes right as she swallowed an impressive bite. "Do you... fear me?" My voice felt hoarse. Never in my life had I needed to ask someone if I caused them fear—I had always known... But Mira...

She took an extra moment to swallow. Her gaze lowered

to her hands, studying them as if the answer was written inside her palm before looking back up to me. "I fear what you've done," she answered numbly, her eyes void and distant. "My brother and his wife... suffered a lot because of you. The men and women in that ballroom are suffering now, and I have no knowledge of what got you banished from your home realm. I fear what you'll do when the rose dies..." She paused to intake a large breath. "But I don't fear you now. And to be honest, I'm not sure you'll even live up to my fears when the rose finally wilts. It's struck me for a while now, that if you truly were as vicious and bloodthirsty as everyone claims you to be, then I truly would have died the night we met."

The air in my lungs dissolved, leaving me breathless as I forced my jaw not to fall open. *She doesn't fear me? But commanding fear is commanding power. Am I truly powerless to this woman?*

"I kidnapped your sister-in-law," I said, my voice steel. "I dragged her through the snow until she nearly froze to death, then delivered her to the beast's leader." I inched onto the edge of my seat, locking my eyes with Mira to ensure not a single word went past her. "I tied your brother to a tree and left him with the same wolf that later destroyed my face." I jeered a finger toward my scarred eye. "And now you're in the same position they were... You are in my castle, under my control, yet you still have the stomach to claim you don't fear me?" I narrowed my eyes, fueling my tone with as much intimidation and malice as I could.

*She has to fear me... Everyone does at some point.*

"I am well-aware of what you've done to my family," she said stiffly, her expression cold and icy. "And as I said, I fear the things you've already done. Because if they had been done even a sliver differently, I may not have that family with me today." She stopped, her eyes darting away from me. "But they are still here, because you didn't kill them, either." She returned her gaze to me, a yearning twinkle in her eyes like she was dying to know more. "So no, I don't think you're as evil as you make yourself out to be. I think you're lost and confused in a realm where no one can understand your voice, and I think you're clinging to your home realm by trying to restore the life you had there, here."

Her words felt like daggers in my brain, digging up thoughts and emotions that were better left buried.

*Restoring the life I once had, here? Of course, that's what I'm trying to do! Because that was the life I was born to live...*

"You've done a lot of awful things, Conan." She nearly whispered my name, as if testing if I would still respond to it. My chest tightened like a wound top, but I remained rigid. "But I don't believe you've gone too far to come back from it. I know I'm still your hostage, but the fact of the matter is, I don't fear that you will hurt me." The depths I could see in her eyes stretched from vulnerable to unrestrained honesty.

*She doesn't fear me...*

My gut twisted as I recalled all the moments I would have harmed her, almost rising up a sensation of... guilt.

**'Guilt is useless. Abandon it or accept that you're just as useless.'**

Father's voice ground against my skull as I swallowed back the invasive emotion. No, I wouldn't feel guilty for the things I almost did to her. They didn't even happen, so there was no use lingering on it. Besides, nothing ever made me feel guilt... not even the worst things I've done.

"You should fear me," I said callously. "Even if I could've done worse to you and your family."

She lifted a brow, her resolve unchanging. "And why is that?"

"Because..." Out of nowhere, my throat began to burn, forcing back my voice for some unknown reason. It was as if something inside me didn't want Mira to know the worst of what I'd done. *But she'll never fear me if she doesn't know...* "I've killed before."

A cold silence swept over the room, and while Mira's expression didn't change, I could see the blood drain from her face, turning her as white as the napkin on her plate. She said nothing for a long moment, only watching me with a steady eye. "Who have you killed?"

My neck tensed, and for the first time in my life, a sense of discomfort rolled through me as I relived the memories. I pushed the discomfort aside, focusing on relaying the facts as bold-faced as possible. "Many men... servants, a neighboring king..." My voice choked, clamping in my throat like a bear's claw. "My father..." Her eyes widened and her thick red lips parted with a tiny gasp. I gripped the edge of the table, fighting the last word that clung to my tongue.

*'Say it, son.'*

I dug my heels into the ground, fighting the seizing pressure in my chest. "And... my mother." Pain seared through my veins as I admitted the last of my sins. It had been a while since I'd been forced to say it out loud; maybe that's why it stung so dang badly.

Mira didn't move, her eyes wide and chest rising and falling rapidly with shortened breaths. She reached for her glass of water, downing nearly the entire cup before gasping for air, and turning to me with a serious glare. "Tell me." She pressed her palms against the table, hard enough that I wondered if she would leave bruises. "Are you proud?"

I rattled. "Pardon?"

She pressed her palms down even harder. "I asked, are you *proud*?" Her voice rose into a crescendo, ending with her standing from her seat. "Are you proud that you took those lives?"

Her question bolted through me, startling my mind as I

wrestled with the answer. Memories of slaying innocent men on the training field and pushing away the nausea in front of my father wracked my brain like a looping nightmare. My thoughts flicked back to the day I had slain the neighboring king in his ballroom, and all the restless nights I'd spent haunted by his son's screams. Of course, I was proud. Father was proud, so that was what I had to be. If I wasn't proud, then what else was I?

*'Certainly not remorseful,'* the voice intruded. *'No son of mine would ever feel guilt over something so trivial.'*

"Was it trivial?" I whispered to myself, just soft enough that Mira didn't hear, but she still noticed my lips move.

My mother's soft gray eyes flicked into my mind, her sweet smile warming me from the inside out one final time as I felt her hand go limp in mine. The pain tore into my heart, shredding it like a wolf's ravenous teeth, until only the raw emotions underneath remained.

*I had felt guilt... it was there. But I would never dare let it out.*

"I was, once..." I admitted, only loud enough that she could hear me. Her eyes gripped me with such intensity, full of questions and concerns that couldn't be expressed by a mere look alone. Why did I want to tell her more? Why did those eyes urge me to open up about things I'd locked away for decades? I took in a breath. "But now..."

A sharp gasp interrupted my thoughts as Mira dropped her fork with what felt like a realm-shattering clatter. With trembling fingers, she raised a hand to her lips, her eyes glued on the meal in front of her as if she had just seen a ghost take a bite out of it.

"C-Conan, did you use flour to make these potatoes?" Her pupils shook like a rattling carriage and her skin turned an unsightly shade of white.

I blinked at her and her meal, with a sudden increase in my heart rate. "Yes, of course. Why? Is there something wrong with it?"

*Why does she look so panicked? Does she think it was poisoned?*

She pushed away from the table without an ounce of hesitation. Her hand was still pressed to her mouth as she stumbled from the table and raced to the nearest door.

"I-I'm sorry," she bumbled, yanking open the closest door. "I have to go."

# chapter eighteen

*I've been eating flour...*

My stomach bubbled like a boiling pot, inflating me with nausea and cramps. It had been years since I'd consumed my allergen in such a high dosage, and now my body was trying to tear itself apart from the inside-out as revenge. I pushed through every door I could find, dashing through hallways, studies, and even a women's lounge filled with lacey trim and rose-colored furniture.

*Where is the ballroom?*

My gut wrestled inside my abdomen with the intensity of dueling boars, causing my steps to stumble and slow. Another wave of nausea overtook me, and I placed a hand over my mouth to try to contain the contents of my stomach. My mind went dizzy as the pain in my abdomen mixed with the sickness lingering in the back of my throat. I pushed through one more door and found myself in what appeared to be the same bedroom I had ransacked earlier in our captivity.

The bed was still stripped of all its blankets and pillows, and the wardrobe's open doors unveiled its empty contents. My attention flew straight to the chamber pot tucked under the bed, and I rushed over to it just in time to spew the poisonous potato cakes. My throat felt raw as I leaned against the edge of the bed, panting, clutching the pot in my lap. I looked weakly over to the nearest door to try to gauge if my quaking limbs could make it that far.

I had hoped to make it to the ballroom where the other

hostages might help me through this nightmare, but now I wasn't even sure I could crawl into the bed behind me.

*Why couldn't he have cooked it with real poison instead...?*

For hours, my body proceeded to drain me of all my fluids in every unpleasant way imaginable. I managed to climb onto the bare mattress at some point, twisting and turning in agony as I waited for my abdominal war to end. Dehydration brought a throbbing headache to my tired mind, which made it impossible to sleep the discomfort away. Even when the nausea ceased and the cramping eased, I still couldn't find the strength to move my crumpled form.

It had been days since I'd had a proper meal or had a sound night's sleep. My eyes stayed glued to the lone window at the far edge of the room, watching as the sun slowly crept from the sky and darkness flooded the space. Without a blanket or fire, the room was dreadfully cold, wracking my ailing body with intense shivering. I closed my eyes in an attempt to sleep and possibly regain enough energy to move, but my unfinished conversation with Conan had left me unsettled and restless.

*He's killed before...*

Another shiver rippled through me, more intense than the previous. His icy words reverberated through my mind like a clanging sword. My muscles tensed as questions pounded through my throbbing brain. He said he had killed both of his parents... and that he had been proud?

*Yet he didn't look proud.*

His dark eyes dug into my mind as their soulless and broken stare haunted me. He had seemed so intent on making me fear him, as if it was the only thing he knew how to do. But in actuality, it made me pity him. A man who could only feel validated by pressing fear into others. What kind of life was that?

*But he's still a killer...*

I nuzzled into the mattress, trying to push away the stinging thoughts. *Have I been a fool for getting so close to him...?* He said he had nearly killed me. Did that mean the other hostages were right? Am I truly a poor excuse for a duchess, who's too bullheaded to be wise? Well, I suppose I was the one laying in an empty bed, too ill to even sit up, while they were waiting on a supper that would never be delivered. It was hard to say who was in the worst situation, but the lingering throb in my abdomen insisted on declaring me the winner.

The beast flooded back into my mind, but with his true name following all my thoughts instead. Calling him *the beast* felt... incorrect, now that I'd learned more about him. He wasn't a mindless, rampaging animal; he was a person. He was Conan, the troubled foreigner with a dark past that intrigued me more than it should have. I closed my eyes and his face flashed in my mind like a flawless portrait, highlighting every curve of his jaw and every shadow of his scars. I knew he received the scars after he reached the Ruby Realm, but somehow, I felt he'd been scarred for much longer.

*But he's still dangerous.*

I rolled over on my back, churning my raw stomach, despite the fact that it was fully emptied. I knew I needed to be careful around my captor, especially knowing what I did now. But even so, I wanted to find out more... He didn't look like a ruthless murderer when he confessed his sins to me; he looked like a man wrestling with an inner beast.

A sudden *click* disrupted my thoughts, jarring me from my scrunched position. I rolled over in the bed with the grace of a bag of lard. I probably looked like a corpse in my current state, but even so, I couldn't imagine that I looked even half as pale as the beast's shocked stare.

"Mira?" He forced the door open the rest of the way and moved to my bedside with a haste that seemed unnaturally fast. "Where have you been? I waited for you at supper, and when you didn't attend, I checked the ballroom and—" His voice snuffed out with a quiet suction of air. He must have just noticed my haggard appearance, because his flustered expression vanished with a soft bulge of his dark eyes.

He gazed down at my sickly state, making me feel exposed. I had never upheld much elegance around him, but even so, being seen in my weakest form was certainly humiliating. Once his shock had worn off, he searched me, as if a clear answer was written on the bedpost as to why I looked so horrid.

"Sorry," I said, my voice raspy and dry. "I don't think I'll be able to make it through a study session tonight." I cracked a weak smile, attempting to feign even the slightest bit of strength so I didn't feel so puny.

"W-what happened?" He pressed a hand to his forehead and then kneeled beside the bed, so his eyes were level with mine. "Have you been ill all day?" His words were breathy, like they were fighting against something he was trying to keep contained. "Is... is that why you ran out of the dining room?"

He pressed his hands into the mattress, digging his fingers into the pillowy top. For a moment I couldn't respond, too enraptured by his overwhelming interest in me. *Does he only care because I am his tutor?*

"Yes," I answered weakly. "I'm sorry I had to cut our meal short, but apparently, some of the food wasn't *agreeable* with me." My stomach lurched just thinking about the potato cakes I had seen one too many times.

He turned his head away from me, shaking with a disbelieving sigh. "All day... I thought you ran out because I'd scared you."

*Scared me?*

I shifted my neck to try to meet his eyes, confusion pulsing through me in tangled strands. "Is that not what you were trying to do?" I knitted my brow, replaying our breakfast chat through my mind. "You told me I should fear you."

He turned back to me, and oddly enough, a spark jolted through my heart. Out of all the times I had seen this beast, I had never seen him look so... somber. His entire face changed under the heavy emotion, causing his scars to appear more pitiful than intimidating, like a wounded animal longing for something I couldn't quite pinpoint.

"I know," he said, his voice heavy and thick. He dug his fingers deeper into the mattress, piercing the top layer and exposing a spring wire. "All day long—" He stopped himself, rolling his eyes while burrowing his hands knuckle-deep into the bedding.

"What?" I edged. "Are you surprised that it didn't work?"

He looked up at me, feeding his mysterious gaze into me like some sort of direct link that made me crave more information. "No," he admitted quietly. "I suppose I was worried it had." The words slipped past his lips with a jolt, as if he was surprised he had even spoken them. He looked away from me, but he couldn't retract the words that were now sifting through my thoughts.

My breath lodged in my throat, and my lips parted with a wordless gasp. His voice lingered in the room like a thick fog, blurring my thoughts as I tried to wrap my mind around what he had said.

*Did he even mean to say it?*

My heartbeat escalated and my stomach squirmed with an odd warmth that made me wonder if I needed to reach for the defiled chamber pot. I swallowed, wetting my barren mouth enough to rasp out a question. "If you don't want me to fear you... then what do you want?"

He didn't look at me, but he didn't move from his kneel, either. For a long moment we sat in silence. The quiet gripped me like an iron shackle, urging me to burst free and ask for an answer. *What does he want from me?* He didn't kill me, and he didn't want me to fear him, but I was still captive to his wicked schemes.

"Conan?" I tested the word as fragilely as a glass snowflake. My eyes pleaded with him, itching to learn more of what he kept chained inside his tattered heart.

He matched my eyes, looking at me with a voided gaze. "You're probably weak from your illness," he said, stepping up from the edge of the bed and starting for the door. "I'll be back with some water and crackers."

Pressure weighed upon my chest as I watched him place his hand on the door. I didn't want him to leave, not yet—not when I had so much more to ask him.

"Conan, wait!" I stretched out my hand, watching it flop limply to the mattress as he spun around, eyes wide. "Please... don't bring me crackers. I can't have them." I bit the edge of my lip, shifting uncomfortably at the thought of admitting my fatal weakness.

He lifted a brow. "Why not?"

"I..." I sighed, "I'm allergic to wheat or have some sort of strange intolerance to it at least. That's why I got so sick when I ate the potato cake you made. I wasn't careful enough and have paid the price, greatly," I groaned, emphasizing my point as I pressed my palms against my eyes.

"My cooking did this to you?" His voice was sharp and filled with horror, shocking me into looking back in his direction.

"Well, yes... but it's not your fault. I needed to be more careful—"

"Wait here," he commanded, swinging the door open with the force of a gladiator. "I'll be back with something you can eat."

He stepped halfway through the door when another

thought prickled my brain. "Also!" I called out, once again causing him to pause. "If you're going to the kitchens anyway, could you take some food to the ballroom?" I bit my lip, saying an internal wish that my request wouldn't be too greedy, considering he was already preparing to help me. "The others will probably get worried if I don't return with their meal..."

He didn't look back, his hand frozen on the doorframe as his shoulders rose and fell with a deep sigh. "I'll return shortly."

# chapter nineteen

*I made her sick.*

Utensils and platters clattered to the floor in a thundering symphony as I shoved everything off the kitchen counters. Flour coated nearly every surface after my sloppy creation of the blasted potato cakes. I snagged a ratty rag from the cupboard, then rushed it to the water pump to drench it. My heart pounded in my ears, flaring up a bundle of iron-clad knots in my stomach as I went to work scrubbing every inch of the counters.

*She had been allergic all along... It's no wonder she was always so weak. She could hardly eat anything I'd provided her with.*

The knots in my stomach twisted tighter, fueling my muscles to scrub with a furious intensity. Sweat beaded on my brow, but I wasn't sure if it was from the labor or the heat of my blood. I must have been angry—there was no other explanation as to why I felt this way. The heat in my veins grew fiercer, and I pumped my arms faster as I scrubbed the back corners of the prep station. Every inch of my body felt as if it had been pumped full of fury... all except for the tangled knots that tore through my stomach and blurred my mind.

*What is this?*

Once the counters were clean, I tossed the rag aside, then began drying the counters with a fresh one. I felt hot, but not in the same way I felt when I was talking to the mirror. It was a deeper discomfort, one that dug into my very soul and urged me to tear myself apart from the inside out. Was I angry at Mira for not telling me sooner? No, that wasn't it. She didn't even blame me, so why would I harbor a grudge against her? There had to be something else that was causing this crushing sensation against my chest.

'*You're feeling guilt.*'

My head crackled as the voice ripped through my mind like a tearing muscle. I whipped around in search of the mouthy mirror, only halting with a lurch as I remembered it was locked in my mind. *Guilt?* Another twist ratcheted in my stomach, flashing images of Mira's curled up form lying limply on the barren bed.

"So what if I am?" I snapped at the voice. I turned my attention back to the pantry and dug through its contents in search of something Mira could eat. "It's just a silly emotion; it doesn't mean anything." My throat tightened, suffocating the end of my words.

'*It means... you're defective,*' the voice hissed.

I rolled my eyes, grabbing a slab of salted meat that had been preserved on a rack. "Defective, failure, worthless... Have you ever considered speaking to me like a person? Or realms-forbid, a son?"

I leaned down to the base of the wood stove to spark a fire, fanning the flames until the heat singed my eyebrows.

'*I speak to you in this manner because you're my son.*' The voice sneered. '*If you were anything less, I wouldn't waste my breath.*'

The heat engulfed me as I threw the slab of meat onto a skillet with a crackle of burning fat and grease. "Then don't," I clipped, my teeth snapping shut with an audible *clatter.* "Don't waste your breath, or don't waste whatever ghastly lifeforce fuels your demonic hauntings. If being your son is the only thing preventing me from being free of your grasp, then you can consider me as nonexistent as your fatherly care." I seared the meat, then grabbed a cleaver from the rack to slice it into smaller portions.

*'Just look at yourself...'* he cooed. *'Look how far you've fallen from the honorable prince you once were. What kind of a ruler slaves over a stove for a useless hostage?'*

My temper shattered, causing me to swing the cleaver around at the empty air as if I could behead the internal voice. "That 'useless hostage' has a name!" I bellowed, my chest rising and falling like a rampaging bear's. "It's Mira, and she is far from useless. The girl you wanted to kill has taught me the beginnings of a language I may have never had the chance to learn. If I had listened to you, I may have won the castle, but I would still be lost..." My body tensed, like an invisible pair of arms were squeezing my torso. "And now she's sick... and it's my fault."

The knots in my stomach returned in full force, crushing me with the undeniable feeling of guilt... A feeling I had managed to ward off for so many years, only to have my efforts undone by one smart-mouthed duchess...

*'A prince admits fault for nothing.'* His words rattled in my brain like a rock shaking around my skull.

I turned back to the stove, my mind burning with images of Mira's crumpled body suffering all alone. "You forget. I'm not a prince in this realm."

*'But you were in mine...'* he hummed like a deadly wasp. *'And I never fail to take action against those who insult me. Let's not forget the last time you developed... an attachment.'*

My gut tightened, rushing me with an unwelcome rise of nausea that I pushed back with a stifling swallow. "You can't touch her... This isn't like the last time."

A dark chuckle resonated through my brain like a painful echo. *'If you keep this up, then this will be even better than the last time.'*

• • • • • • • • • • • • • • • • • • • • • • • • • • • • • • • •

I rolled around in the empty bed for what felt like years. The revenge my body had been enacting on me finally seemed to be settling, but the damage it had already done left me depleted. My stomach growled in a symphony of hunger and pathetic moans. Now that the nausea had passed, I could probably hobble through the castle to try to find my way back to the ballroom. Although, the hope of Conan actually bringing me something edible kept me glued to the bed.

His burning gaze played through my mind on repeat, causing my settling stomach to entangle with odd tingles. He seemed so determined to help me... It was likely because he wanted more lessons. But even so, it was hard to wrap my thoughts around the idea of him running around the castle searching for me. Did he really want to keep learning our language that badly?

Another few minutes passed, which felt like hours as my impatience grew heavier. It wasn't until my eyes had started to drift shut for a little nap that the door began to creak open. At first, I didn't open my eyes, too enchanted by the peace of a blossoming dream. But when the mouth-watering scent of spiced meat and boiled vegetables tickled my nose, my eyes sprang open.

It took me a moment to determine whether I was looking at my beastly captor, or a pack mule. His entire face was hidden behind a mountain of blankets, pillows, and a precariously balanced meal tray on the top. He crouched to the floor in awkward, stuttering movements, setting his load down while placing a steadying hand on top of the silver-domed tray. I watched him with unwavering fascination. He must have been sweating at some point, because his white tunic clung to his arms, leaving not even an inch of his bulging muscles to the imagination. His broad shoulders locked into place, flexing his deltoids as he steadied the tower of bedding on the floor.

He flicked his ebony eyes in my direction, and I jolted as I sucked in a glob of drool before it could escape my lips. *Must have been from smelling the food...* He was looking at me with a more analytical stare than he had before, but not with the scrutiny he possessed when we first met.

"Here..." He grabbed the tray from the top of the pile, never averting his gaze from me as he set it on top of the mattress. "I'm not much of a cook, but this should at least be safe for you to eat." He whipped the lid off the top of the tray, and a savory fog wafted into my face like a heavenly cloud. Seared beef, covered in aromatic spices, sat beside a generous helping of boiled broccoli and asparagus. It wasn't the most soothing meal for a stomach that had been internally shredded, but it wasn't bananas... and it looked safe.

"Thank you," I breathed softly, my cheeks warming, most likely from the steaming meal. "But you didn't have to—"

"Oh, and I brought this, too." Before I could even finish, he bolted around and started tossing aside the mountain of pillows until he had dug out a corked water jug and steel kettle. "I was going to make you some mint tea, but I couldn't balance the full teacup, so I thought I'd just bring the kettle and..." He glanced around the room with an increasing frown. "There's no fireplace in here... is there?"

I shook my head mutely, trying to hide the fascination in my expression.

"I see," he huffed, letting his arms fall with the jug and kettle dangling loosely from his hands. "I suppose I can offer you water then." His frown deepened, and he turned back to the pile of supplies to pick a dainty porcelain teacup from a pillowcase.

"Water would be wonderful," I said with a lick of my cracking lips. My throat still burned from the corrosive fluids upheaved from my stomach, making even the food dull in comparison to the thought of a drink. Conan uncorked the water jug and filled the cup to the brim, then handed it over with a surprisingly steady hand.

I sat up with staggered movements, trying not to fall back down as the pain in my head intensified. Conan's gaze flicked between me and the mattress, his eyes widening as his forehead creased ever so slightly.

"Here." Out of nowhere, he placed his free hand on the top of my back. A bolt of lightning shot through my spine, freezing me in temporary paralysis before his warm touch melted it away.

*What is he doing?*

My lips parted, but I didn't breathe. With the slightest pressure, Conan eased me into a sitting position with the tenderness of a man caring for a dove with a broken wing. My heart hammered in my chest, buzzing in my ears like a brood of cicadas as he mutely placed the water cup in my hands. The moment he passed the cup, he turned back to the pile of bedding, snagging an armful of pillows to bring over. It was a miracle that the cup didn't tremor with my racing pulse pounding in my fingertips. One by one, Conan stuffed the pillows behind my back, not stopping until I was only an inch away from leaning back into a fluffy cloud.

"There." He nodded, his expression remaining dormant. "Now you can eat. It should, hopefully, be palatable. The other hostages didn't waste any time devouring it when I slid it through the door, so it can't taste too horrid."

I paused with my cup halfway to my parched lips. "You fed the hostages?" My throat was dry and scratchy. I raised the cup and chugged it in long, refreshing gulps.

"Yes," he said coolly, turning back to the dwindling pile of supplies to fetch the remaining blankets. "I was already in the kitchen, so it wasn't terribly inconvenient to prepare a few more morsels of food." He tossed the blankets over the mattress, sliding the meal tray to the side so he could cover me from the waist down in the covers.

My heart stuttered, completely dumbfounded that this

man—this criminal—was actually showing me kindness, in his own sort of way. The blanket nestled around me, flooding me with a sense of ease and comfort that I had been longing for all night. How was it possible that this comfort was coming from Conan?

"Why?" I whispered, only loud enough for him to jolt his attention to me. His eyes bulged, looking like a deer in the lamplight, as if he had been caught in the midst of a crime. "Why are you being so nice to me?" I wrapped my fingers around the teacup, gently sloshing the water inside with smooth tilts.

His jaw tensed, and he dug his hands into his pockets while pacing around the edge of the bed. "I'm not being nice," he said with a hot puff of air. "I'm only ensuring that my tutor is still capable of breathing long enough for me to gain a grasp of the language." He clicked his heels together, crossing his arms with a stern scrunch of his brows. He was acting like the rigid beast I had first met, but at the same time, there was something lacking in his ferocious aura. He didn't give off the same hatred or bloodlust he had in the past, but instead, he looked like a child putting on a mask to play the villain.

"But you are being nice," I countered softy, reaching forward to pick up a forkful of the tender beef. The savory smell instantly roused my appetite, even earning a growl of approval from my stomach as I placed the succulent bite in my mouth. I chewed for a moment, too lost in bliss to pay much attention to Conan's arched brow. I swallowed. "I can understand that you would bring me food to keep me alive, but why go to the effort of bringing me pillows and blankets?" I gave him an imploring look, my chest tightening with the longing for a real answer.

*Why is he treating me this way? What has changed?*

He gave me a dull shrug. "You looked cold." He tried to sound uncaring, but the slight draw in his voice left me unconvinced. "You nearly fell asleep on me the last time we studied. If you're not well-rested and at least moderately comfortable, then I'll never advance to real reading material." He waved his hand with a taut flourish, but his aggravation seemed to make his cheeks a lot redder than I had seen before.

*Is he truly this obsessed with learning the language?*

I swallowed a bite of broccoli and washed it down with another gulp of water. With every question I asked this man, it seemed like ten more followed. He was a walking contradiction. He wanted us to fear him, but he got anxious when I did. He wanted to be the villain, but he went out of his way to care for me when I fell ill. It was bizarre, yet... so very fascinating.

"Conan...?" I tilted my eyes up from my cup, catching his gaze with an odd flutter in my chest. "After you learn our language and take over the castle for good, what do you plan to do?" My voice rasped a touch, partially from the lingering dryness and partially from my reluctance to ask. It was hard to say what Conan might do if he succeeded in conquering Dhurin.

"I'll take on the emperor." He wasted no time responding, as if the answer had been well-rehearsed and lingering on his tongue since the moment he waltzed into the castle. "Once Dhurin's army is under my control, I'll overthrow the capital, vanquish the cowardly Golden King, and conquer the entire Ruby Realm." The color in his eyes dulled, changing his glassy onyx gaze to a storm-cloud gray that made me uneasy.

"Why?" I asked. My thoughts swirled like a vicious whirlpool, but I did my best to bite back my burning comments.

His muscles tightened ever-so-slightly, along with a gentle clench in his scarred jaw. "For power, of course." His voice was dead and soulless, like a marionette moving without a puppeteer.

"Why do you want power?" I questioned further. My hands dug into the soft wool blanket, burrowing my nails into the woven stitches.

"Because I was born to be a king." His throat seemed to

tighten, choking his words like it physically pained him to say them out loud. "My father wanted to be the greatest ruler in all the realms, so he instilled me with the knowledge required to follow in his footsteps as heir. He wanted me to be strong; he wanted me to be undeniable. Power is the key to it all, therefore he ensured I always hungered for it, and that I would never fall to weakness. He taught me to—"

"Hold on a moment." I held up my palm to interrupt him, my eyes wide and voice choked. He stopped, but only after flashing me an irritated grimace. "I'm sorry, but I asked why *you* want power. All you've told me is why your *father* wanted power." He blinked at me, his eyes clouded with swirling thoughts, thickening the storm in his dulled gaze. "So, which is it? Is conquering our realm your father's ambitions or is it yours?"

At first, he didn't answer, his brows tightened so tensely that they wrinkled more than an elephant's hide. Finally, he took a seat on the end of the bed. His weight caused the mattress to sink, and my foot slid until it nearly rested against his leg.

He hunched over his knees, his elbows digging into his thighs with his fingers folded together into a thick fist. "For all our lives, my father and I have always shared the same ambitions," he replied, his voice so soft, it was nearly a whisper.

I leaned forward, moving out from the cloud of pillows so I could sit even an inch closer to him. "But you said your father was dead..."

He tapped his chin to his folded hands, his eyes pensive and unbelievably intense. "He's dead, but he's not gone." His tone was cold, chilling my bones even from beneath my new blanket. "Every day I hear him. Reminding me that I can't disappoint him, that I can't risk being a failure."

My forehead crinkled as I tried to wrap my brain around what he was saying, *He... hears him?* I wonder if he simply has strong memories of him?

"Why can't you disappoint him?" I inquired, leaning another inch closer to ensure he could hear me. My heart pattered as I moved closer to him, but I quieted the organ with a swallowed breath. "He's dead. You told me that you... you killed him. So why does it matter if you fail a man who lives only in your head?"

A cold silence swept over the room, followed by the slow turn of Conan's head. His eyes met mine, but instead of being vacant or disgruntled like they usually were, they were ridden with a pain so deep that my chest swelled in stinging empathy that I never knew possible.

"Because I've only truly failed him once." His voice actually shook, a grim fear washing out his features with the pale light of the moon drifting in. He locked his eyes with mine, stealing my breath as he looked at me like I was more than just a hostage, just a tutor, or just a duchess who could be of slight use to him. "And because I failed, I lost the only person I ever cared about."

# chapter twenty

Two days passed before I was fully able to be back on my feet.

I sat in the corner of the ballroom, surrounded by empty meal trays I hadn't bothered to take back to the dining room from my nightly meals with the beast. It easily could have taken another day for me to fully return to my normal self, but I didn't waste any time returning to the ballroom. It was partially because I needed to let the others know I was alright, but mainly because I needed space to think...

*And even space wasn't enough...*

Conan's caretaking had destroyed nearly everything I had assumed about him, while simultaneously confirming many other thoughts. He was a killer, he was a captor, he was a monster... But at the same time, he was only a man. A man who was broken and lost, but a man who still had the capacity to show kindness and express vulnerability, even when he wasn't aware he was doing it. I needed to know more, but no longer knew how to ask.

*Things are different now.*

Something in our dynamic had changed the night he cared for me... I couldn't quite pinpoint what it was, but all I knew was that our captor-captive relationship was no longer supported by fear or authority; and that's what made it strange... For the last two days, he had stopped by to visit me regularly, brought me hot cups of tea, and read stories out loud to me to practice his language skills... or so he claimed. It was nice, in a weird 'he's my captor and he's only caring for me because

I'm useful' sort of way. But even if his motivations for helping me were meant to be selfish, they didn't feel that way on my end... If it wasn't for one teeny, tiny overhanging factor, I might have even thought he cared. But that one factor was far too daunting...

*Our imprisonment.*

My gaze drifted over to the rose, feeling the same bitter twist in my gut that now accompanied my views of it. The stem had grown soft and tipped over, letting the drooping petals collect in a pile beneath its thinning bloom. The leaves and thorns were turning brown at the tips, leaving only the few remaining petals and dark green stem as any proof that it still lived.

There had been no word from outside the walls, other than the occasional crashing of demolition, where we presumed they were trying to break through the exterior walls. It was a clever idea, but I'd done enough exploring around the castle to know that most of its walls were made up of pure granite or other heavy-duty stone. The ballroom was at the center of the castle, so there was no telling how many walls they would have to bust through before they would reach us. Not to mention they had to be cautious of what walls they took down; otherwise, they might collapse the entire castle in on itself. Either way, their efforts made one thing clear: the grand duke had no intention of handing over the province.

The hostages encircled the wilting rose in a tight cluster, still fearful that the moment they moved away, the protection wouldn't reach them and the bloodthirsty beast would come rampaging through the door. After having spent so much time with Conan over the last few weeks, it was hard to imagine that he would burst in on a killing spree. Yet it didn't mean I *couldn't* imagine it, especially when he always avoided the topic of our imprisonment every time I brought it up.

I rubbed my hands along my arms, trying to ward off the

burning frustration that was clawing at my chest. *What is he planning? And why is he being so closed-off about it?* We only had a week at most left before the rose fully withered, and what then? Would he keep everyone locked up until the kitchen's food supply ran dry? Or would he fulfill his original threat and kill everyone as punishment to the duke...

*He wouldn't do that... Right?*

My mouth went dry at the thought, but the usual tightness that came from my anxiety wasn't there. I didn't know what Conan was planning to do at this point, but somehow, I didn't fear that he would prove to be the beast everyone claimed him to be.

*He is so much more than that...*

"No! That will never work; we need to utilize the element of surprise!" Lord Tocken barked loud enough that it tore me from my thoughts.

"How are we meant to surprise him if he controls the entire castle!?" another voice shrieked back.

My curiosity compelled me to investigate, so I started for the center of the room, my attention instantly drawn to the brewing argument.

"Madam Ophelia is right." Lord Illumen pointed at the older woman with a tense glare in his brother's direction. "If we're going to kill the beast, then we will need to—"

"Hold on! Did you say kill him?" I inserted myself into the cluster of bickering nobles, drawing every eye as I blinked at them in disbelief.

*Kill Conan? Wasn't that a bit extreme.*

"Yes. *Kill* him." Lord Tocken drew out the word, sending an oddly painful clench to my chest. "Azura says we have less than a week before the rose dies, which means the beast will be clawing at our throats soon if we don't do something first." His round face burned with a tomato shade of red.

"I say we wait until the rose is fully wilted," Sir Eric chimed in. "That way we can make the most out of the protection spell and prepare a counterstrike for when he comes to attack." He raised his fist in the air, earning a chorus of cheers from some of the other men.

"Why wait?" Madam Ophelia snorted. "What's the difference between killing him now and waiting until the rose finally dies? I'm ready to watch the beast bleed." Her tone turned dark, slowing my blood like it had been replaced with a thick sludge.

"But you can't kill him!" I blurted out, catching myself with a partial gasp as surprise overtook me. *Why did that spill out of me so quickly?* "I mean... you can't kill him because he's too powerful. How do you expect to kill a man like him?" Nerves ripped through me, leaving me anxious and confused as to why they had even taken residency.

*Killing Conan would solve all our problems... But was that how we wanted things to end? Was that how I wanted things to end?*

"We'll attack him as a mob." From the back of the group, Henrietta stepped forward. Her once sweet gaze was shadowed with a bloodlust that genuinely terrified me. *Do they all hate Conan so badly?* "If he's not expecting us to fight back, and we all take him on at once, we should be able to kill him. As long as everyone's on board."

I tore my gaze from the blonde to search the faces of the hostages, desperate to find at least one person who was as uncomfortable with the idea as I was. But no one, not even Azura, who sat silently on the floor beside the rose, held even a shred of reluctance. They had been trapped in this ballroom for weeks, and their manners, common sense, and even possibly their sanity had been replaced with pure hatred toward the man who had kept them confined.

"Excellent," Lord Tocken breathed. His words sent a nauseating chill through me, threatening to make me gag.

"We'll establish further plans in the evenings, while the beast is distracted with his ridiculous lessons." The words pierced me with a bleeding jab, causing me to jolt as Lord Tocken flashed his beady gaze onto me. "And *you*... You must ensure that the beast doesn't hear a single word of this plan. Otherwise, every single one of our lives could be in grave danger. So, keep those pretty lips sealed tight or we'll send someone else to fetch our meals and sing the monster our alphabet."

Fire shot through my veins, rolling my fingers into twitching fists that were dying to blacken his eye. "Who else do you think you'd send?" I shouted, spit flying from my 'pretty lips' with a grit of my teeth. "Because I don't see anyone else volunteering." I looked around the room with a challenging glare, and to no surprise, not a single hostage stepped forward to offer their assistance.

"Mira... please." Azura's gentle voice lilted up from the floor, her big green eyes wide and pleading. "We can trust you to help us survive, can't we?" Her words dug into my skin like a fresh tattoo, carving a contract in ink and daring me to sign.

How could I say no to that? *Sorry, I won't help you survive because I think you're all morons!* That certainly wouldn't go over well if somehow, I still became their duchess...

I bit the inside of my cheek, placing my fists at my sides, but still refusing to uncurl them. "Yes, Azura," I seethed, "you can trust me."

A small smile parted her heart-shaped lips, filling her eyes with a gentle warmth. "See everyone? There's nothing to worry about." Her voice rubbed me uncomfortably, causing my anger to rile up even further, to the point that I couldn't bear standing near the others any longer.

*Why? Why do they always have to undermine me like that?*

I stomped back toward the corner, freezing only just before I pounded my forehead against the stone. Maybe if they spoke to me like a respectable human being, I would be able to understand their line of thought, but right now, it was nearly impossible with all my fuming rage. The thought of the entire group trampling Conan in a furious mob rushed through my mind, flooding my vision with images of a dozen hands around his throat and panic in his dark, mysterious eyes.

I shuddered. *Does he really deserve to die for this?*

He was a killer... He had no issues admitting that to me, but was that enough validation to end this battle with more bloodshed? Soldiers killed men all the time, but they were under vastly different circumstances.

*What were the circumstances in which Conan killed...? Had he even mentioned it?*

I thought back to our conversation, but no answers came to my mind. I looked back at the others, feeling a twist in my stomach as I watched them plot the murder of their imprisoner —the same man who had catered to me when I was ill in bed...

My heart fluttered to life as the memories of him hunched over my bed, refilling my teacup and bringing me trays of food, filled my mind. He had been so sweet to me then... nothing like the man who had first held a dagger to my betrothed's throat. *Honestly, he had become less monstrous than Ian was at this point.* Another image flashed into my mind, this time of Conan conquering Dhurin and me remaining betrothed to the province's heir...

I sucked in a sharp breath, shaking the thought from my mind like it was a bee in my hair. I pushed the warm feelings down to the depths of my soul, shoving them aside until I could think logically. *What am I thinking?* Conan is a murderer and a villain, who has only helped me out of his own selfish gain...

*But still... does he deserve to die?*

I couldn't answer that question without more information, and I couldn't sit by and let the others plan his murder without knowing. I approached the nearest door and swung it open, revealing the familiar shelves of the library.

*I'm not going to squash these feelings unless I have a good reason to.*

• • • • • • • • • • • • • • • • • • • • • • • • • • • • • • • •

Another tremor shuddered beneath my feet, echoing with the sound of crumbling granite somewhere within the castle.

"You're running out of time..." The mirror's cold glass gleamed in the morning light, causing the king's image to shine with an irritatingly bright glow.

"Don't you think I know that?" I snapped, digging my hands into my hair as I paced across the suite's cluttered floors. The soldiers were tearing down more walls by the day, but they had to be careful the further in they got.

"No, I don't think you know." The mirror sneered. "Otherwise, you would have actually done something about it by now."

I stopped in front of the glass, meeting the man's repulsive grimace with my own. "How? All the hostages are cuddled around their precious rose, which still hasn't died yet. I have no means of threatening the grand duke, as long as he believes they're protected."

*But even if they weren't protected, could I truly kill them, too? After how Mira responded to me mentioning I'd killed before...*

"You still have access to *one* hostage." His cold voice cut into my veins, melting into the bubbling heat that was starting to rise. "Haven't you learned enough of the language? You could easily figure out the rest on your own at this point. The girl is becoming a weak point for you, and I—"

"Will you shut up!?" I barked, resuming my pacing as I focused on anything that wasn't the yappy glass. "We've been over this; I'm not killing Mira. She's too valuable as both a tutor and a future grand duchess to her own province."

An eerie quiet followed, sending an unpleasant ripple down my spine that caused me to glance back at the mirror. He was frowning, deepening the wrinkles around his eyes and forehead, and even darkening the sun's glow. "So, is that why you keep her alive? For her province?"

I lifted a brow, turning to face him with a cross grimace. "What?"

"The duchess. You're still hoping she'll marry you, aren't you?" His eyes slitted, mimicking that of a preying viper. "That's why you've been so generous with your time toward her, isn't it?"

A suffocating squeeze clamped around my lungs, forcing my breath down before I could fire back with a denial. My heart drummed against my ribs, threatening to shatter them with the force of my rage and another nauseating emotion that twisted in my gut.

Of course, I wasn't trying to woo Mira. That would be absurd. I was her captor, and she was my victim. Our meetings were mutually beneficial for our current predicament and nothing more.

*Besides, even if I was trying to win her affection, it would never work. She's a beautiful duchess who's betrothed to a wealthy duke, and I'm just a scarred beast.*

"You're being a fool, son," he snorted, actually fogging up the interior of his glass prison. "She'll never accept you. She's been likely plotting to kill you ever since you met."

"That's enough!" I hissed, turning toward the door with an indescribable amount of weight clogging my brain. *Mira wouldn't try to kill me, would she?* "And don't call me son. I'm the spawn of the devil that you are and nothing more." I flung the door open, slamming it behind me with a crack of the doorframe.

My chest heaved as I took in calming breaths, taking in the

musty smell of books and dried ink that saturated the library. This room had become a place of refuge in some ways, because for some reason, each time I was in here with Mira, I could rarely hear my father's voice.

"Conan?"

I snapped my gaze around, wondering for a moment if the sound had come from inside my skull, but then paused as I realized it was far too gentle to be my haggard father's ghost. I peeked around a bookshelf, locking my gaze with Mira's glittering eyes as she met me with a serious frown.

"Mira, what are you—"

"Stop." She held up a palm to my face, crossing the room until it was only inches away from my lips. "I need you to tell me." Her voice was thick, matching her pleading eyes that practically bled with determination.

I blinked. "Tell you what?"

She lowered her palm, taking in a long, heavy breath that sank with her shoulders. "I need you to tell me why you killed your family."

# chapter twenty-one

Conan's dark eyes pierced into mine, wide from my sporadic question. I don't know why, but something about the way he looked at me made my heart beat faster than the wings of a hummingbird. I traced my eyes along his scars, for some reason feeling too anxious to look directly into his entrancing gaze.

"Why do you want to know?" he asked calmly. I had expected him to be stern with me for asking something so intrusive, or maybe even angry. But the tranquil set of his jaw, unpressed lips, and searching glint in his onyx eyes showed only genuine curiosity.

My throat tightened, as if someone had wrapped a scarf around my neck and yanked it. "I-I just need to know." I stumbled on my tongue as I tried to avoid thinking about the hostages' murderous plots. *I can't tell him what they're planning... at least, not yet.* "You wanted me to fear you once, didn't you? Well, this is how I'll know for sure if I do. I need to know why you took the lives you did." I fortified my posture, forcing my eyes to meet his, despite the pounding it brought into my chest.

He stepped past me, his long, slow strides echoing around the books as he stopped by a table to lean against. "Is that what you want?" he asked quietly, his eyes lowered with a dip of his head, showcasing his tussled dark locks. "To fear me?"

The pattering in my chest surged, tensing my muscles and lungs with a sense of what almost felt like guilt. I moved closer to him, wrapping my arms protectively around my torso as I slid into a seat beside him. "I... I just want to do what's right. And the right thing might be to be cautious of you." I gazed up at him, noticing a small twitch in his pupils as a dark smile tugged at his lips.

"Cautious... Do what's right... He was right, wasn't he? You're deciding if you want to kill me." My breath snagged in my throat like a jagged rock as he turned his steely gaze to me. Once again, I had expected him to be angered and explode in a fitful rage, but he didn't. In fact, the cold look in his eyes wasn't filled with hatred; it was filled with heart-cracking disappointment, flooded with sympathy.

"Conan... I—"

"I understand," he breathed softly, turning his focus to the floor. He clasped his hands together, fiddling with the bracelet on his wrist. The charm looked so fragile and dainty when compared to his strong hands. "You have every right to kill me, just like the others in that ballroom. I knew what my fate would be if I failed to overtake the province, so I can't fault you for doing the right thing."

My heart lurched. *The right thing? Does he really mean that?* I dropped my hands to my lap, bunching up fistfuls of my skirt. "I know you've done some awful things, but I was hoping that if I knew why you did them... I would at least be able to make up my mind as to whether or not—"

"If I deserve to die?" He snapped his gaze to me, causing my blood to course with guilt as I realized that I was literally measuring the value of his life. "I can already tell you that I do," he said coldly. "My sins are far past redemption... but if hearing them gives you peace in your decision, then I suppose I can share them with you." He paused, filling the room with a silence that made me almost believe time itself had stopped. "Before I tell you, I want you to know that I've never explained this part of my past to anyone. Mostly because I don't think anyone could stomach it..." An eerie chill slithered down my spine, forcing me to withhold a shiver as he gave me a confirming glare. "Are you sure you want to hear it?"

I nodded mutely, my tongue too entangled by the anxiety twisting around me. I needed to know. Partially so I could validate the others malicious plan, but also so I could finally put an end to the odd feelings that were creeping deeper and deeper within me.

"Very well then." He spoke calmly, but his fingers clasped together with the intensity of an iron fist, as if he was bracing himself for what was to come. "I suppose it all started when I was a child. Growing up in my home kingdom, I had two younger brothers, Killian and Miron. I had always been told that I would be the heir, but the king still insisted that we all train to be worthy of a crown. So, to prevent us from becoming soft, we were never allowed to see each other, except on the training grounds. For most of my life, I only saw my brothers when I had a sword in my hand. The king said it was to ensure that we never developed sympathy toward each other, so we would never hold back in a fight, but truthfully, I think he always wanted there to be a rift between us..." He stopped for a moment, his expression vacant as if he had gotten stuck in a memory and couldn't pull himself out of it yet.

My whole body felt numb. *How different would Zac and my relationship be if we were only together to fight?*

"Anyway, my mother, the queen, despised the way we were brought up," he continued. "She would always fight with my father about how we should be allowed to grow up together and live like regular children, but he didn't believe that was the proper life for a prince. She would try to gather us for dinners or take us on family outings, but each time, Father would stop her. But even so, she was resilient..." He softened his clenched hands as a fond twinkle gleamed in his good eye. "She used to sneak us into her chambers at night—occasionally all at once, but mostly only one at a time. It would usually depend on the guard's patterns whether she could collect us all. She used to read us stories, teach us games, and even spent entire nights laughing with us like she was a giddy child herself." A soft smile twitched at his lip, stirring the warmth in my chest that I had fought to push away before.

"She sounds wonderful," I whispered, my voice almost too light to be heard.

"She was..." His smile fell, infecting his face with a pale, grim shadow. "And then she got sick."

My heart stopped. The pain that inflicted his face was masked, but still raw, proving that this was truly a subject he rarely recalled. "What was she sick with?" I squeaked.

"At first, we thought it was tuberculosis..." he breathed, his lungs sounded tight and raspy. "Doctors and healers from all over the realm spent weeks trying to cure her, but none of their remedies or magic seemed to have any effect. Every night, I snuck into her chambers to do anything I could to help her. It got to the point where she was completely bedridden and could only hold her eyes open for a few hours before drifting back into fitful sleep. I thought it was just a horrid curse—something completely inevitable that nothing in the realms could have prevented—but then my father told me the truth." His face twisted, and his hands clasped with his thumbs facing up, like he was squeezing an invisible victim in a chokehold. "He had poisoned her... his own wife."

My breath hitched, burning in the back of my throat like a searing fire. *Conan's father poisoned his own queen...?* Nausea swept over me, stronger than even the after-effects of Conan's potato cakes.

"When I was thirteen, one of the guards had spotted me being snuck into her quarters. My brothers weren't noticed, so I was the only one who received the blessings of Father's wrath." His teeth gritted, grinding with an audible scrape. "He told me I had failed him by allowing weakness to grow from my compassion toward my mother. As a future king, I wasn't allowed to have soft spots, and he wanted to ensure I was still cold enough to take on the responsibilities of a crown. That's when he offered me a deal... He told me that the illness my mother had contracted was from an enchanted poison and could only be cured by a remedy from the same mage. If I wanted the remedy, I had to prove to my father that I wasn't weak, and that something as simple as an attachment to my mother wouldn't hold me back from being the ruthless king he was grooming me to be. If I wanted to save my mother, I had to kill one of my brothers in her place."

The room went quiet, allowing his words to linger in the air like a toxic fog. I couldn't breathe. It felt as if my very lungs had liquified, sloshing around inside me like the same poison that had infected Conan's mother. How... how could any man, let alone a father, ask something so terrible of his son?

"I would have done it, too." His features tightened, bunching up the scar along his brow bone and tightening the pupil in his damaged eye. "My mother meant everything to me. She was the only person I could go to and be... well, just Conan, not a warrior, or a prince, or a flawless heir. She was the only one I could make a mistake around. I didn't want to lose that. I didn't want to kill one of my brothers either, but despite Mother's intentions to bond us, Father's grooming had worked. I didn't know them like I knew my mother, and if I killed one of them, I would have earned Father's favor as well. It was an easy choice."

I finally took a breath, my head dizzy from the lack of air. Here I was, feeling guilty for weighing the worth of Conan's life, yet he had done the exact same thing with his own family. *But could I blame him...?* What was a thirteen-year-old boy meant to do in such a sick scenario?

"I knew I had to go through with it," he continued, his eyes bloodshot. "Mother was running out of time, and I didn't have the luxury of mulling it over. I was scheduled to train against them both the following day, so I decided that whoever fell first would receive the fatal blow." His breathing slowed, loosening the tension in his eyes as heart-shattering grief sank through his entire being. "That night, I went to visit Mother like normal. I don't know why, but seeing her so sick and weak urged me to give her hope, so I told her everything. I told her about the poison, the remedy, and Father's conditions for her to receive it." His voice quivered, flaring up my heart as he sucked in a sharp gasp. "She begged me not to do it. All night long, I sat in bed with her, pleading to let me save her, but she was as resilient as ever. I feared disappointing my father, but I never knew how much it broke me to disappoint my mother until that night. She made me swear I wouldn't kill them to save her. All she ever wanted was for us to get along, to be like real brothers. So much so that she allowed herself to die to prevent Father from digging a greater rift between us." He placed his hands on his knees, clawing against his trousers, as if the pain of his digging could numb his mind. "But it didn't work. After she died, Father never let me forget it. He ensured that I always knew that my failure was what had ended her life, and I was solely responsible. Once she was gone, he established a new law. It stated that as king, he alone got to select which of his kin became heir. That way any one of his sons had the opportunity to prove their worth to him and gain the kingdom. He did it to punish me... Forcing me to compete every day against the brothers I simply could have sacrificed. The rift between us grew to a chasm, and we fought every day to push the others down and climb to the top."

His voice mellowed, like he had suddenly been possessed by a ghost of his past. My heart drummed so loudly, I feared he might hear it, even in the midst of his turmoil.

"I hated them," he spat the words, but at the same time, he clutched his arms around his chest. His head shook, squeezing his eyes closed as if he was blocking them from his mind as firmly as he was able. "I couldn't look at them without seeing Mother's face, without remembering that they only lived because she had died. They didn't deserve to rule the kingdom, not when they had cost it so much." He sounded agonized, but muffled through the grit in his teeth. "Then they both had the gall to turn against me, and even became traitors to our kingdom. I thought it was my chance to prove that I was the only one truly loyal to the crown, but even so, Father still wasn't satisfied with me. I killed kings for him, kidnapped mages, and performed every vile act possible to earn even a fraction of the affection Mother had given me for free. Any time I got close to displeasing him, he waved my mother's fate above my head like a dangling noose, threatening to make use of it again if I failed. Finally, I couldn't take it anymore. He wanted me to be powerful, he wanted me to be strong, he wanted me to be unrestrained, so I took out the only person who was holding me back... I killed him." He let out a long breath, as did I. It was as if hearing of the king's death had put an end to not only the horror of his past, but the horror of his tale as well. "As for my brothers... they turned against me. They overthrew me from the only thing I had ever earned, and then they had the audacity to fall in love and flaunt their joy in front of my banishment trial. It never seemed fair to me... All those years ago, when I respected my mother's dying wishes, I chose my brothers' happiness over mine. I've regretted that choice every day. Hence why I chose to follow my father's advice instead, because at least through his means, I wouldn't get attached to anything long enough to feel pain when they leave."

When he finally concluded his story, I felt like every piece of me was burning. My eyes stung with unshed tears, my heart flared with cracking remorse, and my fingertips seared with the desire to wrap my grasp around his dead father's throat. *He did this to him... He was the one who had created the beast.* I didn't know what to think. For weeks, I had believed that Conan was a misguided man whose selfishness had ruined his soul, but all along, it was someone else entirely who had destroyed him. My chest ached as I remembered the tenderness he had shown me when I was ill in bed. It wouldn't surprise me if he became so nurturing because I reminded him of the last moments he had spent with his mother... It made so much sense now why he acted the way he did. He played by his horrid father's lessons because his mother's had brought him nothing but grief.

"Does it make you happy?" I asked weakly, my voice dry and gravelly from the choked tears. "Living by your father's advice?" I tried to catch his gaze, but his eyes were solidly fixated on the floor, clouded and broken.

"I've never been happy," he breathed. "Not ever since she died. I don't think I can ever feel the way I did when she was still alive."

I shook my head slowly, feeling my resolve stiffen. "I felt that way too, once." I swallowed stiffly. "Before I found out about my illness, I was planning to learn espionage." His eyes narrowed curiously, but he still didn't look up. "When my health issues were uncovered, I had to give it all up. It wasn't nearly as tragic as what you went through, but I know what it feels like to lose everything you ever dreamed of having." My hand moved on its own, stopping on top of where his hand rested atop his knee. "I only got over it when I decided to change my view on life. Instead of helping others in the shadows, I could now govern them in the light. So perhaps that's where your joy is hiding, too. Instead of following your father's guidance, go back to following the lessons from your mother."

"My mother's lessons aren't applicable now," he snorted softly. "All she ever wanted was for me and my brothers to get along. I suppose it worked for them—considering they're both happily married with castles to call home—but it's too late for me to mend what I've broken between them. Besides, even if I could, they're a realm away. I've missed my opportunity, and now they'll always remember me as the monstrous brother who took after dear ol' dad..." His voice faded with a droop of his head.

I squeezed his hand, my heart flashing on my sleeve as I winced at the thought of him giving up. "You're not a monster,

Conan," I said firmly. "I know that now. And as for your brothers... you made it all the way here, didn't you? Who says a message to them couldn't make it back? If they can forgive each other for the fighting your father had forced them into, then I can't see why they can't forgive you, too." My chest tightened as the words tingled on my lips. My gaze softened on the shattered beast and when my heart opened up to the affectionate warmth brewing within, I didn't stop it. "It's... never too late to forgive."

We both lingered there for an extended silence, my hand still gently wrapped around the top of his. Heat poured through my veins every time I looked at where we touched, but even so, I couldn't pull myself away. His mother had died, but he wasn't responsible for killing her... his father was. I couldn't validate his other crimes, but that didn't mean I couldn't see the remorse thinking back on them brought him.

*I can't kill him for that...*

Out of nowhere, his entire frame sank. He flipped his palm over, catching my hand with a squeeze that nearly made my heart break from the desperation in his touch. Heat inflamed my face as his deep gaze flooded me with an impenetrable look of guilt that sank all the way to the depths of his soul. "Mira, will you help me?" His pupils were as wide as a glass marble, twinkling with a pleading gleam that could only cause me to nod mutely. "I need you to help me write a few letters."

# chapter twenty-two

I signed off the last letter with a slight wobble in my quill. Mira leaned up beside me, her small frame digging into my side like a small crutch. She read over my letters with a detailed eye, inspecting the language to ensure that if any Rubian-speaking citizen found it, they would know to throw it into the Omairan sea. The address was in Rubian, but I had written the main part of the letters in my home language. On the off chance the letters actually found their way to them, my brothers could understand it. My gaze lingered on the drying ink, still not fully believing the words I had written.

They were apologies... Apologies for all the terrible things I had done to them and their families, as well as the real explanation of what happened to our mother. There was also a letter to the son of the king I had slain. That one was both an apology and a thank you, because he was the man who had sentenced me to banishment and allowed me a second chance. Mira's words had stricken me with a guilt I didn't know I could heal. She was right, forgiveness had always been an option, but it was one I had refused to take part in for so many years. When I first picked up the quill, I didn't think I could write them. But the moment my ink hit the parchment, the words simply flew. They had been there all along, just waiting for the courage to try to regain what Father had stolen from me, and what my mother had always wanted. I knew there was little chance of them ever seeing it, and an even smaller chance that I'd even know if they did. But just having it written, having put aside the hatred I had harbored toward them for so long made me feel like I was almost whole again.

"It looks great." She beamed at me, her dazzling smile flowing through me like a burst of energy. "'There's a few tenses that are a little off and a couple of misspellings, but overall, it's perfectly readable. It won't be much longer before there's nothing left for me to teach you." Her eyes sparkled like polished tourmaline, softening my shell to the point where I actually managed a small smile.

*I couldn't have done any of this without her...*

"Thank you," I said the words slowly in Rubian, sounding it out with each syllable to ensure it was accurate. I couldn't remember the last time I ever truly thanked anyone. I had expected it to feel foreign and uncomfortable, but in actuality, it felt completely natural to say. Likely because I had needed to say it long before now. "Thank you for teaching me, and thank you for listening to my story. I never knew how badly I needed to share it until today."

She leaned against me, tilting her head down to hide what appeared to be the edges of a blush from my view. "Of course," she replied quietly. "I'm just happy to see you're finally believing in yourself, in your happiness." She reached forward, folding the dry letters and stamping them with a wax seal. "No matter what happens, I'll make sure these make it to the beaches you washed up on. As soon as this... situation ends..." Her dainty fingers squeezed a little too tightly around the seal's handle.

*That's right... Despite everything that's happened, she's still my prisoner...*

She placed the seal to the side, resting her hand on the table where I took the opportunity to place my hand on top of it. She jolted for a brief moment, but then relaxed when she saw it was a gentle touch. "It *will* end," I said firmly, giving her hand a slight squeeze. "I just need a little time to figure out how."

She tore her eyes away from the table, latching onto my gaze with a hopeful look that sent literal shivers down my neck.

"Alright..." Her voice was barely a breath, her face only inches from mine as we sat side by side at the desk. My heart beat with the intensity of a thundering storm, causing my hand to grow hot where it touched Mira's. She looked warm too, her cheeks flushing a soft crimson, but never pulling away.

"Mira..." I brushed my hand on top of hers, causing her to shudder like a flinching dove. "I just want you to know... my father believes keeping you alive has made me weak." Her dark brows furrowed, lost by my use of the present tense, but I didn't bother to stop and explain. "If he's right... then I don't think I want to be strong." Her brown eyes went wide, sucking in a breath so close to me that it fluttered my hair.

She looked like she was panicked, but even so, she didn't pull away. Her heart beat so intensely that I could feel her pulse throb in the back of her hand. I wanted to soothe her racing heart, wanted to show her just how much I appreciated everything she had done to help me. She had done so much more for me than I had ever deserved... and she deserved the realm and more.

Which is why I pulled away.

My hand slipped from hers with an internal shout from within. Her lashes fluttered in confusion and her lips parted in quiet pants as she tucked a stray hair behind her ear. I pushed away from the table, straining to lift myself to my feet with how heavy my heart felt.

*Mira is the most incredible person I have ever met... Which is why she deserves someone so much better than me.*

"If you'll excuse me." I cleared my throat, trying to hide the agony shredding me from the inside. "I need a little time to decide my next move with the grand duke and the hostages." I started for the door while ignoring the lingering tug on my chest that urged me to go back.

*I need to fix this, and part of fixing it involves reuniting Mira with her betrothed.*

"I suppose I'll return to the ballroom, then," Mira called behind me. Her chair screeched as she pushed out of her seat, followed by the muffled sound of her organizing the letters. "And Conan..." The shuffling stopped, and my heart seized as I froze with my hand hovered above the doorknob. "I just wanted you to know... These letters are really touching. I think your mother would have been proud."

My bones locked together, freezing me in place as I let her words wash over me, as if I was being doused in a rich honey. I had feared that after hearing the extent of my sins, Mira would abandon me and join the others in their quest to end me. But she hadn't judged me at all; instead, she'd listened and then offered to help. The pounding in my chest heightened to a dangerous speed, unlocking my limbs from their stiffness as I pulled my hand away from the handle.

*She told me it was never too late to forgive... But is there even a chance she would forgive me, too?*

"Mira, I—" I spun around to talk to her, but my words fell on empty air. She was already gone, slipped out through the side door and probably already back in the ballroom. I swung my fist at the air before turning back to the door, spitting out a few curses as I burst back into the master suite.

I paced around the floor, kicking fragments of trashed furniture and décor to the sides as I stomped back and forth. *What do I do now...? There is so much that needs to be undone...* I gazed out the glass door, taking in the view of the surrounding army with a clenching stomach. This had gone too far to simply walk away. It was clear to me now that taking over the province wasn't what I wanted; it was what *he* wanted. And I was through with catering to his commands. What I really wanted was to be free from the endless burn for power and to look for the happiness I had once had with my mother... A happiness Mira had reminded me that I once had...

Her vibrant smile flashed into my eyes, framed by her

dark locks, and dotted with her dazzling eyes. If I were being honest, I wanted more than just my freedom... But I'd already spent enough of my life being selfish. Even if I desperately wanted to be selfish once more...

"What took you so long?" The mirror's splintering voice cracked through the room like a lazy bolt of lightning, taking its time, digging its jolts into my every nerve. "I do hope you were busy cleaning up the girl's blood. Otherwise, it will be yours that those soldiers spill next." He directed his gaze toward the window, causing me to question if he could actually see them from his place on the wall.

I ignored him, continuing my pacing as I tried to envision a scenario where I could sneak out of the castle and set the hostages free. Apparently, my silence wasn't well received, because my father's image rattled, shaking the glass's frame.

"Don't pretend you can't hear me, boy!" he barked, his lips snarling in disgust. "I am only trying to advise you on the best way to get what you want, so try to show a little gratitude."

*What I want...*

He'd gotten my attention now. I whirled around on my heels, approaching the mirror with a new energy I hadn't had before. I wasn't going to be his pawn anymore, nor was I going to stand by and accept his verbal beatings. "You know nothing of what I want!" I stopped an inch in front of the glass, my hot breath fogging the mirror like raging smoke. "I want you to leave my head. I want you to have been a proper father. And now I want to be my own man. Conquering Dhurin won't bring me satisfaction; it will only make me crave more. And that's why I'm going to let the hostages go free... They deserve a better ruler than me, anyway." I pulled back from the glass, unmoved by the lethal glare he was skewering into my skull.

"You're filth," he spat. The dark color in his eyes mirrored that of an endless void, so deep with hatred and vileness that I couldn't even see the end. "After everything I've done for you...

after everything you've become, you plan to throw it all away like your varmint brothers? I thought you better than them, Conan. I thought you already learned the lesson of failure from when your mother—"

"My mother was killed by *you*." I jeered a finger at the glass, wishing his body was real so I could deliver something to his face that he would actually feel. "You poisoned her and placed the blame on your thirteen-year-old son."

"I may have poisoned her, but you're the one who allowed her to die," he growled back, his eyes narrowed, stabbing straight through my eyes. "Don't try to play innocent... Let's not forget how many lives you've taken. Shall I remind you of all the tragedy you've caused all on your own?" A dark grin slithered up his lips, causing my muscles to tighten around my bones.

"I can't undo my crimes..." I said firmly, clenching my jaw as I held my arms stiffly to my sides. "But I can beg forgiveness for them, and that's what I have already begun to do. I've already written an apology to my brothers and to the others I have hurt. I don't expect to ever be a man of honor, or even a man who deserves to walk the face of this realm. But no matter what, I swear to be a man who is better than the one you raised." My body strained and ached as the tightness embodying my chest and limbs squeezed one final suffocating breath from my lungs, then dissolved into the air. In that moment, I felt as if a lifelong burden has been shifted from my shoulders, clearing my tainted heart from the black soot leftover from my crimes and opening up to the hope of a new beginning.

*I am free from my father. Free from the dead king...*

Or so I thought.

"You fool!" His sharp cackle flung me out of my internal peace, ratcheting back around me like a ball and chain. "Do you honestly believe that anyone would forgive you? After all the pain you've inflicted? Hah! That's quite the hallucination you've let that little girl trick you into, though I suppose it's easy to deceive the mind of someone so futile."

My breaths sharpened, but it felt as if my lungs couldn't fill with enough air. *Why is he still not gone? What will it take to be free of his haunting!?* "I am *not* a fool! I am—"

"Worthless," he interrupted, clicking his tongue like a snapping limb. "You couldn't even kill one girl, despite the fact that you've had no issue stealing lives in the past."

My mind warped back to the moments my sword had stripped the soul from a body. The shaking in my hands came back in full force, followed by the sweep of nausea I couldn't push away. "I-I killed them for you." My lips stuttered, too disoriented from the gruesome images in my mind. "I-I wanted you to be proud of me, but it never mattered. I'm done trying to please you. I'm done taking lives, and if I could bring back the people I had slain, I would... all except for you."

His features twisted, scrunching his brows and eyes into a demented smile that froze me all the way to my shaken core. "But you can't bring them back, can you?" he tutted. "They're gone... but I'm still here, and I'll always be here to remind you about them." My gut plummeted while forcing bile up my throat that nearly caused me to heave. "I'll never let you forget them... not your mother, not King Garrett, not the servant Drew, or the enchanter Collin..." He continued to rattle off the names of every person whose life I had stolen.

I felt sick, riddled with the horror of my crimes and the painful reality of knowing that no number of letters could ever redeem me for what I'd done. I was a monster; I was a killer. And no matter how much I wanted to change that, some people would never see me any differently.

"That's enough..." I tried to quiet him, but my voice was suffocated by the intense pressure rising inside me. He was echoing in my head now, making me feel hot and dizzy from the control he still had embedded into me.

*When will it stop?*

"It will never stop," the mirror replied, answering the question I had believed to be safe in my mind. He laughed chaotically, his veins and eyes bulging like an unhinged sociopath. "Because I'm never leaving you, son... You're mine. And as long as you disappoint me, I'll always be here to remind you of your mistakes and your failures. My voice will become a regular comfort... always there to tell you that you're a lowly, imbecilic, worthless beast—"

His eyes widened with a horrific look of shock before an ear-splitting crash reverberated around the room. Out of nowhere, a candlestick smashed into the dead center of the mirror, shattering the frozen image of my father into a hundred shards. For a moment I only stared at the empty frame, uncertain if I could trust the eerie quiet or if his voice would sneak back into my mind at any moment.

"C-Conan."

Mira's nervous voice drew me out of my trance, causing me to jolt around and finally, I noticed her standing in the back of the room. Her arm was still frozen in the air from where she had thrown the candlestick. Her entire face was blanched whiter than an Omairan winter. Her fingers trembled, and her breathing seemed to be short and raspy.

"I-I came back to ask if you wanted help preparing dinner, and then I... W-who... who was that?" Her extended hand uncurled into a point, her eyes fixated on the broken mirror, like the image was still there haunting it.

My blood froze as my eyes dilated with fresh realization. "You... you could see him?" I weakly pointed at the pile of shattered glass, still trembling from the final lashings of my father's ghost. Mira nodded mutely, her eyes fixated on the broken mess. "But... he was in my head. He's been there since I arrived in this realm... You couldn't possibly have seen him if he was my hallucination."

She twisted her brows, her lips still parted in disbelief

as she took a cautious step closer to me. "That was no hallucination..." she breathed. "Whoever it was, I could see him clear as day, and hear him, too." She looked up at me with watering eyes, tears sitting on the brim of her thick lashes. She moved closer, slowly at first, and then more confidently as I didn't push back. She wrapped her slender arms around my torso, wrapping me in a tender embrace that cured me of my trembling in a single squeeze. "That was your father, wasn't it?" She whispered her question, her body trembling in fear.

"Yes..." I touched a gentle hand to the top of her hair to smooth it with tender strokes.

She pulled away far enough so she could look at me, her cheeks puffy from the salty tears that slid down her dark-toned cheeks. "You realize what this means, don't you?" She slipped her hands away from my torso, wiping her cheeks as she sniffed her tears back. "I've never seen your father before... Which means, the only way I would be able to see him in a common mirror, would be if—"

"It was enchanted..." Shock split through me like a crack of thunder. Fresh heat flooded through my veins, forcing my mind into overdrive as I replayed all the moments that led up to my discovery of the mirror.

All this time, I thought it was some sort of mirage my mind had concocted to give body to the inner voice that had haunted me... But Mira was right; if she could see it, then that meant it wasn't in my mind. It had to be enchanted.

*But why would someone enchant a mirror to reflect my father?*

I turned back to the empty frame that still contained a few broken fractals of glass. I'd stared at this mirror a hundred times over the last few weeks, but never once had I truly noticed its frame.

*It was made of gold...*

"The griffins," I growled, feeling the pressure rise in my chest like a bursting geyser as I turned back to face Mira. "The griffins were the only ones who knew of my plans to attack Dhurin. They must have gotten here first and enchanted the mirror to somehow reflect my inner demons." I stomped the pile of broken shards, cracking them into dust while piercing the edges of my boot.

Mira looked dazed, her eyes blinking faster than a butterfly's wings. "The griffins? But that doesn't make any sense... Why would they want to enchant a mirror to insult you in the middle of a takeover?"

My anger toward the Golden King's lackeys was instantly eclipsed by a fresh round of panic as the answer floated into my mind. "The mirror did more than just insult me..." I said slowly. "It also wanted me to kill you."

The color drained from her face as if it had leaked out through the floor. "Kill me? But why?" She pressed a hand to the edge of her lips, her eyes flittering in panicked thought.

"I don't know, but if the golden imp is entangled in this mess, then we have bigger things to worry about than a room of grouchy hostages." I gritted my teeth, glaring down at the bracelet I had become so shamefully reliant on.

Mira gasped, "The other hostages! What if one of them is the mage who enchanted the mirror?" She brought her hand to her lips, nibbling on the ends of her nails with jittering bites.

"But that would mean that one of the other hostages... is a griffin." My muscles stiffened, recalling my interaction with the mysterious group when I first entered the province. *Had they really followed me to the castle?*

"It's a possibility." Mira nodded, turning her eyes toward the door. "One that I'm about to look into." Without hesitation, she started for the door, causing my heart to leap in protest.

"Mira, wait!" I reached and snagged her gently by the arm.

"You can't just waltz into the ballroom and ask if anyone's a griffin. What if you're right? They supposedly want you dead, remember?" My chest burned at the thought, causing my grip to tighten on her delicate arm.

She placed her hand on top of mine, giving me a calming smile as she gently eased it off her. "If I'm right, then the ballroom is the best place to call them out." She nodded confidently. "Because no one can kill me around the rose."

# chapter twenty-three

I dashed back into the ballroom with a throbbing heart, pulsating between panic and enchantment. Conan's warm embrace still burned into my skin and caused my body to practically hum with a cozy warmth. A piece of me yearned to go back and be with him for a moment longer—to explore why this feeling followed me when I was in his presence—but the panic of the griffins infiltrating the castle overruled my curiosity.

*They had been here... but how did they get all the way into the grand duke's chambers? And when?*

My thoughts flicked back to the golden key Conan had first used to lockdown the castle. *Had that come from them, too?* It would certainly fit into the golden theme the other objects they had possessed. But why? Why would they go to all the trouble of enchanting a mirror to try to convince Conan to kill me?

*Or the better question... Why did the griffins want me dead?*

When I first entered the ballroom, no one had noticed my presence, as per usual. They were all still collected around the wilting rose. But instead of sitting around in a dismal campsite, they were standing around in the midst of heated arguments. I hurried to the center of the room to try to catch onto what was causing the controversy this time, but when I reached the group, everyone hushed. All eyes fell on me, each with a piercing fury that could have easily speared me to death.

"What," Lord Tocken hissed, stepping forward with a hideous scowl, "did you do?"

Questions filtered through my mind as I waited for him or

anyone else to give me further context, but no one did anything other than scorn me with their beady glares. "I... don't know what you're referring to. Are you talking ab—"

"The mirror," Lord Tocken clipped. "You broke my mirror, didn't you?"

A cold chill dove through my flesh, freezing my blood with a single flick of the lord's tongue.

*H-his mirror? But that's not possible...*

I narrowed my eyes on the stout lord's head, inspecting his salt and pepper comb-over with a soft gasp. There was silver in it... Only a few scattered strands mixed into his natural gray, but even so... I guess Azura wasn't the only mage in the family.

"That mirror was our only way of checking in on the beast!" Sir Eric bellowed with a flail of his arms. "Now how are we meant to know what he's planning or when he's going to come kill us!"

Confusion swept over me like a dizzy spell, causing my head to tilt as it weighed down with all the fleeting questions. "Wait a moment... Is this something you all knew about?" I pointed a wavering finger at the collective group, waiting for at least one person to shrug or nod with the same confusion I was battling.

"Of course, we knew!" Henrietta puffed. "Lord Tocken told us all about how the mirror works and has been relaying the beast's plans ever since you first disappeared into the castle. We didn't tell you because we thought you might accidentally reveal it to the beast, but considering you broke it, anyway, I suppose we were doomed no matter what!" She let out an aggravated squeal, stomping toward the back of the crowd with a swish of her wrinkled skirt.

My head throbbed. "And... what did this mirror do, exactly?" I raked my gaze over the crowd, trying to imagine how casting a projection of Conan's dead father was an act of surveillance.

"The enchantment reflects the image of the victim's worst fears," Lord Tocken explained. His voice chilled as he pulled his pocket watch from his vest, flipping it open to reveal a tiny compact mirror behind the clockwork. "It's technically more complicated than that, but the short version is that my brother and I are spies from Isleen, sent to infiltrate the castle by escorting Azura as a debutant. When we first arrived, I snuck into the grand duke's quarters and used my magic to pair his bedroom mirror to my handheld one. The first person to look into the mirror would have been met with an image of their greatest fear. It was my job to investigate the grand duke's reaction to his fears and study them through the feed on my watch. But the grand duke wasn't the first person to look into the mirror... So, my agenda changed from espionage to survival." He snapped the watch closed, his expression dead and soulless as he met me with a cold glare.

*Azura's uncles... are spies?*

I snapped my gaze over to the quiet caster, her dark lashes downcast so I couldn't see her eyes. "Did you know about this?" My voice was raw with betrayal, nearly as soft as a whisper.

She nodded, keeping her gaze fixated on the rose at her feet. "I did... But I am not a spy. I was merely their 'cover' if you will." She finally looked up at me, her deep green eyes flowing with guilt. "I never meant to deceive you, Mira. I was only doing what my uncles said would keep us all safe. Once the beast took over the castle, Uncle Tocken started monitoring the beast to study what he feared and devise a way to protect us. The only reason we didn't tell you was because you started seeing him so often... We had to protect everyone." Her voice cracked, pleading with me to pause and listen, but I couldn't.

This wasn't right... Lord Tocken being a mage explained why the mirror was enchanted and even why he was always so frustrated with me for getting on the beast's good side. But it still didn't explain the mirror's agenda...

"The mirror told Conan to kill me," I projected, stretching my voice to the far ends of the ballroom to ensure that no ear missed it. I set my gaze on Lord Tocken, noticing a slight twinge in his lip but nothing more. "If it was your mirror... then why would your magic be fixated on convincing him to kill me?"

All attention shifted toward the lord, but the pressure weighed on him as light as a drop of cream. "Kill you?" he snorted, folding his arms with a judgmental twist in his brow. "The mirror never told him to kill anyone. It only riled up his insecurities."

I gawked at him, catching my jaw before it clattered open like a broken marionette. "Riled up his insecurities!?" I charged forward, stopping an inch in front of his fat, ugly face. "That mirror was a monster! Far worse than anything Conan had been! And Conan specifically told me that the mirror had been urging him to kill me. Why would he lie about that?"

"Because he's a beast, of course." Lord Illumen stepped out from behind his brother, shoving in front of him before I could slug him. "Beasts lie, duchess. You cannot trust him simply because he was humane enough to cater to your delicate diet." He folded his arms in front of me, his tall, lean figure towering over me like a willowy tree.

"Griffins lie, too," I hissed, my eyes slitting. "Conan also believed the mirror came from them. Apparently, they were the only ones who knew he was coming to this castle in the first place."

Azura gasped, her face paling like a bleached parchment. "T-the griffins?" She swayed, likely only a breath away from fainting, until her uncle interjected.

"Griffins?" Lord Tocken cackled, filling the room with his painfully sharp voice. "Has the beast also told you about the unicorns? My realms, the duchess has gone mad. She's heard the truth behind our story, yet she still believes the words of our captor." Spit flew from his lips like a thick rainfall as he burst out into another belly laugh.

"It must be her illness!" Madam Ophelia gasped with a clutch of her greasy pearls. "Her ailment, combined with the stress of our confinement, must have diminished her sanity!"

"What!?" I whirled around to face the woman, balling my hands into fists to vent the pure fire raging through my veins. "That's the most ridiculous thing I've ever heard! I'm not mad; I simply trust Conan more than a foreign spy!" My heart jolted as the words spewed out of me, revealing a secret I hadn't even admitted to myself yet.

*I trust Conan... Even in all this mess, I trust him more than the other hostages.*

"Mira..." Azura's soft voice barely swept over my ears. She was reaching out to me as if she had more to say, but once again, it was smashed down by another round of bickering.

"She trusts the beast?"

"The girl's gone mad!"

"Do you think she's already told him about our attack plans?"

"She must have broken the mirror on purpose!"

Panicked voices swarmed around me, all while the hostages circled me like a pack of sharks. "No!" I tried to argue, but my voice was drowned in their anger. "That's not what happened! I'm not... I didn't—"

"We can no longer allow the duchess to visit the beast!" Lord Tocken boomed over the crowd. "It's far too dangerous; he has warped her mind too far!"

I gasped, a searing throb tearing through my heart as they closed in further around me, boxing me in on all sides.

*They're going to try to keep me here... but I can't stay! I need to tell Conan about Lord Tocken's enchantment.*

Without pausing to think, I pushed through the first opening I saw. The group had tightened around me pretty firmly, so I aimed for a gap between Henrietta and the aging Lady Rhonda. I broke through them with no problem, but only made it a few more feet before the group reacted to my attempted escape. Hands snagged on my hair, sleeves, and skirt from every angle. I thrashed against their hold, trying to kick and claw my way free with every ounce of strength I had.

"Let me go!" I screamed. "You can't keep me in here! I'm not crazy! I'm only trying to help!" I tried to yank away with one final charge, but their fierce grasps only managed to tear my skirt, rip my sleeves, and yank my braid with an agonizing yelp.

"Tie her up with whatever we've got!" Lord Tocken commanded. "We can't let her warn the beast of our—"

His voice was muffled by the wall-shaking slam of the ballroom's grand doors. The echo filled the entire room, snuffing out all the arguing and yelling like a smothered candle. Everyone froze. Their grips were still latched around me like iron shackles, but none of them dared to move an inch. They were too fixated on the enraged, bloodthirsty beast at the top of the stairs.

"Get... your filthy hands... off her," he enunciated each word in crystal clear Rubian, snapping his tongue like a barbed whip with each syllable. He was a good deal away, but even from the middle of the ballroom floor, I could see the definition of his steel-clenched muscles and the throbbing veins in his scarred neck. "Now!"

His final command sent everyone scattering like a swarm of bees whose hive had been kicked in. Every hand released me almost simultaneously, leaving only the shredded remains of my dress and the early stages of bruises. They all scattered toward the rose, clustering around it like a shield. Once they'd recovered from the shock of Conan speaking to them in their native tongue, their confidence started to reform. Their hard expressions and battle-ready glares returned to their faces.

"Have you come to kill us, beast?" Lord Tocken barked across the room. "Go ahead and try! You may have infected the duchess's mind, but the rest of us are prepared to rid the realm of your monstrous existence!" The crowd cheered around him, pumping their fists into the air like a proper mob.

He slitted his eyes at them, glaring like they were as insignificant as a stain on his boot. Then his eyes turned to me. "Are you alright, Mira?" He switched back to his home language, ensuring only I could understand him through our connected charms.

Despite my fresh bruises and breathless lungs, I nodded, only a moment before my blood turned cold.

*Bruises... The hostages had hurt me... How far away had I been from the rose when they grabbed me?*

I snuck a glance through the protective group of bodies, only catching the smallest glimpse of only two petals still dangling from its stem. My heart jolted.

"You need to get out of here!" I called to Conan, my blood racing like a rampaging river.

*If the hostages saw the rose was nearly gone, then they won't hesitate to attack him.*

Conan shook his head. "I'm not leaving until you're safe," he called back, stubbornness written all over his tightened brow. "Go! I'll seal off the doors behind you." He tilted his head toward the nearest exit, and I gave him a confirming nod.

I ran. With my heart blazing, a stitch tearing into my side, and panic pounding through my blood, I pulled open the nearest door right as Azura's voice split through the rampaging mob.

"The rose! There's only one petal left!"

# chapter twenty-four

I burst through the door with a lung-tearing gasp, slamming the door to the ballroom behind me at full force. I leaned my back against the door, tilting my head back against the aromatic cedar as I caught my breath. I had ended up in another bedroom, one that appeared to be much grander than the others. Richly embroidered rugs lined the floors, creating a geometric pattern that looked like abstract birds. The lavish furnishings were easily comparable to what the broken ones used to be in Conan's borrowed quarters, so it was likely this was the grand duchess's suite. With my location determined, I pressed my thumbs into my temples to ward off the pounding headache from the litany of unanswered questions I'd accumulated.

*What just happened?*

Somehow, a ballroom filled with the most poised and elegant individuals of the province, had morphed into a bloodthirsty mob. Even timid Henrietta had nearly scratched my eyes out in trying to keep me from escaping. Had being locked up affected them that much? It had only been three weeks... Something definitely wasn't right here, and my every instinct was telling me that it had everything to do with Lord Tocken and his mirror.

*I need to talk to Conan.*

I pushed off from the door to search for him but froze when I noticed the unwelcome breeze fluttering around my knees. My gaze dropped to my tattered dress. Two massive tears had been ripped down the sides of the skirt, leaving a chunk of fabric half dangling around my ankles. My right sleeve had been ripped off as well, now hanging around my wrist like a fabric bracelet. Fortunately, enough of the fabric remained that nothing indecent was exposed, but that didn't mean me tripping on the torn hem wouldn't change that.

I scurried back into the room, digging through the closet and wardrobes in search of anything that could replace the simple dress. As I'd guessed, the room certainly appeared to belong to the grand duchess, considering how overly extravagant each gown was. I tore through the closet racks, trying to find something that would fit my slimmer figure and not possess ten pounds of crystals. When I reached the back of the closet, my hands finally brushed against a soft and surprisingly light satin dress. I shoved the other gowns aside, revealing a dark, plum-colored ballgown with a full, yet airy skirt, and a fitted bodice with small rubies stitched into the shape of a classic Dhurin rose. It must have belonged to the grand duchess when she was much younger, because it was a good few sizes smaller than the rest, and not quite as gaudy.

*Perfect.*

Without wasting any further time, I slipped off the shredded remains of the cotton dress and pulled the voluminous ballgown over my head. It took a little struggling in the mirror to do up my laces, but after a few minutes of muttering curses, the task was accomplished. The dress fit me like a long satin glove, elegant and smooth, with every curve perfectly hugged. The rich plum color complimented my darker skin like I was its perfect canvas, alighting my eyes and rose-red lips against the glittering rubies.

Once I was properly dressed, I turned my focus back on finding Conan so we could unravel the mysteries of the griffins and bizarre hostages. I returned to the door I'd entered, whispering a quiet wish that Conan had actually been able to seal off the entrances to the ballroom before I opened it. I creaked the door open only an inch at a time, peering my eyes through the crack until I was certain I was looking into the library and not a mob of deadly nobles.

"Mira!" I'd barely even cracked the door halfway open before Conan's eagle eyes locked onto me. He rushed over, kicking a chair in his path aside without even blinking.

Relief surged through me at the sight of him, flushing my body with cozy endorphins as I threw the rest of the door open and dashed inside to meet him.

*He's alright… The mob was too slow to attack him.*

When Conan reached me, he instantly snagged me into a tight embrace. He pressed me against his chest, hard enough that I could feel his heart hammering behind his ribs. Comfort enveloped me as I inhaled the warm scent of pine and sandalwood that lingered on him. He moved his hand to gently stroke the top of my head, his grip only tightening as he did so. For a long time, he simply held me there, squeezing me as if I were a flawless diamond he worried would drop into the sea. Our beating hearts slowed in unison, syncing together like a sweet symphony until he finally pulled away.

"Are you hurt?" He brushed his fingers down from my head, tracing them across my ear and brushing my cheek, nearly melting me with its tenderness. "I know the rose was still alive… but the way they nearly trampled you…" He hissed in a breath through his teeth, pulling his hand away to clench it into a fist. "Maybe I should kill them after all."

"What, no!" I reached and grabbed his arm, feeling his muscles loosen under my touch. "You can't kill them… well, not all of them. I'm still debating on what to do about Tocken and his brother." I rolled my eyes, hearing the stout lord's commands replay in my mind.

"Tocken?" Conan scrunched his nose like he'd been fed something bitter. "The balding geezer who always insults you? Yeah, I wouldn't mind taking him out…" He cracked his knuckles with the spread of a sly grin.

"You may not want to kill him just yet," I interrupted over his popping bones. "He claims he's the one who enchanted the mirror. He said that he and his brother were spies sent to investigate the grand duke's greatest fears, but the enchantment fixated on you instead when you took over the castle."

He froze, his expression looking just as lost as it did during our first language lessons. "Greatest fears? I suppose that would make sense why I saw my father of all people, but that doesn't explain why he insisted that I kill you."

I nodded. "That's where it gets bizarre. Tocken claims that the mirror never told you to kill anyone."

His brows furrowed, scrunching up the scar over his brow so it curved more like a bow. "Now that's a bold-faced lie if I ever heard one," he huffed. "I think you're right. If he knew about the mirror's existence, and is lying about the details, then he must be the griffin we're looking for. Perhaps his brother, too."

Fear coursed through my blood at the thought of Azura being escorted by a pair of traitorous uncles working alongside the mythical Golden King. *Does she even know...?* She barely seemed to know about them being spies from another kingdom, so if they were both a part of an underground criminal group, she was likely just as in the dark as the rest of us.

*And in just as much danger...*

"We need to get the other hostages away from the griffins." I bit my lip, trying to vent the tension that was rising in my blood. "The rose is nearly dead. If Lord Tocken was planning to kill me, then who's to say he wasn't planning to kill another one of the hostages as well? The hostages bruised me when they were trying to hold me back, and I was only a few feet away from the rose. If we don't want anyone else to get hurt, then we're going to have to—"

"Let them go," Conan finished for me, snatching the breath from my lungs as his tone turned cold. "You're right. If there's any chance there's a griffin in that ballroom, they're all sitting ducks awaiting slaughter. The only way to protect them is if I open up the castle and let the army free them. If the griffins are anything like the beasts, they won't act in front of an audience. Tocken will likely slip back into the shadows."

His words sank onto me like a hailstorm of gravel, crushing me with a thousand emotions. "L-let them go?" I fumbled over my tongue, fighting between feeling the hope of seeing the sun and the fear of what would truly unfold. *What will unfold for Conan?* "Hold on a moment. If you let the army in, then you won't have any leverage over the grand duke. He hasn't offered you any portion of the province, which would mean..."

"I would be executed." His tone was low and grim, sending a nauseating shiver through my core. *Executed...?* "At least, if I don't escape. Although, the odds of making a getaway are pretty slim when you take a look out the window. There's not a single exterior door that isn't riddled with guards. If I let the hostages go, they'll be safe, but that will be it for me." His eyes lowered, shadowed with grief, but not fear.

As if he had known it would come to this all along.

*I suppose I knew it, too... but still...*

Pain tore through my heart like the polished tip of an iron spear. I shook my head fiercely, biting my lip so hard that I tasted blood as I fought off any tears. "No, you can't be executed. You may have done some terrible things, but you're not that man anymore. I know you're not." A sharp gasp split my lips, forcing me to choke back a sob as I bunched up my skirts in my fists. "I'll go back into the ballroom. Maybe if I try again, I can get through to the other hostages and make them believe that Tocken is dangerous. We still have a little time left before the rose dies, so as long as I—"

"Mira." His voice cut through my panic like a crystal blade, smooth and beautifully painful. He reached out for my hand, pulling it away from where I clawed at my dress and stroked it gently. "It's too late to reason with them. You saw them; they've practically gone savage. Sending you back in there would just give Tocken the opportunity to kill you himself." His eyes were wide and pleading, sending ripples all the way through where he touched my hand to the bottom of my burning heart.

*But by protecting myself, he'll die instead.*

I couldn't let that happen, not after all the struggles he had gone through to step out of his father's shadow and forgive his brothers. I squeezed his hand tight enough to splinter bone. "No, you deserve your own happiness, just like your brothers found theirs." A hot pressure seared against my chest, suffocating my lungs as I shook my head so hard, I thought I might snap my neck. "As the future grand duchess of both Omaira and Dhurin, I forbid you from setting them free! Not while there's still time to talk some sense into them."

Conan's eyes never left mine, latching onto me like he was the wilting rose and I was his sun. "I'm a beast, remember?" He smiled coyly, an aching sadness creeping into his eyes. "I don't follow the orders of dukes and duchesses." His smile faded, and out of nowhere, his eyes widened as if a puzzle piece had clicked somewhere in his stubborn brain. "But you're still a duchess... You may not be able to convince the hostages to listen to you, but perhaps you can convince those on the outside..." He dipped his hand into his pocket, pulling out the glittering gold key I had watched him first seal my suite with so many weeks ago.

I blinked down at the extended key, my brows furrowed. "Those on the outside... Do you mean...?"

"Your family... your fiancé, the grand duke and duchess of Dhurin, anyone who will listen." He turned my palm over, pressing the warm key into my hand and gently folding my fingers overtop it. "You told me once that you had to give up a life of protecting others, so please, allow me to give the chance to finally do it. Leave the castle, leave me behind, and do whatever you must to get the hostages away from the griffins before it's too late. This key will lead you to any door in this castle, so I'll let you decide who you let the soldiers find..." He squeezed his hand around mine, digging the gold prongs into my palm. The golden key tingled against my skin, dulling in comparison to the electricity jolting throughout my chest.

"You're... setting me free?" My voice sounded breathless, too heavy to say what was really on my tongue.

*You're leaving your fate in my hands...*

"I should have done it long before now, but yes." He pulled his hand away from mine, leaving it cold and lifeless. "I'm sorry for everything I put you through, Mira. I'm sorry for trapping you here, for frightening you, and for letting you get so sick and weak. It's my fault the hostages are in danger, and I alone am solely to blame. I regret my mistakes, and I hope relinquishing the power of the key is the first step to doing something right. Whatever you choose to do with it, please know I understand." His eyes fell to the thick key, his dark gaze reflecting the sparkling gold like it was a reflection of his future.

I pressed the key to my heart, feeling my entire body warm and freeze at the same time. "Thank you, Conan," I breathed. "I promise I'll do everything in my power to get *everyone* out alive." His hollow gaze moved up to mine, twinkling with the smallest touch of hope as I gave him a gentle smile. "I meant what I said. You deserve a chance at redemption, just like your brothers. I'm not going to let that chance slip away from you now."

Wonder filled his expression, lighting up his face so brightly that his scars nearly vanished into his skin. He took a step forward, minimizing the distance between us to mere inches as he touched a warm hand to my cheek. My heart flared to life, pounding with the force of a bucking mare as he gently hooked his finger under my chin. He tilted my face up to meet his deep onyx gaze.

"How is it possible that a woman as beautiful as you could have a heart that's even more astonishing?" He pressed his lips to my forehead, causing every inch of me to flood with honeyed bliss. My cheeks flushed and my breath hitched in the back of my throat, a complete captive to my blooming heart. He pulled away, dropping his hand from my chin as he looked at me with the most endearing, yet tragic, gaze. "I'll be in the master suite... if anyone needs to find me."

He stepped toward the door, leaving me completely frozen in time until the *click* of the door jarred me back to my senses. My face still burned from his gentle peck, but I didn't have time to worry about it now. Even if I really wanted to spend the next five hours reliving it and untangling what it meant one word at a time...

*And what does it mean for me...?*

I squeezed the key, reminding myself that, fluttering heart aside, I still had an entire ballroom of hostages to think about. I approached the same door Conan had, pressing the key into the lock as smooth as a flat pin.

*Take me outside...*

I made the request in my mind and instantly felt my hopes flair to life at the thought of stepping outside for the first time in weeks. I pressed the door open and closed it behind me just as quickly, ensuring no guards rushed inside before I had a chance to speak with them. The second I was outside the walls, I instantly gasped as the first blast of fresh air wisped around me like a chilly hug. The evening sun blanketed down on me, kissing my skin with a brush of warmth practically causing me to melt into the ground.

*I did it... I am finally free.*

"Mirabel!?" A familiar voice snapped me out of my bliss, causing me to blink my eyes against the sun until the voice's owner finally cleared in my vision.

Another gasp tore through me, flinging my hand to my mouth as I recognized the sprinting man pushing through the stunned guards. "Z-Zac?" I barely stuttered the words before my brother slammed into me with a bone-crushing hug.

"Mira! Thank the realms you're alive!"

# chapter twenty-five

"Mira! You look so skinny! What did that monster do to you!?" Mother fluttered around me like a panicked goose, switching between checking me over for injuries and flailing around in a panic. "When was the last time you ate anything? No wait! Don't tell me, my poor heart probably can't take it! Don't worry, dear, I'll find you some food right away."

I opened my mouth to explain that I'd actually had a rather hearty breakfast earlier in the day, but fortunately, Zac came to my rescue.

"Mother, relax. She said she's fine." He came up from behind the chair Mother had parked me in, pressing a firm hand on my shoulder. "Besides, she doesn't look thin at all. Mira's not a daffodil; it takes more than a little stress to make her break." He passed me a wink, earning a smile back from me.

*Realms, I am so glad to see him... If anyone will hear me out, it's Zac.*

"I beg to differ. Her figure has certainly... lessened since I saw her last." Ian's crude voice split through the tent as he stepped through the canvas opening. The joy I'd felt from being outside vanished faster than the wilting rose. He eyed me up and down, taking an extra moment to gawk at the elegant gown before giving an unwanted nod of approval. "Glad to see you're alive, Mirabel. This will make things easier going forward. We'll need all the inside intel we can get in order to slay the beast."

My stomach dropped. *Slay him?*

I jumped out of my chair. "Actually, I didn't come out here

to tell you how to stop the beast. I came to warn you about a far more dangerous threat inside." That seemed to catch everyone's attention. My father, who had been sitting quietly in the corner of the tent, took in an unsteady breath, and Mother looked like she was ready to swoon. "Is your father here? He should hear about this, too."

Ian folded his arms, glaring me down as if I had insulted him by requesting the actual grand duke. "He's off meeting with one of the emperor's advisors to gain advice on the situation. I'm afraid you'll have to report your findings to me." A smug grin tugged at the edge of his lips, urging me to crack a few of his pearly teeth.

I swallowed back my irritation, trying to focus on the more important matters at hand. "Alright... Well, Conan and I have reason to believe that there are griffins amongst the—"

"Hold on a moment? Did you just say *Conan*?" Ian sputtered, narrowing his eyes with a humored smirk. "You mean the beast? Why in the realms would you two be reasoning about things in the first place?"

I crossed my arms, eyeing him down with the ferociousness of a prodded lioness. "I was going to explain, if you hadn't so rudely interrupted me," I huffed, tossing my nose in the air while giving him a dirty glare. Being around Duke Ian *almost* made me miss Lord Tocken.

"I interrupted you because you were sounding mad," Ian snapped, impatience wrinkling his brow like a hairless cat. "One doesn't reason with a beast, and for a moment, it almost sounded like you were saying something about griffins—"

"Yes, what about the griffins?" Zac inserted himself between us, his focus on me far more serious than Ian's. "Are you referring to the Golden King's followers? Like, the *real* griffins?"

I nodded firmly, feeling a rush of relief that at least one person had the mind to listen. "Yes, Conan found a mirror that was enchanted to reflect the person he feared most. At first, he thought it was in his head, but then I saw his deceased father in the mirror, so I—"

"Deceased father? Enchanted mirrors?" Ian pushed in front of Zac, his repulsive scowl fixated on me. "Are you certain you walked out of the castle? Or did you tumble out a window and fall on that pretty little head of yours?" He reached out a hand to brush away a strand of hair from my eyes, but I swatted it away faster than a blazing bee.

"Yes, I walked out!" I snapped. "Conan let me out himself! He sent me outside to find help because the other hostages are in real danger!" I stomped my foot into the tent's dirt floor, puffing up a cloud of dust onto the ends of my skirt.

Zac's eyes furrowed. His expression twisted like he had just heard me speak in Conan's language instead of my own. "He really let you out? But why would he do that? I've spent enough unpleasant time with the beast to know he isn't one to have a change of heart." He gave me an inquiring look, almost challenging me to oppose his statement with his curious blue stare.

"But he *did* have a change of heart." I met Zac's glare, focusing all my persuasive efforts on him instead of wasting my time with the duke. "He's different now. He told me himself that he regrets what he's done and wants to find a way to undo it without putting the others at risk. Why would he let me leave if he didn't want to do the right thing?"

"Because he didn't let you leave," Ian interrupted with a commanding boom in his voice. "You must have escaped some other way, and the weeks of confinement and malnourishment have unhinged your thoughts."

If looks could kill, I would have skewered Ian to the tent wall with a hundred daggers. My blood boiled hotter than oil, practically emitting steam off my skin as I dove my hand into my pocket. "If Conan didn't let me out, then how did I get this!?" I flashed the golden key in front of everyone's eyes, their gaze instantly gravitating to it like it was a stolen jewel.

Zac's eyes widened like a glass marble. "Is that the key... The enchanted one he used to take over the castle?" He blinked up at me with a fresh realization spanning across his face, causing my heart to swell in hope that this evidence was enough to convince him.

"Yes, it is," I said softly, lowering my lashes as I gazed down at the glittering embodiment of the beast's apology. "He and I believe that one of the guests, Lord Tocken and potentially his brother, are in league with the griffins. For some reason, they want to kill me, so Conan gave me the key so I could protect myself and get help to save the others." I poured every ounce of my heart into my stare as I dug my gaze into my brother's. *He just has to believe me...* "Conan is not a beast, not anymore."

Zac's gaze never left the key, as if the enchantment upon it somehow had left him in a trance of disbelief. I bit my lip as I waited for him to respond, or at least, to give me any clue that he believed me. He finally tore his eyes away from the key, long enough to shatter me with a solemn expression that sank my heart into the dirt.

"Mira, I'm sorry... I just don't understand how—"

"How she could have lost so much of her mind, so quickly?" Ian's ear-screeching voice shredded through my mind like nails on slate, distracting me long enough that I didn't even notice him swipe the golden key from my palm. The key's warmth faded from my skin, dipping my blood to an icy freeze.

"Hold on! You can't—"

"Hush, my dear." Ian pressed a finger against my lips, causing me to squash them against his fingers. I was nearly about to bite him when he moved his hand to grab me roughly by the arm. "This is not the place to speak about such delicate matters. As the future grand duke and duchess of this province, we should make this conversation a bit more private. I'm sure your family understands." He shot my parents a cordial smile, much like that of a crooked crocodile preparing to snap its prey.

Mother nodded. "We understand, Your Grace." Her face was pale, ashen with a worried twist in her brow and bite on her lower lip.

"Hold on a moment. Why don't we first—" Zac reached his hand out, barely missing my arm before Ian let the tent's flap fall flat in front of his face.

"Pardon you!" I hissed, trying to yank my arm back as he picked up the pace. He dragged me around the back of the campsite, where only a few storage crates and trunks littered the back garden wall. "I don't remember giving you permission to haul me around like a—"

"Quiet." Ian's voice turned steely, and he clamped his hand over my mouth with a tight squeeze. My eyes nearly bulged out of my head.

*What in the realms is he doing!?*

"Mmph!" I tried to push him off me, but he was too strong. His massive hand practically covered my entire face, smothering my nose to the point where I could barely breathe. Yanking on his arm wasn't doing anything, so I tried kicking at his shins. Somehow, I landed one good blow, even without being able to see my feet under the massive dress, but it was no different than kicking a steel rod. He remained completely unfazed, only squeezing my jaw tighter, as if silently warning me to strop struggling. I darted my gaze around the gardens, desperately searching for any onlookers I could wave down for help, but there was no one around. He had perfectly lured me away from the crowd to do... what, exactly? What kind of ludicrous plan was he crafting?

"You should have learned by now that cooperating with me is always your best option," he said coldly, his frosty eyes intense enough to house their own blizzard. "I don't know what nonsense that beast has been filling your head with, but it certainly won't be spouted around my province." He tightened his grip, cutting off my air flow and making me wheeze. "So, here's what's going to happen... Do you think you're finally ready to listen to me?" A vile smirk spread across his lips as he patiently waited for me to respond.

I only manage to cough into his palm, once again ready to fight and claw his clamped hand off of me by whatever means necessary.

"Excellent, now that's a good girl." He grinned. "You're far more tolerable when you only let those pretty eyes do the talking." He traced his free hand across my brow and trailed it behind my ear like the slither of a serpent. I spat into his hand, causing his face to twist in repulsion before he could regain his composure. "You've had a rough visit so far, and I understand that," he cooed, clearly in no rush to grant me more oxygen. "But don't worry, my dear duchess, I'm going to take care of *everything*."

An unsettling ripple spread from where he gripped me, racing waves of nausea through my organs. *Take care of everything...? What horrors does that entail?*

"I really must thank you for delivering the key." He raised the trinket to the light, catching the dwindling sunlight on its sparkle with a twist in my gut. "Now I can finally be the hero Dhurin is in desperate need of. Once I kill the beast and free the hostages, we'll throw our wedding right away to celebrate. Of course, you'll need to spend some time with some shrinks to help sort out your trauma from the whole situation, but there will be plenty of time for that. All that matters is that you keep your ludicrous ideas about humane beasts and infiltrating griffins to yourself. I already have enough damage control to do without your nonsensical stories stirring everyone up in a frenzy. Now, in the meantime..."

He pulled me further back into the creeping shadows, stopping in front of one of the many storage trunks that littered the castle grounds. The trunk was already flipped open and empty, nearly the width of a standard coach. Judging by its depth and width, it was likely used to carry weapons or other supplies brought in for the soldiers. Ian pressed his free hand against my shoulder, knocking me off balance so I fell back into the crate with a bruising thump on my rear.

I gasped in a breath, finally free of his sweaty hand. "Ian? What do you think you're—" He slammed the lid down before I could finish, forcing me to duck into the bottom of the trunk to avoid being smacked in the skull by the lid.

Darkness enclosed the tight space, leaving only a tiny keyhole along the side to drift in a fragment of light. "Ian! Let me out!" I kicked against the trunk as hard as I could, but I could already feel the weight of something heavy press down on the lid.

*Did he put another trunk on top of me?*

"Don't worry, dear, this is only a temporary arrangement," he whispered through the keyhole, riling up my fury as I kicked even harder. "I know it's not the finest room I could offer, but I need to protect my province from your wild thoughts. I'm sure you'll thank me someday."

"Thank you!?" I screamed, cracking my voice with a painful strain. "You'll be lucky if I don't kill you once I get out of here!"

A dark laugh echoed from outside the trunk, growing quieter as he moved away. "That beast truly rotted your dim little mind even further. Don't worry, dear, I'll avenge your suffering before morning..." My thrashing stopped. Every fiber of my muscles clenched as my fears clawed into me like the iron teeth of a bear trap.

*Ian still has the key, which means...*

"I'll be back. As soon as I kill myself a beast."

# chapter twenty-six

"No! No! No! Someone let me out!" I thrashed like a wild animal, bunching up my skirts around my waist. My knuckles and toes bruised, screaming at me to stop, but I didn't let up.

*Ian is on his way to kill Conan... and I gave him a ticket inside.*

Sweat trickled down my face as I stirred up the hot air with another kick. This wasn't how things were meant to happen. I was supposed to get everyone out safely, *including* Conan, not send a bloodthirsty duke in after him. My heart sank to the bottom of the trunk, clattering against its wooden frame like shattered stone.

*What will Conan think when he sees Ian? Will he think I wanted him dead all along? That I had tricked him?*

Another droplet slid down my cheek, but this one wasn't sweat. The hot tear rolled down the side of my face and caught in my hair. This was all my fault... I should have never let that key out of my sight. Conan's face flashed in my mind, his dark eyes fading back into the lost beast that had first locked everyone inside. It had taken him so long to open up to me, to learn that he could trust more than just himself.

*And I handed over the one thing he trusted me with...*

Hot tears flooded down my cheeks, mixing with my salty sweat. I let out a frustrated screech and kicked the trunk's lid with all my might. One thing was for certain, if Ian killed Conan, it would be his neck next.

"Mira!?"

I sucked in a dingy breath, the air humid from my sweat and tears. It took a moment to register the voice I'd heard, but the moment it clicked, my heart recollected and jumped for joy.

"Zac! Can you hear me!?" I pounded my fists against the lid, scraping my knuckles against the coarse wood.

Running feet echoed from outside the trunk, skidding to a stop right in front of me. "Mira!? What in the Realms—" His voice was cut off by the clattering of him shoving aside whatever junk Ian had piled on top of the lid. A moment later, the lid popped open, rushing me with the freshest burst of air I had ever felt.

"Zac! Thank goodness you heard me!" I jerked upright, wrapping my arms around his neck with a breathless squeeze before pulling away. "Now, if you'll excuse me, I have a beast to save and a fiancé to murder." My face twisted in pure severity, clenching my jaw hard enough to crack diamonds as I stepped out of the trunk.

Before I could go wring Ian's neck, Zac snagged me by the arm and pulled me back. "Hold on a moment! Are you saying that the duke locked you in there?" His expression instantly reflected mine, tight and fierce with the power to kill on sight.

I yanked my arm away. "Yes! The monster took my key, too. If I don't get it back soon, then Conan will—" A sinking horror cut off my voice as I suddenly noticed the lack of soldiers. My eyes scanned across the grounds until they caught sight of the nearest servant door.

It was wide open, with a hundred soldiers funneling inside...

"No..." I placed a hand to my gaping mouth, feeling a wave of nausea sway in the back of my throat.

Zac placed a hand on my shoulder. "It's what has to be done," he said coldly, his tone shattering me as if my bones were made of glass. "I'll deal with Ian when he comes back out. He has a lot of explaining to do after locking you in a trunk, but now isn't the time to—"

"So, you're just going to let Ian kill him!?" I swiped his hand off my shoulder, whipping around with stinging in my eyes. "He doesn't have to die! He's not some savage animal that needs to be put down; he's a person!" My chest cramped from the intense pounding of my heart.

*He didn't let me die... Even when every voice around him was telling him to kill me. I'm not going to let him die, either.*

"A very *dangerous* person," Zac emphasized, his eyes tightened with a commanding glare. "Face it, Mira, you've been through something really traumatic, and you're not thinking straight. You'll feel better in a few days after this has all blown over."

"No, I won't!" I snapped. "Not if Conan dies! I promised him I would do everything I could to get him out. To get everyone out!"

"Why do you care so much?" He thrashed his arms up in the air, his patience finally snapping from my childish tantrum.

"Because I care about him—" My words broke as my gasp split them apart, widening my eyes larger than the rising moon. Zac went quiet, shock paling his face as the tension in his shoulders dropped faster than a lead weight.

*I care about Conan.*

The realization froze me, stiffening me like hardened clay that had molded a truth I wasn't prepared to uncover. But it *was* the truth. The pounding in my chest, the swirling blood in my cheeks, and the breathless gasps that followed my words only confirmed it. Conan had proven to me over these last few weeks that he had become more than just a jailer or even a snarky student. He had taken a piece of me with him inside that castle, a piece I truly hoped he wanted to cherish. Maybe it was the way he cared for me when I was ill, the way we teased each other over picture books, or how he had set me free... But it happened, and I couldn't simply move on now that part of my heart clung to his.

"Do you mean that...?" Zac's eyes were vacant, lost between utter disbelief and a softness I couldn't quite interpret.

I nodded, tears leaking down my cheeks. "I do," I rasped through my tense throat. "And I may even be foolish enough to believe that he cares for me, too." I clutched my hand over my heart and scrunched the bodice's fabric.

*Would Conan have set me free if he didn't care for me?*

Zac's gaze searched me as if checking to see if Ian had been correct about my mental instability. Finally, he let out a long breath, clenching his fist until his knuckles paled. "I'm going to have to kill that beast for choosing my sister of all people..." he huffed. "But I'll need him to be alive in order for me to kill him..." He raised his vibrant blue gaze to me and a soulful twinkle sparked a light within me.

"Are you saying...?"

"Go," he urged, gesturing toward the open door. "Find him and keep Ian off him for as long as you can. I'm going to grab some soldiers I can personally trust to help investigate this griffin issue."

Gratitude couldn't even begin to describe the feeling that exploded inside me. I snagged his hand, giving it a smothering squeeze with the biggest smile before whirling around for the castle. "Thank you, Zac!" I called back.

"Be careful!" I could barely hear him over the swishing of my skirts. "If anything happens to you, I'll take my rage out on that beast!"

His voice disappeared behind me, blurred by my feverish adrenaline. A few soldiers still lingered around the stone walls and were patiently waiting their turn to funnel through the narrow door. Patience was the last thing I had. When I reached the cluster of guards, I instantly shoved and elbowed my way through them, and even made use of my dress's wide girth to push them aside.

When I finally clamored through the doorway, the all too familiar sights and unpleasant smells of the dingy ballroom smacked me in my senses. At first, this sight washed me with relief, assuring me that the hostages would be rescued and dealt with before Ian could smoke out Conan. But when my eyes finally adjusted, the small flame of relief was snuffed. What I was looking at wasn't a rescue attempt; it was a full-fledged battle.

The clanging of metal echoed with a sickening *crack* as the soldiers' swords met candlesticks, dinner platters, serving knives, and anything else the hostages had scavenged as weapons. Confusion dotted the faces of the soldiers as they half-heartedly fended off the hostage's attacks, unsure of whether they could harm them. This seemed to empower the raging group and their bloodlust thickened. It was as if they had truly lost their sanity, driven only by the vengeance their confinement had made them long for.

*But don't they see they're attacking their rescuers?*

A sharp thought pricked my brain as I dodged a flying candlestick to catch a glimpse of the hostage's precious rose. *If it's still alive... then at least everyone who's close to it won't get hurt.* I ducked to the floor, leveling my eyes with the wilted flower, just in time to see the last blood-red petal fall lifelessly to the floor.

*No...*

As if reacting to the end of the flower's protection, the hostages went wild. Henrietta clawed at a soldier's hair, Madam Ophelia was attempting to lock another in a chokehold, and even Sir Eric was chasing down a panicked young man with a butter knife.

*What in the realms happened to them...?*

Panic flooded me as I realized that I didn't see Lord Tocken or his brother. I darted my gaze around the chaos, hoping I'd just overlooked them. But as I searched, I quickly realized that Azura was missing, too. Had her uncles dragged her away before they got caught for being with the griffins?

"My realms... They've all gone mad." I shot my gaze in the direction of whomever had just voiced my inner thoughts, landing on none other than my putrid betrothed.

Ian's sword dipped to the ground, his eyes scanning the wild group with an astonished gape. *At least I'm not the only one who finds this absurd.* He sheathed his sword with a slick scrape of metal, then dove his hand into his pocket to produce the key he'd stolen from me. My heart jolted at the flash of gold, and I stepped back a few feet to try to slip out of his direct view.

*I need to get that key back.*

"First, the duchess, and now everyone else..." He squeezed the key in his palm, tensing up his oversized muscles enough that I could see his veins prodding through his sleeves. "It must be the beast's doing... He must have cursed them, somehow. Once I slay him, their minds will surely be restored."

*No!*

With his new self-assurance in place, he bolted for the nearest door with the key held ready. I had backed too far away from him in my efforts to stay hidden, so I was too far to try to tackle the key from his hands. Without pausing to think, I hiked up my skirts and bolted after him, muttering pleas that he wouldn't get away. My heart throbbed against my ribs, tearing a killer stitch in my side as I pushed my legs to move faster. I was only a few feet away when he pulled the door open. My legs fumbled, nearly causing me to trip as I recognized the wrecked remains of the master suite through the open doorway.

*That's where Conan is!*

With my last push of energy, I urged my legs to go faster, feeling my blood drain with each inch the door swished shut. My hand reached out for the brass knob only a second after it clicked closed, causing my blood to run cold.

"No!" I yanked on the doorknob, praying it would lead back into the master suite, but as I pulled it open, only a dim hallway with iron wall sconces that hadn't been lit in weeks greeted me.

I dashed inside anyway, desperate to search every door until I found one that led back to Conan.

*I can't let Ian kill him... Whatever is happening in the ballroom isn't his fault. It has to be some sort of madness, or something to do with their obsession with the—*

"The rose worked splendidly."

My legs halted, nearly shattering my knees as I stumbled to a stop. I paused, stifling my ragged breaths as I pressed my back against the opposing corner of where the sound had stemmed. The voice rang in my ears like a lingering chime, infecting my brain with its familiarity in the most unsettling way.

*Is that... Azura?*

"I knew the power would strengthen with the flower's death, but I hadn't imagined it would be quite so spectacular." Azura's calm voice numbed me like a deep winter chill. It was her, there was no doubt about it, but the way she carried her tone sounded so much more sinister than the sweet caster I'd grown to appreciate.

"Yes, the enchantment worked, but I believe that's mostly due to the way you fibbed about its effects." Lord Illumen's shrill voice tore through me with another chill, causing me to press my back firmer against the wall. "By convincing them the rose would protect them, they all clung to it like an infant to a rattle. A lot of your success was also due to luck. My illusion could only hide injuries, not prevent or heal them, so we were fortunate that no one else tried to test its power."

A thousand thoughts scrambled like cockroaches in the sunlight. *The rose's magic was an illusion? By Lord Illumen?* My mind whirled back to the moment I had cut my hand on the castle window at the beginning of our confinement. When I had returned to the ballroom, the injury was gone, but I had still felt the pain...

"Luck or not, His Majesty will be pleased," Azura snarked, startling me with her sudden rough tone. "The experiment was successful. My enchantment infected the hearts of every victim in that ballroom with a murderous hatred toward first the beast, then the guard, and soon, each other. The rose acted as an excellent vessel to introduce the spell slowly, therefore, the magic had the optimal effect."

*A slow infection... But that didn't make any sense. Azura is a caster and casters can only place magic into living things... So how did her power grow stronger if the rose was dying? Unless...*

Azura was an enchantress.

Nausea wracked my stomach, nearly causing me to double over as I put the pieces together. The rose had never protected us at all... It had been spreading an enchantment of hate. One that only grew as Azura's magic spread to the wilting parts of the rose. Enchanters could only cast magic into non-living things, so by picking a pre-picked flower, she had essentially created a magical time bomb.

And now it was completely wilted.

"Yes, yes, you did well, but how are you going to explain the issue with the duchess to His Majesty?" I snagged a breath, instantly recognizing the scraping voice of Lord Tocken. *At least I was correct to assume he was a part of all this.* "Your spell never worked on her, and despite my noble efforts, the beast was too bull-headed to do away with her."

My body stiffened, clamping my muscles around my bones. *So, he had been trying to kill me... because I was somehow immune to the rose's enchantment?*

Azura groaned, earning a jump from me as I snapped out of my thoughts. "You and I both know your *noble* efforts were unnecessary," she snapped, her voice slick and oily like a black viper. "I told you, the duchess *was* affected, but not to the extent of the others. It likely had to do with the fact that she spent most of her time out of the ballroom while the others hovered around the rose. I even intentionally sent her away to test my hypothesis, and by the looks of it, I was correct."

*Of course...*

I sucked in a shallow breath, barely filling an inch of my lungs. Every time I entered the ballroom, I felt like I was being suffocated in a fog of negativity. All this time I thought it was the other hostages' insufferable attitudes that were riling me up, but it was so much more than that... It was Azura's enchantment.

"Even so, I still think it would have been wise to kill her," Lord Tocken hissed. "His Majesty wants us to drive a rift between Omaira and Dhurin, after all. The beast was an excellent start, and the mad hostages an admirable touch, but killing off Omaira's duchess truly would have sealed their feud."

"Is that why you went behind our backs with the mirror?" Lord Illumen huffed. "You were only meant to drive the beast mad as punishment for denying our divine ruler, not go off and insert the idea of murder into his head."

"Oh, please!" Lord Tocken snorted. "The Golden King would have been pleased, and you know it, so don't act all high and mighty by—"

"Ladies, ladies, quit squabbling," Azura groaned with a sharp growl in her tone. "Save it all for your reports to the king. We need to get out of here before those savage hostages break out of the ballroom."

A few muffled arguments echoed from Lord Tocken, but not a moment later, I could hear their feet rushing back down the hall. All urgency remained dormant in me as I pressed my spine against the cool stone wall. I felt like I might collapse, my head dizzy and heavy with the bulk of information that had been crammed into it.

Out of all the chaos that had just unfolded, only two things managed to crawl to the front of my mind.

The rose had been enchanted with a rage-inducing magic.

And I had definitely found the griffins.

# chapter twenty-seven

I stared through the stained-glass doors, watching the army trickle in like a deadly virus that was slowly stopping my heart.

*Mira had let them inside...*

A piece of me still clung to the hope that she had only sent them after the griffins, but deep down, I knew their rushed entrance wasn't due to a stealthy extraction.

It was a beast hunt.

I paced the crumbled remains of the suite, crunching the broken glass of the mirror as I stared into the empty frame. For once, I was disappointed that I couldn't see my monstrous reflection. Perhaps seeing my disfigured face would remind me of why I wasn't deserving of someone as perfect and genuine as Mirabel Brantley.

*This is the ending I deserve... At least I got to make my peace before my time came.*

I thought back to the letters I had stashed in the library, wondering if Mira had meant it when she said she would do her best to toss them into the sea. Maybe it was foolish of me to believe she had been earnest in her promise, but even if it was, I was content with being foolish one more time. I had told her I wouldn't blame her for whatever she chose to do with the key, and I meant that. She had every right to decide my fate.

*I just wish she'd chosen a fate where I'd get to see her just one more time...*

Perhaps Father was capable of hurting me all along... Even

in death, his lingering soul still found a way to separate me from the one other person in the realm I'd learned to care about.

"There you are…" the oily voice echoed behind me like a call from the grim reaper. He spoke in Rubian, but his words had clearly reached my mind. My heart tensed at the reminder of my lessons with Mira, and how proud she would have once been when she saw what I could understand. "This ends now, beast."

I turned away from the empty mirror, meeting the furious glare of the flawless duke with a stare as shattered and empty as the frame behind me. He was handsome, much like a proper prince would have been in my home realm. He was just the type of man I would expect a girl as beautiful as Mira to marry.

Perhaps she would be happy with him someday…

"My, don't you look pitiful?" The duke sneered. He drew a long steel blade from his hip, flashing the jeweled hilt in the moonlight that drifted in from the glass doors. "What's the matter, beast? Not feeling so chatty now that you don't have all your precious trinkets?"

It took me a moment to translate his voice in my mind, but he made it easy to fill in the blanks as he dangled the enchanted gold key from his fingers. My chest tightened like it was being pressed by an anvil.

*So, Mira had given him the key after all…*

All hope I'd had of the duchess caring for me shriveled like the wilting remains of the ballroom rose. She had feared me all along, though I can't say it's surprising, not for someone as horrid as me.

"That's right, beast." He lashed his tongue like it was prodded with venom, taking a tedious step forward with his sword raised. "I control the castle now. There's no use in trying to escape."

I pressed my hands against my side, lowering my head in pure submission as I took a stuttering step forward. "I wasn't planning on running," I replied in choppy Rubian.

The duke paused his pursuit, shock wisping around his eyes as he took a moment to digest the words I'd spoken. "So... the beast has learned to babble." He let out a belittling chuckle, brushing off his surprise with another step forward. "Did my darling bride teach you that little trick? She definitely seemed keen on convincing me that you had *changed* and that you were showing signs of humanity. How juvenile."

My head jolted up, replaying his voice in my mind as I ensured I had translated it right. "What?"

*Mira told him I'd changed?*

"You really did a number on her and the others," he tsked darkly as he admired his reflection in the blade with a lick of his teeth. "I must say, I'm curious to know how you did it. I wouldn't mind learning how to manipulate minds myself, especially after I marry that bubble-brained duchess. She'll look stunning in our family portraits, but otherwise, she doesn't need to be too involved in our province's affairs." He laughed to himself as if he had told the funniest quip in all the realms, completely unaware of the raging fire he was stoking within me.

"Pardon?" I clipped, just short of a full-on growl. My fists balled firmer than any brass knuckle, only a blink away from cracking the duke's blabbering jaw. "What did you just *dare* say about Mira?"

His eyes narrowed and a mischievous smile slithered up his face. "Why so bothered, beast? Did you actually end up taking a liking to my doll?" He tilted his head back with a split of skin-crawling laughter. "She is quite the temptress, so I can't say I blame you for appreciating it. But I'm afraid I've already marked my claim on her. I was in need of a quiet trophy wife, and her illness made her the perfect candidate since I could use it as an excuse for her common absences. That, and she's perfectly stunning, so I think she'll amuse me just fine. Once you're gone, her head will clear from this madness, and I can get to work grooming her into becoming the perfect bride for me. That's one of the perks of being a charming and influential duke." He leveled his gaze to me, just begging for me to rip his throat out as he let out another demented chuckle. "The province is mine to command."

He thrust forward, spearing his sword straight for my heart with pride swelling in his bulging eyes. But all I saw was red. The inferno raging inside me was intense enough to peel my skin from my bones. When his sword approached my chest, I snapped a steel grip around his wrist, stopping the blade's momentum with raw strength. The confidence drained from the duke's face like a spider sapping his blood. He tried to jar his wrist free from my grip, but it was far too late for him to fight back.

*And far too late for mercy.*

I twisted his wrist, causing him to yelp in pain until he released the sword. The steel blade clattered to the floor, and I released his fragile limb only a moment before it would've snapped. He jolted his hand free from me in a moment of panic, leaving his neck entirely exposed for another latch of my clawed grip.

"W-wait!" I squeezed the air from his throat, choking his words until his skin paled. He tried to pull at my hands, but my grip was steel.

"You... vile, squirming maggot," I hissed, my vocal cords sawing against each other in the deadly tone. I dragged him toward the balcony doors, kicking them open with a single strike that shattered half the glass. My entire body felt as if it had been dipped in tar and lit aflame. I stepped out onto the short balcony and thrust the duke over the edge, while still gripping him by the neck. "You don't deserve this province."

*'Yes, son...'*

His legs dangled freely over the balcony's edges. He kicked and thrashed against the air, struggling between clawing my hands from his throat and trying to latch onto my arm if I let him fall. My entrance onto the balcony had caught the attention of the soldiers below. Desperate shouts and panicked orders drifted through the air, all rushing to rescue their pathetic excuse of a duke.

*'Let him fall, my boy... Show them you're no coward.'*

Rage blinded me, pounding my heart directly in my ears and blurring out every other sound. My muscles burned from hoisting all the duke's weight on a single arm, but my adrenaline was happy to compensate for the extra effort. This man was a disgrace to Dhurin and an insult to Mira; he deserved to die. If I had to perish for my crimes, why shouldn't I take another monster with me?

*'Yes, Conan, be the monster... Be what they fear most.'*

Father's voice cracked through my mind, causing my brain to spin. He wanted me to kill him; he wanted me to be powerful. He would be proud of me if I did this. If I killed one more time, then maybe he would be appeased. I just have to let him fall... just the lift of a finger...

*"You're not a monster, Conan."*

I flinched, nearly allowing the duke to slip through my fingers as Mira's words resurfaced in my mind. For a moment, everything went quiet except for the rushing of my blood in my ears. My breath hitched in my throat, burning all the way to the bottom of my lungs as I realized what was happening.

*I am still hearing Father, but how? The mirror was shattered. He was dead. The griffin's enchantment was gone, all except for...*

My eyes flicked to my clenched wrist, widening on the glittering gold charm.

*'Let him fall, Conan... Kill the brat.'*

"It's the charm..." I breathed hoarsely, drawing the duke in a few inches to inspect the trinket. "Ever since I entered this realm, I've been plagued with my father's voice... I thought it was his ghastly way of taking revenge on me, but it was never truly him at all..."

I pulled the duke another inch closer. His eyes were beginning to flutter shut from the lack of oxygen but shot open when he felt me move.

*'What are you doing, son! Kill the duke! Now's your chance to take Dhurin as your own!'*

I clenched my free hand, fastening my piercing gaze on the dirty talisman. "No..." I drew my arm in closer. The duke's legs scrambled to hook on the edge of the balcony. "I'm done being a killer, and I'm done being manipulated by you."

I drew my arm in the rest of the way, placing the duke's thrashing feet solidly on the ground before releasing my clasp on his throat. He collapsed onto the balcony and gasped wildly. With my hand now free, I snapped the woven band off my wrist. Instantly, I felt a lingering tug vanish from the back of my mind, as if there had been a leash tied around my subconscious. A thousand eyes gaped at me from below as their frenzied rescue attempt settled. I dangled the bracelet from my fingers. I gave the cursed gold charm one final spiteful glare before letting it slip through my fingers and crack on the ground below.

*It's done...*

But my victory was short-lived, when out of nowhere, an iron fist slammed into the back of my spine. I doubled over from the shock, then whipped around to catch the red-faced duke in a complete rage. He held his fists close to his chest, his eyes narrowed and level, ready to break my jaw in return for my tender treatment of him. He swung again, but this time, he was sloppy. He threw all his weight forward with the punch, likely eager to place a fatal blow to my temple. I stepped aside at the last moment, causing his eyes to widen like a glass marble. His momentum was too much for him to stop, and he stumbled over the edge of the balcony.

His scream split through the air, and my body reacted

entirely on its own. I threw my arms over the edge and barely snagged him by the ankle. My arms burned with the pull of his plummeting weight, nearly tearing my arm from the socket.

"Hold on, you idiot." I'm not sure what language I cursed him in, but he seemed to be content with not arguing as I hauled him back over the edge. Cheers erupted somewhere along the ground, but it all faded as I tossed the squirming noble down to the balcony floor. "Try that again, and I'll let you fall," I growled, narrowing my eyes like an irritated predator.

He didn't answer me, his face still ashen with his brush with death, though he still managed to give me a bitter frown. I wonder if I had been this obnoxious when I first arrived at the Ruby Realm. If so, it was no wonder why the Golden King wanted to spend all his time tormenting me.

"Conan!"

My gaze darted back into the room just in time to see Mira's sweat-slicked face burst inside. Her dark curls sprung tightly around her face, frizzy from her perspiration and frazzled sprint. My heart cracked open, unveiling the hope I had tried to seal away of ever seeing her enchanting face again.

*She came back... She came for me.*

The duke clamored to his feet beside me, eyes beady like a flaring cobra. "Mirabel..." he growled, stepping past me with wobbling steps to approach his undeserved bride. "What do you think you're doing here? You should be—"

With the most flawless form I had ever seen, Mira punched the duke square in the face. He fell back like a rag doll, knocked out cold, leaving Mira standing proudly with a loose shake of her hand. "The wedding is off," she spat at his crumpled form.

I don't think I could have adored her more...

"Mira..." I stepped into the room. "You're here."

She threw herself straight into me, wrapping her arms

around my torso with enough strength to nearly crack my ribs. Light rippled through my dark soul, finally feeling fully whole now that the last of my father's ghost and the Golden King's infection was gone. I squeezed her back, digging my hands into the back of her hair and sliding my hand around her waist. I felt so warm holding her, so peaceful, so... so happy.

"Thank the realms you're alright!" Her voice was muffled against my chest, but I could still hear her clear as day. It was getting easier to understand the language with each passing word. I hadn't realized quite how similar our languages were until I had been entirely forced to forgo my old one.

*Like the Conan who once spoke it, that language is now dead to me.*

"I'm more than alright," I said slowly, giving her one final squeeze before allowing her to peel away. "I'm me again... all of me. The last of my mental curse had been trapped inside the charm bracelet." I pulled her hand upward, catching the light of the second charm in her widening eyes.

"Your charm... of course." She pulled her hand from mine, and instantly yanked the bracelet off, tossing it to the floor. "Realms... what *haven't* the griffins enchanted?" She stomped her slipper on top of the charm, shattering the golden bead with a satisfying *crack*. "It turns out being a griffin is a family business."

My forehead wrinkled, tensing my brows as I tried to follow what she was implying. "Are you saying that Lord Illumen was in league with the griffins as well?" I clenched my teeth, growing angry at myself for ever locking Mira in with those monsters to begin with.

"Yes, and Azura, too," she hissed, her expression twisted in betrayal. "I overheard them in the halls when I was searching for you. It seems like this entire mess was some sort of experiment for their magic. Azura isn't a caster, she's an *enchantress*. The rose wasn't growing weaker as it died, it was growing stronger. And instead of protecting us, it was infecting us with a deadly rage, capable of turning us against everyone, even those we trust."

My body stiffened, locking my joints in place except for the mechanical shake of my head. "No... that can't be possible. I watched Azura slice her own hand. If the rose hadn't been protecting her, then how had she managed to go uninjured?"

Her pupils dilated for a moment, widening like a perfect black pearl. "Because she *was* injured... which would explain why she kept to herself so much at the beginning of the takeover. Her uncle, Lord Illumen, supposedly placed some sort of enchantment on the ballroom, hiding all physical injuries. I never saw any silver in his hair, but if he could truly create illusions, then I suppose he could have hidden that, too."

Every piece came crashing together like a hailstorm of boulders. All the times Mira had been frustrated after returning from the ballroom... The reason why the hostages had attacked her so aggressively and ignored her warnings... They were also victims of the Golden King's mind games.

"Are they still in the ballroom?" I asked, a new haste flooding my blood.

She bit her lip with a soft nod. "When I left, they were still there, but it's not good. The rose is dead, and its enchantment is at full power. If we don't do something soon, they'll tear each other to shreds."

"Then we need to destroy the rose." I stiffened. The idea of rushing into the horde of soldiers flickered images of chains and gallows in my eyes. There was no chance I'd be able to escape them if I ran right into the center of their rescue, but that was a sin I was ready to pay for. "You stay here. I've been wanting to crush that blasted flower for weeks." I started for the door, but her nail-digging grab clamped into my wrist.

"If you go, they'll arrest you!" She flung my arm, forcing me to whirl around and face her panicked expression.

"And if you go, you might get killed!" I bickered back, the new language flowing easier off my tongue in the heat of an argument.

"So could you!"

"Yes, but I'm the beast who started this mess; you're the duchess—"

"Yes, I'm a duchess," she snapped. "But that doesn't make me weak!"

"Of course, it doesn't!" I shouted back, my breath flaring hotly. "You're the strongest woman I've ever met. Which is why you need to stay safe! Omaira needs you, this realm needs you, and I need—" I choked in a breath, barely stopping my next words before they burst free.

"You need what?" She flailed her arms, face crimson. "What do you need?"

I held my tongue, feeling it burn in my cheeks until I couldn't bite it back any longer. "You." I moved forward, cupping my hand around her velvety cheek as I pulled her face into mine. My lips pressed down on hers with a ravenous hunger that had been starving me for weeks. She leaned into the kiss, sending waves of bliss through my pulsing heart as she wrapped her arms around my neck and pulled me closer.

When we parted, her eyes were wide and wistful, cheeks flushed, and ruby-red lips still parted with soft puffs of breath. "I need you too, Conan," she whispered, rushing shivers down my neck and arms. "So don't you dare leave me without you." Her voice intensified with the sharp command of a true duchess.

I nodded breathlessly. "Then let's face the army together."

# chapter twenty-eight

*I kissed Conan.*

My heart blared in my ears as I waited for Conan to swipe the enchanted key from Ian's unconscious body. Once he had it, he pushed open the suite's door, allowing the chaotic shouts of a self-contained war to waft around us. My stomach tightened, twisting my gut as I saw the fresh anger spilling into the eyes of the feuding soldiers.

*The rose is starting to infect them, too.*

"We have to hurry." Conan reached his hand out to me and held the door open. "You destroy the rose, and I'll watch your back." His expression turned to stone, putting on the mask of an unwavering protector that I had no doubt would take an arrow for me.

*I just hope he doesn't have to...*

Before following him, I darted over to the side of the broken master bed and grabbed a candlestick that still harbored three tiny flames. *The rose is already dead, so I'll need something to truly destroy it.* "I'm ready." I nodded, then swept through the door with him a half-step behind me.

My heart flew to my hand, throbbing where I held the candlestick as I watched the flames wobble. The sound of clattering iron tore through the ballroom as swords and other weapons clashed. The air was thick and heavy with the smell of sweat, and the entire ballroom sweltered with the heat of unfiltered hatred. A flash of silver flickered in the corner of my eye. Before I could react, Conan whipped out his dagger and parried the blade of a hostile soldier.

"The duchess has turned against us!" the soldier cried out, pressing his long blade against Conan's stout dagger. "She's aligned with the beast! She—" Conan swung his free hand square into the soldiers' jaw, knocking him out cold with a harmless flop onto the ballroom floor. I snapped my gaze back at him, horror spreading in my eyes.

"He's fine," he explained, urging me forward. "Trust me, I've spent enough years sparring with my brothers to know just the right angle to give someone a nice nap."

My anxiety eased at this notion, but also flared with my curiosity as to what else he learned from his years of battle-training. I continued forward toward the center of the ballroom, keeping my head low to avoid flying dishware and other odd projectiles. Conan ended up drawing more attention than I did, attracting vengeful hostages like bees to honey. He fended them off one by one, cautious not to do any real damage to them. When we reached the center of the ballroom, my eyes fixated on the small water vase we had used to prolong the cursed flower's life for so many weeks.

*But it was tipped over and it was empty.*

"Where's the rose?" I called back to Conan, who was currently busy wrestling a fork from Lady Rhonda.

He snapped his gaze around, prying the fork free from her wrinkled fingers with a firm yank. His eyes narrowed on the empty vase. "Did the griffins take it?"

I shook my head, dodging to the side to protect the candlestick's flames from being doused by an incoming spray from a flying water bucket. "If they had, would they still be this angry?"

My heart rattled my chest like a realm-shaking quake. My blood burned as the familiar sensation of the magical rage slowly began to integrate into my system. I had avoided the worst effects of the rose by keeping my distance from it, but now that it was at full power, it was wasting no time in clouding my mind.

*I'm running out of time.*

I swept my gaze around the room, scanning every inch of the cluttered ballroom for a wilted bloom. Panic seeped into me, causing my muscles to shake and limbs to tense. Frustration brewed inside me like a thick poison, forcing my nails to dig into my fists.

"Get the beast!" Out of nowhere, a soldier jumped on Conan's back, wrapping his neck in a chokehold, while a second soldier wrestled his weapon from him.

Fear tore through my chest, parting the frustration out of the way like oil to water. "Conan!" I hadn't realized how far I'd wandered away from him in my hunt for the rose. I darted around, wrestling nobles and squabbling men, stopping right in front of the soldier who gripped Conan. I beat my free fist on the first soldier's back, trying to do anything I could to get him off.

"Let him go! He's not a beast! You're just under an enchantment!" My frustration returned, burning inside me like a growing pile of embers.

*They can't kill him! I won't let them!*

My chest tightened, ready to combust with a spew of rage as I raised my flaming candlestick to hit the soldier in the back of the head. My arms made it halfway through the air when a choked gasp from Conan interrupted my fury.

"Th-the rose." While struggling to pry the soldier off his throat, he pointed a shaking finger toward the corner of the ballroom.

My eyes locked onto his point, following it until I saw the crumpled flower rolling aimlessly around on the ground.

"I see it!" I pulled away from the soldiers, feeling my heart bleed for leaving Conan to their mercy. I darted for the smashed flower, pressing every ounce of adrenaline into my muscles as I bobbed and weaved through the raging crowd.

I slid onto my knees, my fluffy dress cushioning my slide as I snatched the barren rose from the ground. It was barely a stem since the petals had fallen, so shriveled and trampled that it was nearly black. I placed the candle stick on the floor, only now noticing that all but one of the flames had blown out from my sprint.

"This is for Dhurin," I hissed. I held the dry stem in front of the flame until the fire engulfed it. The black stem lit like a perfect wick, absorbing the fire and burning with a puff of silver smoke. As if the flame had been lit inside my chest, the anger that had been pressurizing dissolved with a soft burn. I placed the stem on the stone floors, watching it do the same as it turned from a hate-inducing talisman to a pile of black ash.

The clattering of steel went quiet and the shouting ceased, leaving only the echo of twisted confusion ringing through the deafening silence. It was over. The rose was gone and the enchantment with it.

The castle was free.

"What did you do to us, beast?" The first voice that split the air came from a decorated soldier, likely a general or lieutenant. I whipped my neck around so fast, it audibly cracked, blinding me momentarily until I could blink my eyes to life. The soldier had Conan at sword point, the blade drifting eerily close to his throat. "What mad trick is this!?"

I clamored to my feet, heart in my lungs as I sucked in a stuttering breath. "It's not his trick!" My voice reverberated off the walls with a painful echo. "It was an enchantment by the griffins." Gasps echoed around the room, followed by a stiff silence that rattled my bones.

"The griffins?" A familiar voice cut through the quiet, causing my muscles to stiffen as I turned to see the disheveled grand duke of Dhurin. His hair was tussled, coat half-unbuttoned and torn, likely from being swept up in the battle. But it was definitely him...

The grand duke's gaze shifted between Conan and me, his eyes narrowed. "Are you claiming that the Golden King's followers are involved in this mess?"

I nodded viciously, swirling my brain into a headache. "Yes. They enchanted the rose so everyone near it would spiral into an endless cycle of rage, while also tricking us into a false sense of security with an illusion. I overheard them myself. It almost sounded like it was all an elaborate test to play with each enchanter's individual magic." I approached Conan, my skin burning as I took my place next to him. "And Conan was another victim of their mind games."

Whispers fluttered around the room as wide eyes gawked at my placement by the horrid beast. He may have given the griffins the opportunity to make this mess, but I wasn't about to let him take the fall for it all. Not now, not after how much he'd done to fix it.

*And how much I want him to stay with me.*

"The beast!? A victim!?" Ian's voice reached my ears like the yowl of a whining cat. He pushed through the crowd with a frown almost as ugly as the black eye darkening his cheekbone and lid. "The beast is the cause of all this! Griffins or not, he is no victim. He's a monster, deserving of the most severe punishment!" He jeered a finger at Conan's unmoving expression, causing my blood to boil hotter than when the rose was tainting it.

"He is not a monster! And he doesn't deserve—"

"Mira, please..." Conan's soft voice jarred me out of my rage. He called the attention of the entire room as they furrowed their brows at his choppy Rubian. "Thank you, but he's right." He lifted his chin, sawing my heart in two as he met the eyes of the grand duke with a humble sink of his shoulders. "I did not curse the minds of anyone in this castle, but I am solely responsible for imprisoning them here." He lifted his hands, offering his wrists for any chains they had ready.

"Conan, no..." My voice was too weak to be heard, only shattering me as he kept his eyes locked on the grand duke.

"You aren't even going to defend yourself?" the grand duke scoffed, eyeing him down with a contemplative lift of his brow. "You trap my people for weeks, and for what...? A useless endeavor to try to swindle my province from me?" He folded his arms, expression tight and scathing.

"I made a mistake," Conan replied grimly, his head lowered. "A terrible, unforgivable mistake where I risked the lives of your people. I let my demons get the better of me, and for that, I am truly sorry. I will accept any punishment you see me deserving of, but first..." He turned his focus to the gawking crowd, fixating his gaze on the scattered hostages speckled around the room. "Please, allow me to apologize to all of you for the horrors I put you through. I was cruel, spiteful, and downright... beastly. I am entirely undeserving of your forgiveness, but before I face the gallows, I shall beg for it, anyway. When I first entered the castle, I sought to become your leader, but I know now that a leader doesn't command with unrefuted power, but with compassion and assurance. I'm glad I failed, because your province deserves so much more than I could have ever given you."

Tears spilled from my eyes as I watched the light drain from his. My lips quivered. "W-what are you doing?" I asked him, catching the edge of his heartbroken gaze. "I told you... I told you that you deserve a chance to find happiness, too..."

He turned to face me, being cautious of the blade at his throat as he gave me a tragic smile. "But I did find happiness..." he breathed. "I found a love for you... my smart-mouthed duchess who taught me how to read." He winked at me, but I barely saw it through the blurring in my vision.

*He loves me...*

And the worst part was that I loved him, too...

"There! He admits he's at fault!" Ian bellowed. "Now chain him up and take him away! I don't want to see his ugly scars in my province ever again, unless they're six feet under."

My cheeks flared with anger as I shot a deathly stare in the duke's direction. I opened my mouth to give him a piece of my flaming mind, but was stopped by another interjection.

"I didn't think it was *your* province yet." The sharp sneer resonated from the back of the crowd, and the group parted, revealing none other than a stern-faced Lady Henrietta. Her thin brows were knit together with a scowl that could peel paint. "You weren't here for the last cluster of weeks, so who says you get to decide the beast's fate?" She looked around the crowd, gaining the attention of the other hostages as they slowly clustered around her. "I'm not going to speak for everyone, but I'm fairly sure it's safe to say that none of us are *happy* with what had happened." She twisted her mouth, aiming her disgruntled stare at Conan. "But as someone who was only a moment away from stabbing a Dhruin soldier with a spoon, I, for one, am grateful that he risked being captured to save us. I may have been seeing red, but I still saw what he did. Mira destroyed the rose, but she only got to it because he guarded her." Her gaze softened, easing the slightest smile up her plump lips. "And I appreciated your apology."

Conan's eyes widened, and for the first time since kissing Conan, I smiled. *Did she really just say that?*

"I agree with the debutant." Sir Eric stepped forward with a slight limp in his right leg. His coat sleeve was torn, dangling around his wrist, and his hair was matted like a long-haired cat, but otherwise, he looked unharmed. "What the beast did was wrong, but I respect that he had the courage to admit his mistakes and sacrifice his chance at escape to save us. He never truly harmed any of us, and even worked alongside the duchess to ensure we were fed and cared for. I'm not saying he should go free, but I do believe a trial is in order."

Soft nods and murmurs of agreement resonated from the rest of the crowd, each one swelling my heart another size bigger.

"That's absurd!" Ian sneered, throwing his arms up in the air like a child throwing a magnificent tantrum. "He's guilty of kidnapping and imprisoning an entire castle! There is no use for a trial when he clearly deserves to die for such heinous crimes."

"Oh? You mean like the crimes you committed to my sister?" Zac's trumpeting voice bellowed from the back of the room, shifting all gazes to where he stood alongside my parents and a few guards I recognized from Omaira. "Kidnapping... Imprisoning... Locking someone in a trunk...Will you tell them what you did to Mira? Or shall I?" He stepped into the room like a cold shadow, suffocating the duke's voice with a murderous glare.

"I-I... that wasn't— That's an entirely different—" His bumbling quieted as Zac stepped in front of him, towering over him with the authority of a man willing to slaughter a fellow duke.

"Here's how I see it..." Zac said coldly, his voice grim and sharp. "Since you committed the same crime, you deserve the same punishment. Unless you want to bring down the full wrath of the Omairan military on your province... Oh, and did I mention it's headed by my darling wife now. You know, the one with the gift to control wolves?" He flicked his eyes toward Conan's scars, hinting at the torment he would happily inflict on him. "So, what will it be? Trial...? Or execution?" He unsheathed a blade from his hip, inspecting his reflection in the glint with a sinister smile.

Ian went paler than a bleating lamb. "But... he's a beast! He's in league with the Golden King!" he argued between nervous gulps, keeping his gaze trained on the blade.

"Not anymore," Conan stated, diving his hand into his

pocket to pull out the magical key. "I'm through playing around with his tricks and letting him play with me." He dropped the key to the ground with a sharp clatter, stomping his boot straight on its golden shaft until it cracked in two. A vibrating hum filtered through the ballroom, causing the floor to tremble and walls to buzz as the magic drained from the castle doors. "The Golden King is as much of a nuisance to me as he is to you. I won't say that you should spare me, but if you do, I swear to expose every piece of knowledge I ever gained about him from my time with the beasts."

Father stepped forward, gaze steel, yet vibrant with fascination. "Do you swear that?" he questioned.

Conan nodded. "I do. Anything I can do to rid the realm of his golden blood, I will do."

The room went quiet, thoughts and questions fluttering in the air as the tension tugged me in every direction. Finally, Dhurin's grand duke stepped forward, shifting his gaze between his pathetic son and where Conan and I stood firm.

"A trial it is."

# chapter twenty-nine

"Tell me, my griffins, how was your trip to the castle?" The golden-eyed king stood just beyond the shadow of the trees, the forest wind brushing his dark blonde hair across his furrowed brow.

The trio of former hostages stood in the front of the group, with the other six members in a neat line behind them, awaiting the king's judgment. The once stout lord stepped forward, his round features now sharpened, his dark eyes a pale blue. His balding head was replaced with his true thick brown curls and his extra weight and age had vanished.

"It was highly informative, Your Majesty." Lord Tocken bowed, his brown curls fluttering over his brow. "Illumen's enchanted cloaks did an excellent job of disguising our true appearances, just as efficiently as when we first encountered the beast in the forest. He also did well in enchanting the walls of the castle's ballroom to ensure our lies were well disguised."

The Golden King's eyes scanned over to Illumen, inspecting the older man with silver strands tucked amongst his gray hair. "An excellent shield..." The king's voice lilted like an unfinished poem, tilting his head with squinted eyes. "But do I need a shield when what I desire is more violence...?" His eyes slitted at Illumen, like he was silently calculating the man's value. "Tell me, what came from his mirror?" He directed the question toward Illumen with a jeer of his head in Tocken's direction.

"Tocken's enchantment on the mirror and the charm proved to be... mostly successful." Illumen paused, ignoring the lethal side-eye Tocken gave him.

The king quirked a brow. "Explain."

"You see, Your Majesty..." Illumen swallowed, his eyes darting to the panicked look of his fellow enchanter. "Tocken was successful in infiltrating the former beast's mind, that much is true. But he took his actions too far and veered from the agreed upon plan."

The king's eyes narrowed, ice flowing into his yellow stare. "How?"

"He took it upon himself to sway the beast into killing the young duchess," Illumen continued. "The duchess had become an anomaly due to distancing herself from Azura's enchantment, and Tocken felt she would become a threat to our test."

The king shifted his eyes to Azura, a gold fire burning behind his glare. "Was she?"

Azura shook her head, her long locks shifting like a dark rippling wave. "No, Your Majesty. The girl was actually rather useful in determining my power's range and efficiency."

The king turned back to Tocken, who had tensed tighter than the gears on his watch. "I was only trying to help, Your Majesty," he bumbled, sweat beading down his brow from the burst pressure. "The girl appeared to be a hazard, and you said that you wanted there to be strife between the provinces. Killing off Omaira's heir would have accomplished that, while also removing the risk of her—"

"Did I *tell* you to kill anyone?" The king's snarl resonated across the forest, silencing even the chirping birds hovering above the trees.

Tocken gulped. "No, Your Majesty."

"Correct," he said coldly, taking a long step toward the tense enchanter. "Consider this as a lesson, my children." The king slid a blade from his hip, catching the glint of the morning sun in the steel as he trimmed the edges of his nails. "My plans are absolute. My requests bear no room for flux. If I request a test be performed, it shall be done without misstep, else the consequences be severe." He plunged the blade into Tocken's heart, and he fell to the ground without as much as a gasp.

No one flinched, each griffin as rigid as stone.

"Azura..." The king turned to the enchantress, while wiping his blade off with the edge of his cloak. "That isn't your true name, is it...?" He made a long stride in her direction, pointing the blade at her as he used the tip to brush aside a strand of hair from her eyes.

"It is not," she said coldly, turning her head to meet the golden eyes of her king. "But you already knew that, Your Majesty."

An impish smile crept up the king's face, curling his dry lips like cracked serpents. "Indeed, I did," he mused, lowering his blade to investigate her closely. "Your gift is rather unique, my dear. The power to sway a heart's temperament is something that suits my arsenal well."

An eerie chill swept through the trees, ruffling the edge of her skirt like the wings of a black raven. "You know the reason for my loyalty, my king," she said starkly. "Help me achieve what I want, and I shall wield my gift as your flawless sword."

The king's smile broadened, twisting into a wicked grin that sparked an eerie cackle. "And that I shall do, my dear." He backed away, keeping his eyes trained on his followers as he sheathed his sword. "But not here... Dhurin is no longer the place to run my tests, not while there are so many more delectable provinces to sink my teeth into." He steepled his fingers, tilting his chin down to where the forest shadows darkened his face in a villainous glow. "The griffins are dead. Much like my beasts, their time has come to disappear and move to grander explorations. But don't worry, your end shall not be nearly as tragic. Most of you shall join me in Sonal with the leviathans, but you..." He turned back to the enchantress, crinkling his gold eyes with a skin-crawling grin. "Welcome to the basilisks."

• • • • • • • • • • • • • • • • • • • • • • • • • • • • • • • • • • •

I ran my fingers through my thick curls for the hundredth time as I paced the castle floors. It had been two weeks since I'd returned to Omaira with my family, but the familiar castle walls were doing little to ease my anxiety. Conan had been escorted back with us under the joint custody of the Dhurin and Omairan guard, with an overseeing judge sent from the capital, Shainee. I'd only been permitted to visit him a handful of times through barred windows ever since our departure from Dhurin, but today was the day that could all change.

*For better or worse...*

"It will be alright, Mira." The calming words of my sister-in-law, Roisen, barely reached my ears through the sound of my grinding teeth. "The trial should be over by now. Zac should be back any moment with the verdict." She leaned back into the velvet sofa, pressing her hands down on her knees to vent her poorly concealed tension. "If Zac and I can look past the things Conan has done, then I'm sure the jury will, too."

I spun around on my heel, meeting her warm gaze that resembled so much of her darling grandmother. "But what if they don't?" I breathed hoarsely, my throat already tightening at the possibility of Conan being sentenced to something far worse than imprisonment. "You and Zac forgave Conan because you had multiple chances to speak with him and observe how he's changed. The jury only gets one day, and that one day is partially filled with Ian blabbering his accusations." I pressed a hand to my chest, attempting to press my rampaging heart back into my skin before it burst free.

*What if they can't look past the scars of the beast?*

Ro stood from her seat, crossing over to me with an easy smile as she pulled my hand from my chest to give it a squeeze.

"If anything, having Ian there should give you all the more assurance that the jury *will* listen. From what I've heard, he isn't much of a crowd pleaser."

I rolled my eyes. "He is in his head," I scoffed, squeezing her hand in return.

Despite being so close to the situation, I hadn't been permitted to testify in the trial due to Ian's insistence that my mental stability was still in question. Of course, we tried to argue this ludicrous claim, but we ended up settling in order to keep peace between his family.

We meandered around the parlor for what felt like hours, when in actuality, it was only about three and half minutes. When the servant pulled open the tall birch door, I thought my vision would black out before I had the chance to see who was standing behind it.

*Please be Conan. Please, please, be Conan!*

The doors parted, revealing only Zac... My heart sank to the bottom of my shoes, splintering and cracking into a thousand shards as heartache flooded my face.

*Where's Conan? They didn't... He couldn't have...*

"The verdict has been sealed." Zac's tone was void of emotion as he stepped into the room, his empty gaze tearing me to shreds like the claws that had scarred my beloved beast.

"What... what verdict?" My voice quaked as I pressed my trembling hand to my lips, eyes already fighting back the tears.

*They couldn't possibly have executed him... He must only be imprisoned... How could they kill a man who showed so much remorse for his actions?*

Zac folded his hands behind his back, his head low as he averted my gaze. "The jury came to the decision that holding innocent captives against their will is a crime that is lawfully punished by imprisonment." I sucked in a breath, feeling a small ounce of relief that he was at least safe from the claws of death. "Although Conan's crimes were greater, we did convince the jury that Duke Ian should receive an equivalent sentence since he directly abused his power to detain you. But the duke has a portion of diplomatic immunity that lowered his sentence to only three years of guarded supervision with an appointed official."

My jaw fell open with a literal crack as my joints popped. "What!?" I threw my fists to my sides, eyes blazing. "So, Conan apologizes and goes to prison, and Ian maintains his pride and gets sent home with a slap on the wrist and a babysitter?" My blood raced faster than a flaming geyser. I was beyond angry. Ian had done nothing but throw tantrum after tantrum ever since he was called to stand trial, while Conan had been cooperative and respectful. If Ian didn't have to rot inside a steel cage, then neither should Conan.

"Hold on, there's more." Zac cleared his throat while still keeping his tone soft to avoid provoking my anger further. "After the verdict was decided, I approached the judge and asked if diplomatic immunity could be applied, even after a trial had concluded. He said typically not, but in this case... there was a window of opportunity, in a sense."

The heat in my veins simmered to a buzzing tremble as I lifted an inquiring brow. "What are you talking about...?" I don't know why, but an eager throb started to flare in my heart as if the pieces of his clue were starting to form together, but I couldn't quite see the picture.

Zac lifted his gaze to meet mine, his blue eyes crinkling with a fresh smile. "I'll let him explain..." He stepped aside, revealing the tall, dark-eyed man, raked in scars who had stepped into the doorway.

"Conan!" My heart soared nearly as fast as my feet as I launched myself into his arms, only to be blocked by the chains still binding his wrists. I stumbled back a step, my eyes widening as I finally noticed the two guards who stood on either side of him. "Conan... what's going on?" My gazed darted between the guards and chains, fearful this was all going to end with him being dragged away from me.

"Mira..." His dark eyes twinkled like obsidian, warming my heart despite the cold chains that prevented me from crawling into his arms. "Do you remember the first time we spoke? When you barged into the master suite and demanded I hurry up and kill you?" He stifled a laugh, his cozy smile imprinting in my vision so I would never forget it if it disappeared.

"Of course..." My voice choked on an insistent tear, but I swallowed it back. I wasn't going to cry, not if this might be the last time he saw me. "I must say, I'm rather glad you denied my insistence." I laughed wryly, my throat tense and dry.

"As am I," he breathed. His hands may have been bound, but I could practically feel his caress from his tender gaze alone. "But there's one other thing that happened during that conversation... A question I had asked you that I assumed would solve all my problems if you said yes." With his hands still bound, he lowered himself to his knee, wobbling slightly from the iron shackles on his ankles. My heart burned as the memory of that day slowly drifted into my mind like a distant dream. Conan reached out for my hand, lifting his chains until he had me in his grasp. "Mira, the beast asked you to marry him because he wanted to be powerful. The prisoner is asking to marry you because the title he'd share would grant him freedom. But the only request I truly want you to consider is from the kneeling man who loves you more than any castle, kingdom, or crown. I want nothing more than to save the realm with you again and again, watching you prove to the realm that a title is nothing more than a novelty. Mirabel Brantley, will you marry me?"

Pure, heart-healing bliss flooded me to the core, pushing away every ounce of fear, grief, and tragedy that had haunted me for so many weeks. I nodded mutely, my smile too broad to even force my lips to make a proper reply. I squeezed his hand, choking on a breath long enough to squeak out, "Yes."

Unfiltered joy flooded Conan's ear-to-ear grin as he leapt to his feet and pulled me into an awkward, chain-entangled embrace. I ducked under his shackled wrists and settled myself between his arms with a crushing embrace that I had been waiting to give him for weeks.

"Well, you heard the duchess." Zac's humored tone cut through the moment as he strode up to the pair of guards who remained at attention. "The prisoner is intended to become a duke; therefore, according to the court's ruling, he is now under my direct watch. I'll be taking the keys now." He held out his hand, flicking me a cocky grin.

"Wait a moment..." I gawked, mouth ajar. "Conan is under *your* watch. You're the appointed official who has to monitor him for the next three years?"

Zac accepted the keys from the guard and waved them off, turning to unlock Conan's cuffs with the most brotherly mischief in his eyes. "That's right. It only makes sense that the previous heir to the province chaperone the new one." He gave Conan a malicious grin, dropping his shackles to the floor. "So, it looks like you'll be under my tender care for the next three years... That will give us plenty of time to reminisce about those good times we had together in the forest... You know, with the wolves and all." He twirled the key in his fingers with a taunting toss, only for it to be caught midair by Ro.

"But he will only be around when diplomacy calls for it," Ro interjected, giving her husband a glare of warning. "He wouldn't *dare* unnecessarily intervene in your new marriage."

Conan wrapped his arm around my waist, his eyes narrowed on Zac in silent victory. "I'm sure he won't," he said through a sly smile. "But in all seriousness, Your Grace. Thank you for accepting responsibility for me. I cannot begin to express my gratitude for what you have done for me." His intensity softened, unveiling the warmth that lingered beneath that I had come to adore.

"Yes, Zac." I nodded, giving Conan another squeeze. "Thank you."

Zac ran a hand through his hair, averting his eyes as he stared at the floor. "It was nothing. You've dealt with a lot ever since your illness was discovered, Mira. I just didn't want you to lose anything else."

Ro swept up beside him and planted a kiss on his cheek. "You're too sweet," she cooed, slipping her hand in his as she started dragging him out of the parlor. "Now bring your sweetness elsewhere before we spoil their happy engagement any further." She pulled Zac through the door, passing me a sly wink before calling back, "Welcome to the family, Conan. Thanks for kidnapping Mira and me, so we could all come together!"

They disappeared through the doors, leaving us alone in the parlor to laugh at her wild humor. Conan pressed his hand to my cheek, the smile still planted deep enough on his face that I didn't think it would ever leave. I leaned into his touch, entirely mesmerized by his captivating gaze as he inched my face closer and pulled me into a tender kiss.

"I love you, Conan," I whispered as we pulled away, my heart melting as his warm breath brushed against my lips.

"I love you too, Mira." He pulled me in for another kiss but paused midway as a curious twinkle swept over his eyes. "Oh, I meant to ask you... Did you ever send those letters we wrote? The apologies you were going to throw back into the sea?"

A soft laugh fluttered in the back of my throat as I caressed the edge of his scarred cheek. "Not yet. I was hoping that if you were granted your freedom, we could do it together." I trailed my hand down his shoulder and arm, taking his hand into mine.

He smiled his flawless pearly grin. "I'd like that. Can we go now?"

"Now?" I giggled.

"Yes." He smiled assuredly, bringing my hand to his lips for a gentle kiss. "What better way to start our engagement than with a walk on the beach and a send-off of apologies for a new beginning?"

I smiled, nodding softly as I led him toward the door. "Alright then, let's go."

# epilogue

The warm sea water lapped up the sides of the white sand beach, frothing into a thick foam as it slid up the cove. The warm sun baked the sand in its golden rays. Sea mist filled the air with its salty spray, luring the king and his pregnant wife to the edge of the water for a leisurely stroll. The waves picked up, splashing in a soft tide that carried something small and reflective in its blue caress.

"Dear, what's that?" The queen tucked a long strand of her silver tresses behind her ear while pointing at the bobbing object with her free hand.

The king quirked a brow, stepping away from his wife's side to inspect the glistening object. "I'm not sure. Hold on..." He walked down the beach, sloshing his boots into the frothing tide to chase after the foreign object. He dove his hand into the warm sea, pulling it out with a victorious chuckle. "It's a bottle! And it looks like there's a note inside."

The queen clasped her hands together with an excited giggle. "Oh, how exciting! Shall we open it?" She approached her husband with her curious eyes gleaming eagerly.

"Well, I don't see why not," the king exclaimed, already fiddling with the cork on the bottle. "I don't think someone would have sent it so far adrift if they hadn't hoped someone would read it." He laughed warmly as he popped the cork off the top, tossing it onto the sand as he yanked out the stack of papers. "Realms, there are quite a few letters in here, and it appears that they're addressed in two languages..."

"Two?" The queen peeked her eyes over her husband's shoulder. "What other language is there aside from the ancient scripts of our ancestors?"

The king flipped through the papers, his eyes furrowed. "I'm not sure..." He skimmed over the documents quickly at first, but then his skimming slowed. His bright eyes widened, his pupils dilating larger than a blot of spilled ink. His breathing slowed, and he lowered the letters with a distant gaze.

The queen stared at her husband in wonder, catching the small glints of moisture clustering in his eyes. "Miron? Are you alright? What did it say?" She pressed a tender hand to his arm, giving him a worried squeeze.

He shook out of his trance, turning to his wife with a reassuring smile as he wiped the droplets from his eyes. "Yes, I'm fine, dear. Better than fine, actually." He pressed the letters to his chest, taking in a shuddering breath before turning back to his queen with a tear-jerking smile. "We need to get in touch with Killian and King Jasper... There's something I need to show them."

# Thanks for Reading

*Ready for more fairy tales? Keep reading for a sneak peek of The Ruby Realm book three.*

*Sole of Secrets: A Retelling of The Twelve Dancing Princesses*

# Sale of Secrets

## Prologue

The emperor leaned back in his throne with a *creak* in his aging spine. His steward read off the monthly reports in a tone so slow and drawn that the emperor nearly drifted into a late-afternoon doze. He tuned in and out of the reports as the steward recapped the events of a failed castle takeover in the Dhurin province and the increased number of bizarre bandit attacks in Isleen. He didn't have time to bother with so many trivial incidents, not when he already knew the cause of all of them.

"Your Majesty," a strong voice disrupted the steward's report, and the emperor glanced up through his drooping eyelids long enough to see that one of his footmen had entered. "I apologize for the disturbance, but you have a visitor who urgently requests your presence."

The emperor shifted, sitting up in his throne with a lift of his thick brow. "Who dares request an audience with me uninvited?" His voice boomed through the wide space, echoing off the glittering mosaic floor all the way to the domed bronze ceiling.

"He says, 'I've come to collect your gold,' Your Majesty." The footman's voice grew stiff with skepticism. "I apologize. The man insisted I use that exact phrasing."

The emperor's dark eyes widened larger than a black pearl as his boredom instantly dissolved. He stood from his throne with a straightened spine, resting as little of his weight as necessary on his jewel-encrusted cane.

*He's back.*

"Show him in," the emperor commanded.

The footman startled at the stern command, then without further hesitation scurried out of the room to fetch the visitor. The emperor tightened his fingers around his cane's golden head as he waited, feeling his fingertips go cold as he stifled the blood flow.

*He has some nerve coming back after all this time.*

The footman returned, guiding a hooded figure who was cloaked from head to toe in black. The emperor didn't have to see the man's face to recognize him by the unmistakable jingle of coins. His cloak parted slightly as he walked, revealing the bulging sack of gold coins that always marked this particular guest. He kept his head low to shield his eyes, but his eerie grin was impossible to mask.

"Leave us," the emperor instructed coldly, his eyes narrowed on the visitor with a sharpness that could dull any blade. "All of you. I wish to speak with this man in private."

His guard shared a nervous glance, looking less than eager to leave their emperor alone with this stranger. However, they knew better than to argue against their ruler, so one by one, all the servants, stewards, and guards funneled out of the room. The door sealed behind them with a deafening *thud*, leaving the two men locked in eerie silence for a cold, quiet moment.

"Come to collect my gold, have you?" The emperor sneered. "Does that mean you're finally here to bring me a son? Or have you merely returned to play another trick?"

The emperor's grip tightened on his cane, bulging the veins in his hands and stiffening his arms beneath his rich silk sleeves. The visitor chuckled, a low dark sound, one that only halfway filled the massive room in a way that made it feel voided and hollow.

"Oh, Your Majesty..." the man pulled his hood down, revealing his unforgettable golden eyes and sinister smile, "since when have I ever tricked you? Forgive me if I'm mistaken, but I do believe the deal we made was that you would pay me gold in exchange for a child. Twenty years later, and now you have not only one, but twelve, flourishing princesses."

The emperor locked his jaw with a tight scowl. "You know perfectly well that I made that deal because I needed an *heir*. My daughters are a blessing, but they cannot inherit my realm. I know that our deal doesn't specify the number of children you can bring me, but I simply cannot accept another daughter. I refuse to give you any more gold unless you bring me a *boy*." His voice boomed with a finality that burned in the edges of the echo. "You may be the fearsome *golden king*, but I am still the prime ruler of the Ruby Realm. I will no longer uphold a deal I'm not receiving any benefit from."

The golden king's eyes darkened, though his eerie grin remained unchanged, much like a lifeless puppet with a painted smile.

"You think you can simply break off a deal with me?" The golden king chuckled under his breath. "Need I remind you what happened the last time you tried to break off a deal? The poison my beasts infected you with would have killed you if I hadn't so graciously given you another chance. Don't forget that our contract is one of the few things that keeps me and my followers from tearing your precious realm apart. I bring you a squirmy toddler every few years and you replenish my gold, that's the deal—and a rather fair one, if I do say so. The girls I acquired for you are the finest the realm has to offer. You should be begging me for another, not acting *ungrateful*."

His golden glare caught the king's with an icy warning, one that caused the ruler to stiffen.

*Smug little imp...*

"What's the use in having so many children if none are suitable to take over my rule?" the emperor countered bitterly. "Only a male can inherit the crown. Is this your way of preventing the Ruby Realm from ever having a successor?"

The emperor's anger flared at the thought. He'd known it was foolish to make any deal with the man who ruled his empire's underbelly, but he'd been so desperate for a son after his queen died that he never considered how their bargain would work long-term.

"I wouldn't go that far," the golden king mused as he casually wandered around the throne room. "I may be this realm's true king, but I still need a proper figurehead to deal with all the finicky details. So, no, I have no intention of allowing your empire to go without a ruler."

The emperor glared at him, burning with the urge to have him beheaded for downplaying the power he held as emperor. But despite how much he hated this man, their contract prevented him from interfering with his affairs.

"Then where's my *son?*" the emperor growled with an empowering lift of his trimmed beard. "Unless you have an infant swaddled in that cloak of yours, I'm not certain we have anything else to discuss."

The golden king wandered to the edge of the room and toyed with a decorative vase like he was casually exploring a market. His eyes flicked discreetly back to the emperor, sparkling with that nefarious glint the emperor knew all too well.

"You don't need a son..." The golden king's voice darkened like an eclipsed moon. "You only need an heir."

The king's thick brow furrowed, wrinkling his forehead with a furious blood vessel on display.

"I've gifted you eleven stunning jewels to stud your crown." The golden king smiled. "Now all that's left is to flaunt it and see who fits it best."

*Eleven jewels?*

"Are you implying that I should seek an heir by marrying off my daughters?" the emperor asked with a steel tone.

"Not all of them, just whichever one your victor selects," the king explained.

"Victor?"

"Ah, yes! You see, that's the fun part." The golden king pressed his fingers together with a giddy look that made the emperor's skin crawl. Nothing good ever came from this man's excitement. "You'll need to hold a competition. One where only the finest men in the Ruby Realm may compete for the hand of a gorgeous princess of their choosing and the opportunity to be crowned your heir."

The king nearly fell back into his throne as he steadied his wobbling legs on his cane. "What kind of absurdities are you babbling about? This wasn't our deal! I cannot simply let the empire go to some random individual based on a game of *chance*."

The golden king's eyes narrowed, digging into the emperor in a way that felt like he was peering past his soul. "Oh? But you were perfectly fine with the empire going to a random infant, so what's the difference?"

The emperor gritted his teeth, fighting the urge not to swing his cane in a fresh rage. "The difference is, I would have raised the infant. Not just any man has the skills required to rule over an entire realm."

"Then ensure that the competition selects someone who contains the proper skills," the golden king stated with ice in his tone. "Instead of arguing my genius, look at the benefits. You have twelve striking daughters who will lure out any man of value to join the competition. Once they're here, you can test them as you see fit and select a ruler you won't have to wait another eighteen years to become competent. *This* will mark the end of our contract. Once you have your heir, I will no longer have any need to bring you children. Our deal will finally be satisfied, and you'll have the strongest, wisest, most perfect successor a ruler could hope for."

Suspicion snaked through the emperor's blood like a squirming viper—no, more like a *basilisk*.

"You're planning something, aren't you?" the emperor glowered. "Who are you intending to place in this competition...? I'd gamble you already have a candidate in mind for my throne."

The golden king only responded with a toothy grin, the kind that seared into your mind with the crushing memory of regret later on.

"Why should I even bother to do a single thing you suggest?" The emperor tapped his rings on top of his cane, his stomach twisting as he already felt the answer burn into his heart.

The golden king's grin lifted with the pride of an undisputed victory as he tugged his hood back over his eyes to leave. "Because it's your only chance to be rid of me. I'll look forward to the first event."

# Follow me

for more updates on the
Chronicles of the Ruby Realm

 Abigail Manning, Author

 Abby Manning Author

Abigailmanningauthor.com

Special Thanks to Jada for inspiring Mirabel.

Made in the USA
Middletown, DE
11 July 2023

34856286R00166